Highland Temptation

Highland Pride, Book 3

Highland Temptation

Highland Pride,
Book 3

Lori Ann Bailey

Entangled Publishing, LLC
2614 South Timberline Road
Suite 105, PMB 159
Fort Collins, CO 80525
rights@entangledpublishing.com

Amara is an imprint of Entangled Publishing, LLC.

Edited by Robin Haseltine
Cover design by Yellow Prelude Design, LLC
Cover photography from Deposit Photos, Shutterstock, and Period Images

Manufactured in the United States of America

First Edition June 2018

For: My daughter, Bailey, as you start on your new journey, know that you are loved and your dad and I are proud of the woman you have become. You will do amazing things and I'm honored to watch from the sidelines as your story unfolds.

Chapter One

C'mon, open.

Kirstie Cameron fumbled with a hairpin she prayed would give her access to the locked door. After falling through her trembling fingers, it hit the floor. She cursed under her breath. Her brother's life lay in the balance, and she couldn't still her frayed nerves.

Scanning the darkened hall, she surveyed the shadows then bent. As she swiped her hands across the cold stone floor in search of the pin, her finger managed to knock into and push it beneath the locked door.

Breaking into the most dangerous man in all of Scotland's room was not her brightest idea, but it was her only option, and now the opportunity was lost. She stood and looked around to see if there was anything else she could use to dislodge the lock on the Earl of Argyll's door. Nothing but the bleak gray stones and scattered flickering sconces down the hallway of the castle stared back at her.

Wait. There was a shiny scrap of something just under the dancing flames a few feet away. Stepping away from the door and bending to inspect it, she froze at an unwanted familiar voice.

"Miss Cameron."

Kirstie rose to see a shadowed figure glide toward her. *How'd he do that?* She'd not heard the man approaching. She shivered but plastered a smile on her lips to face one of the men who might hold answers to the Covenanter plot. "Hamish, how are ye this evening?"

"It's a beautiful night now that I've found you." He bowed like English gentry, and she was, as usual, at a loss for how to respond.

Knowing she was too tall and far from the fairest lass around, his words fell short of their intention. Even Hamish was shorter than her. Sure, she had other attributes men liked. Her breasts were large and she was fair of face, but as soon as a man stood next to her and realized he had to look up to catch her eye, he turned and bolted the other way.

Hamish's flirtatious comments were commonplace, and she'd learned to take them as what they were. Practiced words to woo and seduce. Despite the urge to pull away from the man set on converting her to Presbyterianism, she would lead him to believe it possible, at least until her family was safe.

"'Tis many a bonny lass in residence this week. I'm fair certain ye could have yer pick."

"Ah, but what if I have already chosen the lady I wish to court?"

Her gaze traveled from his hair down his form to make certain he knew she was looking and doing her part to gain his confidence. She was not unpracticed at flirtation as well. She glanced back up to see his lips curve in an appreciative smile. His shoulders straightened, and he moved closer.

I bet the English lasses are all prim and proper and dinnae spar with him this way.

"May I escort you to the hall? I've wanted to dance with you since we arrived." He gently laced his arm through hers and turned her in the direction he'd approached from.

Her heart sank as she realized there was no way to get out of it. Breaking into the Covenanter leader's room would have to wait for now, but she couldn't delay long as more guests would be arriving soon. She would have to try again before the castle became crowded and the chance of discovery was too great.

"What brings you to this part of the castle?"

Her steps faltered, but she recovered quickly. "I was told that Malcolm arrived earlier. I cannae wait another minute to see him."

The lie slid easily from her lips because it was also the truth. Too much time had passed, almost a year since she'd seen her younger brother. The urge to wrap her arms around him and know he was safe clawed at her.

The threat against her older brother, the Cameron laird, was the only reason she was here spying in this overcrowded, suffocating castle, and despite her desire to be back on Macnab land and tending to the horses in the stables, she was thankful Lachlan had not come to Edinburgh. If someone was after Lachlan, would they use Malcolm to get to him?

"It is not proper for a lady to be seen in the men's quarters."

A chuckle escaped her lips, and he turned a disapproving gaze on her.

She was reminded again of how different they were. His family had ties to the English aristocracy, so as a youth he'd gone to live with relatives in England and attend school there. She'd spent her whole life in the Highlands and couldn't imagine calling any other place home.

He was but a year older, and she'd met him back in the

fall. It was late June now, and in those few short months, she'd come to the conclusion that the only thing they had in common was an uncanny ability to turn any conversation into a flirtatious combat.

This was the first time she'd seen disapproval in his eyes, however. They were dark and held a hint of something dangerous beneath the surface. A chill prickled at the back of her neck, and she shuddered.

She wasn't going to let a man tell her what to do, but she thought it best to pacify him. If for no other reason than to reinforce her half-truth.

"I was just hoping to see him before he was swept up by all the lasses who will be clamoring to be at his side. Ye will have some competition now that he is here. Ye will have to pick a lass and pursue her before he sets his sights on her."

"The only lady I wish to woo is you, but you are correct. Apparently I am already at war with him for your attentions." As they passed a sconce, she noticed the merriment had returned to his hazel eyes.

Kirstie pulled her skirts high with her free hand as they rounded the corner and started down the stairs. Slowing her pace, she kept her gaze focused on each step before her foot touched it.

Not much embarrassed her, but her awkwardness had caused many moments of humiliation. It was why she felt so at ease with her animals. They were graceful and lithe. Riding horses had been the perfect antidote to her inability to not walk a straight line without falling on her face.

As they reached the bottom of the stairs, she dropped her skirts. A lively tune floated on the air, and as they stepped into the hall, she swallowed. The warmth of the crush of people wafted over her, along with the smells of overly perfumed ladies and sweat.

Her mouth was suddenly dry. Just the thought of being

next to the hordes of people she didn't know made her head spin. Where had they all come from? Most of them must be staying in the city, because the castle still held many empty rooms, waiting on visiting lairds and their clansmen who were due to arrive in the coming days. She stopped at the edge of the floor as Hamish attempted to guide her out into the dancing crowd.

"I must have something to drink first."

"How silly of me. I will get you a refreshment, and we can step out for some air. It is stifling in here, but I will not let you desert me until you have honored me with a dance."

"I would never think to deny ye." *But oh, how I wish I could.*

"Stay here. I shall return shortly, and we can go for a stroll."

Hamish moved to the refreshment table. To keep herself busy, she scanned the crowds. She hoped for a glance of Malcolm, but she also stopped on each unfamiliar face and studied them for any signs that could give her a clue as to who was behind the plot against her older brother.

A flash of her cousin Fiona whirled by laughing in the arms of an attractive man who swept her away as soon as she'd appeared. It was nice to see her cousin enjoying herself. Since the man she was interested in had disappeared several months earlier, the lass had been miserable. Kirstie smiled at the thought that her friend might again find happiness.

Hamish appeared through the throng of people holding two cups. "Adam's ale." He winked at her. Her brow crinkled until she took a sip and realized it was water.

"Just what I needed."

"Come." He threaded his free arm through hers and guided her toward the exit. The smell of fresh air washed away the tightness that had enveloped her in the great room. She was made for outside and wide open spaces. Confined areas always left her with an unsettling rumbling in her belly. She inhaled deeply and let it out slowly.

"'Tis a bonny night." She glanced up at the stars.

"Only matched by your beauty."

He took her free hand in his and stared deep into her eyes. "You should join me tomorrow. Robert Baillie will be speaking at Greyfriars Kirk."

"Nae, ye ken 'tis no' where I belong." She tried to look accepting but at the same time stern in her own beliefs. His hand tightened slightly.

"I will entice you to join me one day." He smiled, but she had the sense he was only indulging her.

He really believed she would renounce her religion for his. He treated her as if she were a child who had not been able to comprehend a lesson he was attempting to teach her. It was the one quality about him that angered her. Of course she didn't like that he was too English, but what really got under her skin was that he would not accept that she was Catholic and wanted to stay that way.

Pulling her hand free, she raised the other holding the cup to her lips to swallow the last sip of her water. "I am anxious to find Malcolm. Will ye please escort me back in to look for him?"

He perked up like a strutting peacock and resumed his position at her side. She regretted losing the cool night air, but it was the fastest way to change the conversation. He'd not tried to force his faith on her like the fanatics, but the last thing she wanted to do right now was talk about the Covenanters when they were out to kill her brother and force their beliefs on her clan.

Strolling back into the hall just as the notes of a song rose up in the air, he took her cup, set it near the wall, and whisked her straight out to the dance floor.

A familiar face appeared in the crowd. "Malcolm."

Hamish twisted to follow her eyes.

"Ah, he looks like ye." She smiled because Malcolm glanced over, caught her eyes, and grinned from ear to ear.

"We have often been told we look alike." Being away from her family had been hard on her, but she had purpose on the Macnab's land, a position that made her feel needed and fulfilled. Back at Kentillie, she felt as if she was always under someone's feet.

"I shall direct our movements that way. Why did the Laird send him? I thought he would want to be here for the meeting."

"Aye, Lachlan would have come, but his wife is having their first bairn any moment. He chose to send Malcolm to represent the Cameron clan."

For the first time, it occurred to her that she might have to make a trip to Kentillie. Maggie may not want to bring the babe to her, and she had to see her first niece or nephew.

Just as they were skirting around the last couple, the crowd parted, and the face of her oldest brother's best friend appeared. Her heart dropped, and her feet faltered. The room started to spin, and she tripped over Hamish's boot. She braced for the worst, but strong arms closed around her before she hit the floor.

"Still as graceful as a newborn foal." Alan's teasing voice invaded her ears and held her captive.

Warm, joking eyes from her past fixated on her as he held her so close she could feel the warmth that radiated from him. Soul-shattering embarrassment assailed her as a tremble of recognition rushed through her. And yet at the same time, she fought back the desire to sink into him.

"'Tis good to see ye, Kirstie." Alan's gaze softened to the sincere gray that reminded her of cool overcast evenings, of home, and for a moment, she thought she saw longing in their depths. But she'd been wrong before.

She should move, but her muscles had gone as limp as an overcooked cabbage. And she could feel her breasts rise and fall as she fought to catch her breath. They had conveniently landed just under his eyes, which darkened for just a moment before amusement lit them again.

"I see there is a bit more to ye now, though. Those would throw anyone off balance." Her face had surely turned pink from the heat in the room and the embarrassment, but now, it most likely reddened with outrage.

He had no right to look at her, because she'd given him the chance once and he'd turned her away. "Let me go, Alan." She tried to impart anger into the words, but she could feel her voice shake in protest.

A warm hand took hers and pulled her up and away from Alan's arms. Hamish positioned himself between them.

Good, she needed the space.

She was not going to acknowledge that it had felt right to be in his arms and that her body still tingled where he had touched her. She was not going to admit he still caused strange stirrings in her that left her speechless and wanting to beg for things she'd never experienced.

Damn, after all these years. Why was he still the only man who made her turn to mush and forget her defenses?

Chapter Two

Curiosity and a small spark of anger catching him off guard, Alan Mackenzie studied the Covenanter with his hands on his best friend's little sister. Although he should be looking upon her as a brother might, he had a hard time reconciling the image of the lass who had left with the woman she had become. He blinked to clear the image of the last time he'd seen her from his mind.

He wasn't here to dredge up old memories of his laird's sister. He was here to look after Malcolm and discover who was behind the plot to assassinate the Highland chiefs who wouldn't convert to Presbyterianism and acknowledge the Covenant put forth by the Church of Scotland. Rumors were floating around that the plot would be carried out soon, and the only way he would be able to discover who was behind it was to ingratiate himself with the Covenanters.

Tempted to shelter Kirstie behind him and lecture her on who she was keeping company with, he refrained from lashing out just as the weasel took her hand and pulled her from his grasp.

Biting back the protective retort that was stinging the back of his throat, he held out his hand. "Alan Mackenzie." He ignored the tilt of Kirstie's head, and her narrowed eyes as she took in what he said, and he hoped she had enough sense not to question the use of the name he'd denounced years earlier.

"Hamish Menzies." Although the Covenanter's features were hard to read, Alan could sense the man already viewed him as a threat.

Hell, I'm supposed to make these men like me.

Distrust still reflected in the Covenanter's eyes, but as Alan had hoped, the mention of his former clan, the Mackenzies, who fought for the Covenanter cause, had apparently tamped it down a bit.

"I've been in Edinburgh for days and didnae ken my former sister was here." The lie rolled off his tongue. He'd arrived early to put distance between himself and his clan so that it would seem he and the Camerons were at odds. When he'd heard the clan Kirstie had been living with the last three years had brought her along, he'd avoided the urge to seek her out.

Hamish still held on to her hand, so Alan made a show of looking at the place where they touched and then at the man. He had to gain the man's confidence, but Hamish's familiarity with her couldn't be overlooked.

Kirstie solved the problem by pulling her hand free and running to give her brother Malcolm an embrace. "'Tis been too long. I expected ye here yesterday."

Alan listened to the conversation but moved to put distance between Malcolm and him. They couldn't appear to be on friendly terms, especially not with a Covenanter present and their ruse well under way.

"Aye, the rain delayed us. Ye look well Kirstie."

That's an understatement. Alan had to fight to rend his

gaze from her. Her large doe eyes were a deep shade of blue like the darkest of skies before a storm. Funny he'd never noticed that before. She had dimples on both cheeks that appeared as she graced Malcolm with a lovely smile.

Why had her older brother Lachlan ever let her leave Kentillie? She belonged there. If she'd been his sister, he'd never have let her go.

The Covenanter moved toward her again.

I swear when this is over I will take her home. If the Laird willnae put his foot down, I'll convince Malcolm to make her come back.

"How is Maggie? Has she had the babe? How is Mother? Did she come with ye?" she asked.

"Nae, the babe wasnae here when I left, but Maggie looked like she would deliver at any moment. Mother stayed with her and Lachlan."

Keeping one ear on the conversation, he took the opportunity to speak with Hamish. "Are ye here for the meeting?" He knew the answer already but needed to start the conversation somewhere.

Everyone was here to see if the Royalists would acquiesce to the Covenanters' demand that clans unite to support the English Parliament in their bid to take power from King Charles. It was a battle best left to the English, but the Scottish Parliament wanted every able-bodied Scotsman to travel to England to help defeat the king's forces. In return, the English Parliament would help the Covenanters spread their Protestant religion throughout the Highlands, pushing out those who would remain faithful to their Catholic upbringing.

"Yes. A unified Scotland is a better Scotland."

"Aye. I'll drink to that." Alan didn't drink, and his vision of a unified Scotland didn't include the Covenanters forcing their beliefs on others. His was more of tolerance.

Hamish nodded and smiled, his shoulders relaxing a bit.

"After the lady retires for the evening, would you like to accompany me to The Full Cask? It's in walking distance and serves the best ale in Edinburgh."

"Aye, I could use a good drink after the long journey here," he lied again.

Kirstie broke in, "Hamish, this is my brother Malcolm."

Alan attempted to seem cross, knowing how important it was that they be seen as enemies.

Backing farther away, he eyed Kirstie's ringlets bob as she turned her head. The deep chestnut curls had grown, and she wore it pulled back at her temples while the rest fell like unruly waves to her waist, beckoning to him. He wanted to touch one of the spirals to see if it was as soft as it looked.

He shook his head. This was Kirstie, Lachlan's little sister. She'd changed. On top of that, instead of following him with those blue eyes like she always had at Kentillie, she studiously avoided his gaze and turned her attentions to the man he was quickly developing an irrational loathing toward. He didn't know why, but it annoyed him that she was no longer infatuated with him.

What the hell was he thinking? He blinked and turned his attention back to his target. And what was she doing dancing with the enemy, anyway?

A tall, sturdily built man with a regal bearing approached Kirstie. "May I have this dance, Ms. Cameron?"

"Aye, Mister Campbell, but I must warn ye. I am no the picture of grace." She smiled, and her dimples peeked at the man.

Why did she even ken a Campbell?

"'Tis perfect. 'Twill give me the opportunity to hold ye close and keep ye safe."

Alan's breathing became quicker. Was she flirting, and with a Campbell no less? They were sworn enemies to the

Royalist cause and her clan. And was the man eyeing her breasts? Alan was going to have a talk with her about her lack of judgment and putting on some proper clothing.

A short blonde lass appeared by Malcolm's side and drew him in for a hug. He overheard snippets of the conversation as Kirstie was whisked out to dance with another Covenanter. If Lachlan were here, he'd tell his laird to bend the lass over his knee.

Hell, he might do it himself.

"When did ye and Kirstie get here?" Malcolm asked.

The lass must be Blair Macnab. *That* was the problem—the Macnab was a Covenanter. And it explained why Kirstie was consorting with the enemy; she'd been allowed to live with them. Lachlan should never have let her go to stay with that set of cousins.

Blair and Malcolm continued to talk, but Alan lost track of the conversation. His eyes had focused on the Campbell with his arms wrapped around Kirstie. The brute was entirely too close, and he vowed to find out who the man was.

Beside him, Hamish watched Kirstie's partner intently as they sashayed around. The weasel's face remained passive and unreadable, the clenched fists and white knuckles at the man's side the only clue that something ominous lurked beneath the surface.

She laughed and said something, then smiled and looked down to concentrate on her steps. The unknown Campbell's eyes focused on Kirstie's chest as if she were thick, creamy custard to lick from a spoon. She seemed unaware, or worse yet, not bothered by the arse's perusal of her ample bosom.

Did she even ken what kind of effect she had on the arse?

The man beside him still didn't express anger, but his fists pounded on the side of his leg. Hell, did she ken what kind of effect she had on Hamish?

"And ye must be Alan." Blair's high voice cut into his

thoughts. She was a pretty lass, probably a year or so younger than Kirstie.

"Aye, 'tis a pleasure to finally meet ye, Blair."

Who was this lass Kirstie had given up Kentillie for? He'd often wandered through the stables and wondered why she would leave her home.

He had never been asked to accompany Lachlan or the rest of the Cameron family when they had gone to visit Kirstie, and the couple times she'd come home, he'd been with his cousin on the Isle of Skye. He had never before acknowledged the part of him that felt the loss of Kirstie's presence, a lass he'd always considered a sister.

"Ye are as handsome as Kirstie said, but ye are much larger than I expected."

She said I was handsome?

Blair studied him with a mischievous glint in her eyes that seemed to indicate she was privy to secrets he knew nothing about.

"Has she filled yer ears with me, then?" At one time, Kirstie had followed him around with stars in her eyes, a silly childish infatuation. It had been flattering at the time, but now he stilled and swallowed waiting on Blair's response. The girl bit her lip then looked down.

"Nae, only when she first came to live with me."

Hamish, who had been watching silently, pretending to observe the conversation, broke in, "Mackenzie." He almost didn't realize the man was speaking to him until he remembered his reason for using the name he'd been born to, a name that invoked anger and rejection.

"Aye."

"I must be off. Will you join us tonight at the pub?"

"Aye, I look forward to trying some of Edinburgh's brew." He attempted to look enthusiastic.

The Covenanter gave a curt nod and turned to go.

Losing sight of Kirstie, he swiveled to follow Hamish's movements as the conversation between Blair and Malcolm continued. He was barely aware of what was being said when he saw the Covenanter approach a man wearing a gaudy yellow military-style coat.

It was the captain of dragoons of the English Parliamentary army and an Anti-Royalist. The two men headed for the door together. Yes, Alan would be meeting with the right crowd tonight. If he could pull this off, in the morning they would think he was one of them.

When he glanced back, Kirstie was standing next to Blair. But the vision before him was not the lass he remembered. Cheeks flushed a warm pink, she was winded, and a sudden wave of irritation that he'd not been the one to make her look so ravishing gnawed at him. It was irrational.

"I need to get some air," she said, looking at Malcolm, but he took the opportunity and jumped in to answer her.

"I could use some time under the stars. 'Tis stuffy in here."

Despite the disapproval in her gaze, he took her arm before she could utter an objection and hastened toward the door. He might be able to see where Hamish and the army captain were headed if they made good time. Afraid he might lose sight of them, he took the most direct route, straight through a throng of guests, dragging Kirstie behind him.

"Alan," she protested as she tried to pull free from his grip, but he ignored her as his prey disappeared then reappeared again.

When they reached the door, he scanned the courtyard. Kirstie jerked free of his grasp as he looked down the corridors, to the left and right, then across the open space. People loitered, but there was no sign of the yellow jacket.

Hell, they'd been too late. If she hadn't fought him, they may have made it. He turned his frustration on her. "Ye didnae need to…" He stopped when he saw her face.

The courtyard was well lit with sconces, and the full moon shone high and bright. Kirstie's smooth golden skin had turned green. She was standing by—no, leaning against—the wall as she held a hand to her mouth. Her eyes were squeezed shut, and her breaths were rapid and unsteady.

His hand rose and stroked her cheek. "Are ye going to be sick?"

She froze and then flinched back as if his touch burned her. Then she moved to put more space between them. "Ye have no right."

Her long curls bounced rebelliously as she fisted her hands on her hips. The candle caught her eyes in a way that turned the blue darker; a glimpse of a spark of anger bubbled to the surface of their mysterious depths. Her shoulders were held high, which not only made her look like a conquering goddess in the moonlight, but pushed her chest up for his display. He licked his lips. His gaze dropped to take in her small waist and large hips. They were just asking for a man's hands—no, his hands—to hold them and pull her down on top.

What the hell was he thinking? Breathing in sharply, he gulped.

Her dress left little to the imagination. He'd never noticed her figure back home at Kentillie when she'd worn a plaid draped over her shoulders.

When had the little doe-eyed brat who used to follow him everywhere turned into a woman? And why was he having this reaction to her?

She was forbidden.

He'd never risk harming her in any way. Her family had taken him in when he had no one else. Lachlan and he had sworn oaths to each other. Where was his honor?

He beat back whatever he was feeling. It belonged locked away in a box he couldn't get to—there were enough complications and risk in his plan already. The less Kirstie was involved, the better. Her brothers were already in danger. He couldn't think of protecting them if he was distracted by her.

"Ye and Blair should leave Edinburgh."

"Are ye mad? I amnnae going anywhere." Her head jerked angrily. The defiant stance made him want to wrap his arms around her and cart her off. He stepped closer but didn't risk touching her. She didn't back down.

"Edinburgh isnae safe." He spoke in a quieter tone and enunciated each word slowly as he clenched his plaid to keep his hands from reaching out to shake her.

"Nae, 'tis being around ye that isnae safe." Her haughty tone seemed to indicate any childish feelings she'd had for him were long forgotten. He sighed. The knowledge should have made him happy.

Lightening his tone, he motioned toward the door. "Come, I'll take ye back inside."

"Nae, 'tis time I return to my chamber. I dinnae wish to go back in there." He almost missed the tiny shudder that ran through her.

"Then I will escort ye back to yer room. Ye shouldnae be alone."

She pursed her lips and studied him then nodded agreement. "We are in the east wing."

They fell into step together as they strolled silently through the courtyard. As they took the stairs, Kirstie's foot must have caught on her dress, because she pitched and careened toward the stone. His arm was able to catch hers before she hit, and they stood there a moment, as if they'd both been rattled by the contact.

"Thank ye," she said, and if it had not been so dark, he was certain a blush would be on her face.

For some reason, it made him smile. "Ye will have to watch yer step in the dark."

"Nae, 'tis this silly dress. They are made so long that steps are impossible to navigate."

She ran her hands down the length of her skirts, taking the material and pulling it up, then stilled and looked at him with questioning brows. He felt a tightness in his chest as he stared back.

Her eyes darted to his hand. She was waiting for him to let go of her arm. Forcing his fingers to loosen, he let his hand fall limp to his side.

"How is Maggie?" she asked as she started up the steps again.

He stayed a pace behind her. There was still a chance she might tip backward with all that material trailing behind her. "She is going to have the babe any moment. I have never seen yer brother so worried over something before."

"He'll be a good father, and Maggie is so perfect. I'm glad they found each other."

"Aye, 'tis so easy to rile him up with her around."

They crested the top of the stairs, and she turned to the right. He followed, noting the lighting as they walked the hall. One of the sconces was out. She walked past not noticing, but he found himself scanning the shadows.

It was too easy for someone to hide in the dark.

He'd have to have someone take care of it. There was no reason to think she was in danger, but since her brothers weren't with her, the responsibility fell to him to be certain she was safe.

After stopping in front of a door, she turned to him. She looked timid, like a cautious cat. It was quite a change from the tiger he'd seen just a few moments earlier with claws drawn, ready to strike. This demure side of her was just as appealing as the fiery one. He found himself leaning in and trying to read those soulful, mysterious eyes.

She sank back into the doorway. "Will ye be certain Malcolm gets Blair to the room? I amnae sure where her brother has run off to, but she shouldnae walk back alone."

"Aye, 'tis no' safe for any lass to be roaming these halls alone. Too many men drinking." The words reminded him, he couldn't be seen with Malcolm, so he'd have to ensure Kirstie's friend had another escort, because he'd be pretending to be one of the men indulging in spirits shortly. She said nothing. "Be sure to bolt the door, kitten."

Her eyes narrowed, and a flash of something unreadable hinted at hidden currents that lay buried beneath a calm facade. If he'd not been like a brother to her since she was but a wee thing, he would think she was afraid of him. What had possessed him to call her kitten?

She fumbled behind her back then pushed the door in and silently took a step backward. He didn't move. "Good night, Alan. 'Twas nice to see ye."

It was the first kind thing she'd said to him. Some pent-up dam of emotions cracked inside and relieved a pressure he was only vaguely aware of. He was able to breathe a little easier, but then a memory of the last time he'd seen her crept in unwanted.

The hurt on her face that day had been a source of guilt for years. He squashed it down because there was nothing he could have done differently. He still wouldn't change the past even if it were possible. He'd done what he had to.

"Sleep well. Dinnae forget to bolt the door." She disappeared into the dark room, closing the door without looking back at him. He stood there until he heard the lock click in place.

He headed back to the great hall to ensure John Macnab was present to take care of Blair. Not knowing the man and unable to find the lass's brother, he escorted her back himself.

Then he would be on his way out of the castle and down the hill to The Full Cask to become one of the enemy.

Chapter Three

Kirstie leaned against the back of the door as she fought to control her pounding heart. Her hand touched her cheek where his had so tenderly caressed it.

Damn him.

He'd touched her arm, too. It still tingled where his bare skin had warmed hers.

Damn me for being such a fool. He never wanted me and never will.

Then why did his touch still affect her so?

Alan had called her kitten. No one had ever called her kitten. He had never called her anything but Kirstie or brat. She preferred brat; at least that wasn't confusing.

Had she imagined the interest in his eyes?

She was going daft. All the time and distance between them had dulled her desire to be near him, but if he touched her again, she was afraid her silly, childish infatuation would return.

Why had she insisted on coming to Edinburgh? She hated crowded places, and this had to be one of the worst.

And she should have known her brothers wouldn't have left home without Alan. Now, despite her desire to be anywhere else, she had to be here.

But she knew well why she had insisted on accompanying Blair's family. Her friend Isobel, a member of the Royalist Resistance, had warned her that the Royalist lairds in attendance at the upcoming meeting in Edinburgh were at risk and that the Resistance was working to quell a plot to murder them all. She'd expected Isobel to make an appearance this week, but so far, there was no sign of her.

Tamping down her besotted childish dreams to be with her brother's closest friend, she shook her head. The soul-crushing fact was he saw her as nothing more than a little sister. It was the furthest thing from what she had felt, and if she wasn't careful, those feelings she thought long ago gone might awaken. She was the worst kind of fool.

Alan was a complication she didn't need or want. It would take all her strength to avoid him and the way her heart fluttered at the sight of his gray eyes. She had more pressing matters than a foolish infatuation. It was imperative she discover who was in on the plot to eliminate the lairds.

Taking a deep breath, she stepped away from the door. The sound of Alan's boots echoing down the hall had faded, and the air returned to her lungs.

The night had netted no evidence. Her attempt to get into Argyll's room had been thwarted, and her dance with Niall Campbell had given no clues as to who wanted to murder her brother. She had put on the charm, too. He didn't let anything slip, but he had become quite comfortable with her, even putting his hand dangerously high on her ribs, his fingers inching toward the underside of her breast. Twice, she'd had to physically pull his hand back to her waist. And he was unapologetic about it, the treacherous rogue, giving her a sly smile as if it were a game and he thought she was happily playing along. He would be dangerous.

Sweet, unsuspecting Hamish had a viper's nest of friends. She'd be happy when this business was over and she could return to her peaceful life in the Highlands with her horses. Maybe if Alan remained here a while, she could go to Kentillie to see Maggie and the babe. And Mother. She desperately missed her mother and her own room and the comforts of home, but she'd built a comfortable life at the Macnab's, and now they depended on her.

Pulling at the unfamiliar gown, she undressed as quickly as her fingers could fumble with the confining ribbons. The coolness of the night air was a balm that reminded her of home, and although the room was small, she felt as if she could finally take in a full breath. After removing her shift, she put on the thinner of the two night rails she had brought. As she sat on the bed, visions of Kentillie floated in her mind, just as they had a thousand times before.

Damn, I miss home. She thought of the river, the rolling hills, the snow-topped mountains, and the green and purple meadows as she waited on Blair to get to the room. Living the last couple years on the Macnab's land had been bearable because she had a purpose and felt needed, but it wasn't Kentillie.

A quiet but firm knock jolted her from her memories. She jumped up and padded toward the door, the chilled stones refreshing on her bare feet. The latch creaked as she lifted it. The door swung in, and in an attempt to get out of its way, she tripped, falling back flat on her ass.

A hulking silhouette stalked into the room, and Blair's small shadow followed.

"Kirstie?" The smooth burr she'd recognize anywhere washed over her.

"Down here."

"What?"

"Ye nearly pushed the door into me."

"Are ye hurt?" Alan sounded concerned.

"'Tis only my pride that will be bruised."

He reached forward with both arms, but she stared at them, not sure if she should take his hands. Feeling vulnerable on the floor, she took them and he hefted her to her feet.

"Ye should ask who's at the door before ye open it." His protective gaze met hers without letting her go.

"I was expecting Blair." She yanked her hands free and took a step back. "And look, there she is." Kirstie pointed at her friend. Blair remained silent but looked as if she was stifling a laugh.

"I told ye 'twas no' safe here. Never unlatch that door without first being certain of who is on the other side." Even though it sounded like a plea, he was acting like a brother again, and it brought back the rejection and anger he'd inspired in her youth.

"I will be sure to do that in the future, because I will ken 'tis ye, and I willnae give ye entry." She balled her fists at her side.

He went still and audibly inhaled, staring at her as if he'd never seen her. Her grip slackened.

"What are ye looking at?"

Movement caught her eye. It was Blair, coming to stand beside him. She lifted her hands up to her shoulders and swept them down her body like she wanted Kirstie to see what she was wearing, then she pointed back to Kirstie.

Och, her back was to the candle, and she had put on the thinnest piece of clothing she owned. It was a garment that over time had worn down to become almost transparent. It dawned on her that she was near naked in front of him.

"Och, Alan, close yer eyes." Rushing to the side of the bed, she grabbed a plaid, wrapping it around her before glancing back up to see him shift his gaze to the floor.

"'Tis time for ye to go." Her face burned with a mix of embarrassment and anger.

"Aye, I've had a nice view. Tempts me to walk Blair back tomorrow." His gray, teasing gaze returned to hers, and flames erupted in her cheeks. She bit her lip and looked away.

"Ye shall no' see it again," she snapped back.

He shook his head as if trying to dislodge the memory. "Good. Ye shouldnae have any men up here."

Why was she so calm and clear headed when other men flirted with her? She could match innuendos with them all, but something about Alan threw her completely off balance. Most likely it was because she was well aware he didn't want her.

And that's why it stung so badly.

"I think 'tis best if ye leave. Thank ye for the escort," Blair said.

"Aye. 'Tis time I'm on my way."

Kirstie turned toward the window, determined to not let those old feelings surface; they were both different people now. She couldn't face him. If her gaze met his, he would see the tears stinging the back of her eyes. She had sworn to herself that he would never see her cry again, but she was dangerously close to letting that happen, so she said nothing.

"Bolt the door behind me."

"Aye," replied Blair.

His boots clacked on the floor as he moved to the door. They stopped.

"Kirstie." The room was quiet until she looked his way. "Please be cautious and dinnae open this door again without knowing who is on the other side."

He sounded every bit like the overprotective "brother" he claimed to be, and that shouldn't still hurt, but it did.

Seconds ticked by, his gaze locked on hers, as he waited for a reply. She finally managed, "Aye, I will be certain 'tis bolted." The words were soft, her throat aching at what felt like a concession, but he was correct to be worried about the people roaming these halls.

"Good night, ladies." Alan's regard broke from her and traveled to Blair. He smiled then pivoted and strode toward the exit. Stopping with his hand on the knob, his back to them, he paused as if he'd say something else but shook his head then pulled on the handle. A *whoosh* of air sent a hint of sandlewood floating her way as his broad back and shoulder-length dark blond hair disappeared.

Rushing over, she dropped the latch in place and fought to collect her calm.

"'Twould seem ye were wrong about him." Blair's words brought Kirstie back from her silent contemplation of the back of the door.

"What is it, then?"

"He does have strong feelings for ye."

"I've told ye what he thinks of me. There is no reason to believe he has changed his mind."

"He may have told ye that, but 'twas a lie. He looked at ye as if he were starving and ye were one of yer cousin's famous tarts laid out on a platter before him."

"Nae, he's just playing some game with me. 'Tis best if I avoid him while we are here." After moving to the bed, she eased down, not wanting to acknowledge that her knees had been trembling with his nearness. No, it was her anger; that was why her hands still shook.

"Ye should tell him and yer brother what Isobel told ye. They will help. 'Tis too dangerous for ye to be spying on those men."

"Nae. If I tell them, they will tell Lachlan, and he will come to Edinburgh. His absence may be the only thing that keeps him and Malcolm safe."

"Ye must tell someone." Blair slid onto the bed just to her

side, picked up her hair to separate it into three sections, then started to braid. The ritual was comforting, and although her confusion over the appearance of Alan and her reaction to seeing him was abating, worry for her family was taking root again.

"I will consider telling yer brother if things get dangerous. He will help," Kirstie conceded with a noncommittal shrug.

"I dinnae ken that he would be able to do anything about it." Blair peeked over Kirstie's shoulder and raised a brow, reminding her that Blair wasn't sure which side John would come down on, but she was certain that despite their father's changing allegiance, he remained steadfast in his belief the Covenant shouldn't be forced on those unwilling to change their religion.

"I dinnae want to tell anyone until I have proof." She yawned.

"If I didnae like Edinburgh so much, I would beg ye to leave. 'Tis madness to get mixed up in this." Blair finished the braid, tied it off with a band, and turned. Kirstie shifted and took Blair's long golden tresses in her hands.

"What shall I wear tomorrow?"

"Doesnae matter what ye wear. Ye are the bonniest lass in all of Edinburgh." Finishing her work, she yawned. "Now, I wish to go to bed. I need sleep."

Blair climbed in next to her. And it wasn't long until her world turned black, dreams of being caught spying on the Earl of Argyll and heart-wrenching screams and shouts tearing through the air.

· · ·

"Wake up." Blair's voice pierced through the fog as hands shook her shoulder.

Stretching, Kirstie pulled back and was surprised to see

daylight streaming through the window. "What time is it? I cannae believe ye are up before me."

"Ye missed everything. Did ye no' hear the commotion last night?" Blair sat cross-legged on the bed, holding her pillow to her chest, rocking and hugging it. Her friend looked like a small, frightened child clinging to a doll.

"Nae, ye ken how heavy I sleep." Yawning, she rubbed at a little itch on her temple.

"There was a man murdered. Just at the base of our stairs." Blair's voice shook.

Bolting up to a sitting position, she felt her mouth fall open as she looked to Blair for more information. "Who?"

"'Twas one of the Marquess of Montrose's cousins. He was stabbed."

Och, nae, no' the Royalist leader's kin.

Blair seemed to gulp before biting her lip and continuing, "Several times."

"Are ye certain? That would mean someone may already be attacking Royalists."

"Aye, I saw him." Her friend's gaze misted.

"What were ye doing out there?"

"When I heard the shouts last night, I dressed and went to see what was going on." Closing hazy blue eyes, Blair shook her head as if trying to dislodge the image. "There was so much blood. I froze, but yer brother's friend Finlay calmed me down and brought me back. He told me to lock the door. I couldnae sleep after."

She hadn't seen Finlay yet; he must have come to Edinburgh with her brother.

Kirstie said, "We have to get down there to see what's being said. Do ye think it has something to do with the plot?"

"I dinnae ken, but the dead man was a favorite of the Royalist leader. Do ye think the Earl of Argyll could have had him killed?"

It was likely, with the tensions between those loyal to the king or to the Covenanters, but she could only guess. Shaking her head, she said, "I dinnae ken."

Only moments later, they were dressed and making their way down the stairs with Blair pointing out where the body had been and what the scene had looked like. Judging from the layout of the steps and the alcove just behind them, it appeared as if someone had been waiting for him or someone else to come along. She shuddered, and they moved toward the great hall.

Dreading the crush of faces and sweaty, smelly bodies as she and Blair made their way into the large room for breakfast, relief flooded her to see the crowds had dissipated, apparently choosing to sleep late or were aware of the murder and sticking to their rooms for safety. Tables sat at the places where dancing couples had brushed against her the evening before. As they strolled toward a sideboard filled with meats, eggs, summer fruit, and fresh baked rolls, she let go of the apprehension over meeting the same crowds again.

Now, it was fear that Isobel had been correct about the true purpose of this gathering that held her in its grip. Before they had a chance to enter the short line, she and Blair found themselves surrounded by Malcolm, Finlay, and another old friend from Kentillie. Dougal nearly knocked her over when he slung his arms around her in greeting, then Finlay embraced her fondly, but his eyes peeked through his lashes, seeming more interested in her friend. Another wave of relief claimed her as she realized Alan wasn't with them.

Finlay released his grip, and her gaze lit on her brother. "Ye didnae tell me Finlay and Dougal were here." She tapped him on the shoulder to get his attention, because it seemed focused on an entryway. She followed his stare but only caught sight of two men's backs as they disappeared.

"I barely saw ye last night. And 'twas so loud in here I

coulnae tell ye anything." He pushed back at her gently.

Finlay's head was tilted down as he covertly watched her oblivious friend. Always so serious and secretive, she'd never seen him take interest in anyone. Blair was always unaware of the effect she had on men, and a stab of pity for Finlay pinched her as she thought of Blair's interest in another man. She would have to warn him that the blonde beauty's affections were already claimed.

"What happened last night?" She pierced Finlay with the question.

Finlay's gaze met Malcolm's, and the two exchanged a pensive look before her brother turned to her. "Nothing. Seems the man had been drinking and angered someone."

She wanted to ask if it could have something to do with the threat Isobel had told her of, but if she revealed what she knew, Malcolm might send her away. Especially if he found out she'd been doing some investigating on her own.

"Do they have the person who did it?"

"Nae, so dinnae go about on yer own. Ye two should have either Finlay or Dougal with ye at all times."

Well, that was going to make her plan more difficult. It was already hard to find the evidence she was looking for; now she would have to find a way to dodge guards placed on her. Glancing toward Dougal and Finlay, she wondered how hard it was going to be to disappear; at least the crowds would work to her advantage in the evenings.

Changing the subject, Kirstie turned her attention to Malcolm. "I want to go for a ride today, see more of Edinburgh. We'll be trapped here in the castle again tonight. Will ye come with me?"

"Aye. We shall all go."

As they made their way to the table and sat, she found herself thankful for Malcolm's appearance, a chance to get out of the stifling castle, and the absence of the man who somehow still made her heart race faster.

• • •

Alan's head pounded as he sat next to Hamish Menzies and listened to Robert Baillie's oration on the virtues of Presbyterianism as rays of sun burst through the window and heated the church to a sickening level; maybe it wasn't that hot, but he felt stifled all the same. Baillie was the newly made Professor of Divinity and had come to Edinburgh for the special meeting that had been called here with many clan leaders in an attempt to come to some peaceable conclusion regarding the dissent among the Catholics and Presbyterians.

Overall, he respected the Presbyterian religion. His problem was with the overzealous and power-hungry leaders, the ones who would stop at nothing to prove their way was the only one.

Wanting to jump in a loch and bathe, he'd felt cheap and sick after the evening spent with them, needing to cleanse himself of the venom spewed around the table as the men boasted of their superiority. Just to play the part, he'd choked out some of the foul words himself.

The evening had been a success. Not only was he still alive, but he'd been able to get through the night without having to drink one ounce of that putrid brew. An involuntary shudder ran through him.

When the sermon was over and they got up to walk out of Greyfriars Kirk, the conversation turned to a subject he didn't want to discuss.

"How long have you known Kirstie?" Hamish asked.

"Since she was a wee thing."

"I attempted to talk her into coming to the service today. I have made it my mission to see to it that she finds the proper place in heaven."

Alan nodded.

"Do you think she will listen to reason and convert when it is time?"

"Aye, she is a sensible lass." *But,* he was thinking, *'tis no way on God's bountiful earth ye will ever get that stubborn lass to change her beliefs.*

"I would be so pleased to be able to save her. She has such a sweet soul." Hamish's eyes projected the sincerity and conviction born of not truly knowing Kirstie. The Covenanter actually believed she would forsake her religion in favor of his.

Were they talking about the same lass?

A vision of her sparring with him last night popped into his head. It was followed by the image of her curves and the near transparent shift she'd worn, the one that had let him see how truly shapely she had become.

His lips parted and words spilled out. "If only we could save them all." A good response for someone pretending to be a zealot; he'd pat himself on the back if he could.

"How was it you were able to keep your religious beliefs all these years while you lived with the Camerons?"

"I did a lot a praying."

He had, but only that he wouldn't turn out to be like his father, and thanked God every day that the Father had put the Camerons in his life. He would never be able to repay all the kindness they had shown him through the years. These Covenanters were fools to think he would betray the Camerons just because his given name was Mackenzie.

They were almost back to the castle when a familiar figure with dark ringlets and flowing skirts riding through the city caught his eye. Hamish missed the glimpse of Kirstie as the man prattled on about the importance of Jenny Geddes's actions in St. Giles Cathedral when she'd thrown a stool at the priest in objection to the use of the Anglican Book of

Common Prayer.

"Thank ye for allowing me to join ye for the service," Alan said, cutting him short.

Hamish beamed at him, and he continued before the man could start up again. "I need to check on my horse and see it is cared for."

"Yes, of course, you must care for all of God's creatures." Hamish ran his tongue back and forth over his teeth.

"'Twill see ye tonight at the pub?" Alan tilted his head in the direction of the tavern.

"Nae, I shall not be there this evening, but you can meet Niall there. I will tell him to save you a place at the table." Niall, the Campbell who couldn't keep his hands off of Kirstie. It would be a chore to drink with that Covenanter and not be tempted to drive a fist into the man's face.

"And why can ye no' join us?" He made it sound as if he'd really miss Hamish's company, although the man had bored him almost to tears.

"I plan to spend the evening wooing Ms. Cameron."

His chest felt heavy, as if a cow had just trampled him. He missed a step, but Hamish didn't notice.

"Ye will have to watch out for her brothers. They are a protective lot." Maybe he could find a way to scare the Covenanter from her without giving away his true feelings.

Alan was walking a thin line. He had to prove he wasn't loyal to the Camerons and the Royalists, but at the same time, he had to look out for Kirstie.

Besides, this man was too English for her, too boring, too stiff. Hamish wouldn't go for rides with her, or walks in the hills, or lay her down and make love to her in the heather in the shadow of Ben Nevis. The man would preach to her and make her miserable.

Hamish peered at him and did that thing with his teeth and tongue again.

Watching to see how I'll react.

The man's tongue stilled. His features remained eerily unreadable except for a small, almost unperceivable smirk that slowly curved up one side of his lip.

Hamish said, "Let me worry about that."

Alan fought to hide the chill that ran through his body as he caught a hint of something that almost felt evil beneath the calmly spoken words. This man was either the naive zealot he appeared to be or the devil incarnate. Either way, he would have to keep Kirstie far away from Hamish Menzies.

Managing a smile, he slanted his head as if to say *do what ye wish.* Hamish's grin widened. Relaxing in the knowledge that he'd just garnered a point in the game of treachery, he rounded and walked toward the stables while he wrestled with the unease that swelled in his gut.

Cursing to himself as he strode away, he grappled with the fact the zealot was fully intent on wooing Lachlan's sister. How would he keep an eye on her and rendezvous with the Covenanters tonight?

Malcolm, Finlay, and Dougal were the only people he could trust with her, but his laird's brother and friends might be in danger as well, and under the guise of their estrangement, he couldn't risk being seen with them.

After hearing of the murder early this morning of the trusted cousin of the Marquess of Montrose, leader of the Royalist cause, Alan had decided that even though the threat was supposed to come after the meeting, someone was getting a head start on attacking those loyal to King Charles. If these men were daring enough to attack the leader's kin in a crowded castle, there was no telling how low they would stoop.

He might just have to shove Kirstie and Malcolm in a wagon and ship them back to Kentillie. That was the only place they were safe.

The smell of dried grass and grain floated in the air as he entered through the main stable door. Malcolm and Blair stood guard at the entrance, waiting on Kirstie to join them, but he skirted around, making no eye contact with his adopted brother.

Where is she?

Hurrying to find her, he looked into each stall crowded with the horses of all the visiting clan chiefs. Dozens more belonged to curious Scots who had come to Edinburgh to see what would come from the meeting.

He saw her just ahead. Stilling, he slid into the shadows. She brushed the horse he'd seen her riding moments earlier. As she stroked, she whispered in its ear as if telling the beast her most intimate secrets. The steed nickered and nudged in to listen. He tilted his head but couldn't make out the words.

She'd always had a way with horses. It was like they understood each other on some fundamental level no one else could see. They had a secret language.

There had always been something soothing about watching her with the horses. Maybe it was the calm, nurturing way she cared for the animals or the quiet, lilting tone she saved for them alone.

She'd always had bonny eyes, but now he saw that with one heated gaze, she could send a man down to his knees begging for her touch. But it was more than that. She was more confident and knew how to wield her feminine charms. She had become dangerous.

Hell, what was he thinking? She'd always been dangerous.

He shouldn't have followed her here. Something hidden down deep drew him closer to her, pulling him toward the peaceful ritual he'd lost when she left.

"The animals at Kentillie have missed ye," he said as he rested his arm on the beam at the entrance to the stall. Leaning against it, he took her in and hoped to give off an air of nonchalance.

"I am sure Wallace has taken good care of them." She stopped brushing and looked up at him. He liked that she was tall and didn't have to crane her neck to meet his eyes.

"Aye, but he's no' ye."

"I'm fair certain that he has treated them well."

"Why did ye go?" He stepped into the stall and shut the door, cutting off her escape.

She angled her chin up and stiffened, but her tone remained calm. It was as if they were discussing someone else, not her, not him. "Ye ken why I left."

"But ye didnae have to be gone so long." He reached out and fingered a ringlet of her hair. She didn't retreat, but she didn't encourage him to move closer.

"Aye. I did. I was not going to follow Brodie down that path."

How could she compare herself to Brodie? The man had nearly gone mad when Skye had left him. Kirstie had just been a girl. There was no way she could have had those types of feelings for Alan. He'd done the right thing by telling her there would never be anything between them.

She backed and reached to hang the brush on a hook. It seemed a natural movement, but it was her attempt at putting distance between them. Once, he'd been the one to push her away, so why did it bother him now that she retreated from his touch?

"Skye is back, and they are happy," he said.

"Aye, that may be true. But ye of all people ken that 'twould no' be the same outcome for me. 'Tis better that I found my own way."

No one had ever told him she had left because of him. As far as he knew, her departure had been planned for weeks. He just woke up one day and she was gone to Blair's for a visit with a story that the Macnabs were in need of her assistance with their stables. He had never imagined that trip would last for years and she wouldn't even come home to visit.

Time went by and life had gone on, but had it for her? Even if it hadn't, circumstances would never change. Even if he had had feelings for her, she was Lachlan's sister. The one man on earth he would never betray.

Kirstie shrugged past him in the small space, her skirts swishing across his legs; he had to fight the urge to coil his arm around her waist and draw her to him. The proximity felt intimate, or maybe it was the conversation.

She opened the door, went through, and waited for him to follow. He did, and she continued down the corridor to the main door with him trailing behind like she had followed him as a youth.

"Yer family has missed ye."

They came out into the fresh air, and he had to squint from the brightness of the midday sun. Thankfully, Malcolm had already retreated with Blair.

"I see them." Her hands were fisted in her skirts.

He wished for the days when she wasn't afraid to talk to him, the days when her thoughts and emotions were laid bare on her face for him to see. Now, he realized how he'd enjoyed her fixation on him. He missed her affections. Why? Maybe because he felt undeserving.

"But do ye miss Kentillie?"

He read the longing in her eyes. It seemed the more they talked, the more their old familiar ways were returning. It was comfortable and easy. He felt the urge to take one of her hands in his. When they had been children, they had held hands frequently, but as they grew, he'd pulled back. Being several years older than her, he'd come to the conclusion sooner than she that a relationship between them was impossible.

"Aye, I do. With all my heart." She released her skirts and

clasped her hands together behind her back as they continued to edge their way toward the castle.

"Then ye should come back." His thumbs slid in circles over his forefingers.

"Nae, 'tis better this way. I am needed where I am now." A resigned sadness appeared in the depths of her eyes.

She'd moved on. Strangely, it felt as if the air had been knocked out of him.

"'Tis time I marry soon. I am sure my husband would take me away from Kentillie anyway."

His steps faltered, but she was focused on something ahead and didn't notice. Recovering, he caved to the temptation and reached for her hand, urging her to a stop. Her long, delicate fingers were warm as they lay motionless in his grasp. Freezing at his touch, she shifted her gaze slowly back to him. Her cheeks reddened to the hue of a mountain bearberry bush as their leaves burst into a crimson shade with the coming of cooler weather.

"Ye should come home and find a Cameron."

"Nae, I have plenty of options. I just have to choose." She pulled her hand free and clasped it to the other in front of her skirts.

"Who are they?" He heard the edge in his voice and despised the traitorous tone that reverberated in his chest. Lachlan needed to keep a closer eye on her.

"Why should I tell ye?" Her tone taunted him.

"Because I want to ken ye will be well cared for."

"I willnae let ye choose my husband for me." She laughed.

"Then ye should let Lachlan."

She indulged him with a smile but turned and kept walking.

"'Tis Blair and John." She picked up her stride.

"Are ye considering John, then?"

"For what?"

"Yer husband?" He growled.

"Oh, aye." She shrugged. She was almost at a run now, but he kept pace.

"Ye dinnae sound enthusiastic. Do ye love him?"

She stopped, turning back to face him, her brow crinkled. She had to think about it, then.

"He will do."

What did that mean? She deserved someone she would be happy with. But some part of him was happy she didn't love John Macnab. He would be just as bad for her as Hamish. No one knew for sure where the Macnab loyalties lay.

Her tone took on a tinge of annoyance. "Stop this talk of husbands. 'Tis the last thing I want to think of on such a beautiful day."

Did she just roll her eyes at me? She pivoted and started walking again.

He couldn't let it go. "Hamish. Are ye considering that peacock?" his voice rumbled.

"I thought he was yer friend. I saw ye with him today."

Wanting to deny the claim, he clamped his teeth shut to prevent the truth from spilling out, because he had to pretend to like that stuffy, poor excuse of a Highlander.

Reaching the Macnabs, he opened his mouth to ask for her answer, but Blair grabbed Kirstie's arm, guiding her toward the hall as she broke into excited chatter. "What took ye so long? I'm famished."

Without another word to him, Kirstie followed, leaving him to trail in their wake with John in tow.

John's gaze lit on him as speculation and accusation swirled in the distrustful depths of his eyes. "Ye have been seen with Hamish Menzies at Greyfriars. Ye should watch what company ye keep." His brows rose disapprovingly, and the lines around his lips tightened.

"Ye should keep Blair and Kirstie away from him," Alan

countered, hoping the man held some sway with the lasses.

"I will look out for my sister, but shouldnae Kirstie's welfare be the job of a Cameron?" Dark eyes peered at him. "*Mackenzie*?"

As Lachlan and Malcolm trusted John to keep an eye on Kirstie, which meant he was likely a Royalist despite his father's political vacillation, Alan took his use of the Mackenzie name as a direct challenge. Everyone knew the Mackenzies were Covenanters.

"My family was exiled by the Mackenzies. The Camerons raised me." It was evasive but would give the man an idea of where his loyalties lay without having to admit them.

John clasped him on the shoulder. "I'm happy to hear that."

A group of unattended little boys ran into the hall tossing a potato around. One threw too hard and missed his target. Landing on a table, the vegetable knocked over a cup of ale, causing it to splash onto a man seated on the bench.

Despite the man's large girth, he had an elongated neck, big beady eyes, and rounded ears that reminded Alan of a weasel. The ale-soaked man stood and wobbled around the table, starting toward the lad who had thrown it. Rushing, Alan got to the child just before the other man's palm connected with the boy's cheek, catching and holding his wrist midair.

"What the hell?" Face reddening, the weasel jerked free from his grasp and backed, taking in the size of the threat that stood between the man's rage and the small child.

"'Twas an accident. There is no need to harm the lad," he managed to say with calm even though every muscle in his body twitched and urged him to escort the man outside and take him to task for raising a hand to a defenseless child.

"'Twill teach him to no' do it again." Spittle flew from his mouth.

"Touch him and I will take ye outside and show ye what it looks like when someone bigger than ye picks a fight with someone weaker."

The man's gaze roamed over his solid frame to assess the situation, then eyes darting down in defeat, the weasel let out a frustrated growl. Backing off slightly, but returning cold fury to his gaze, the man huffed, "Ye do him no' favors by protecting him."

"Aye, I believe I do," Alan said.

The man pinned him with a defiant stare then turned on his heels and stalked away.

Alan watched to make sure the man wasn't a threat before looking to the boy and pointing, indicating a spot where he wished to talk to the lad. He stopped to retrieve the potato along the way. The other boys joined them, appreciation showing in their faces as he knelt down to their level.

"'Tis probably a good idea to save this"—he nodded toward the potato he held in his hand—"for outside play."

The youngest of the three stared at him wide eyed, while the middle child nodded and the oldest studiously avoided his gaze. "There are a lot of men and women in here who have forgotten what 'tis like to be a child." Alan tossed the makeshift toy from hand to hand.

"Will ye be giving us that back?" The oldest, who stood with feet braced shoulder width apart, crossed his arms.

"Aye, but ye must ken since yer are the biggest, 'tis yer responsibility to look out for these two."

The child pouted but nodded.

"Can I rely on ye to keep them safe and out of trouble? Ye look verra capable." The boy straightened his shoulders but also seemed less tense, obviously realizing Alan was not a threat to the younger boys.

"Aye," the leader said.

He tossed the potato back to the oldest and winked. The

boy finally gave him a smile.

"Now, make sure ye avoid that man. He willnae be happy I didnae let him strike yer friend."

"'Twill no' let him hurt Artair. He's me brother."

"Good. Take care of them both. Now run along and stay out of trouble."

The trio brushed by him and headed straight for the open door.

When he turned his attention back to the room, the first thing he noticed was that John Macnab was no longer by his side; the second was that Kirstie's gaze was fixed on him. She looked away, but a small part of him rejoiced until he noticed she had gone straight to the table where the Campbell she'd been dancing with the night before sat. The one whose arms had been all over her as they'd danced.

Hell, she cannae be considering him.

Kirstie gave the rogue a smile and dipped low enough to entice him with a peek at the round globes of the top of her breasts. The corner of the man's mouth went up, and even from this distance, he could see the arse's eyes spark with interest. He was a dangerous man. What was she doing?

Sitting just on the other side of him was The Earl of Argyll. Did she know the vipers she was getting mixed up with?

As soon as the midday meal was over, despite the plan to keep his distance, he would find a way to get a message to Malcolm. Someone had to tighten the reins on the man's sister.

If Malcolm didn't put an end to it, he would.

Chapter Four

Kirstie easily shook her guard and spent the afternoon exploring. The last thing she wanted was to waste the day hidden away in that stuffy castle. After learning earlier he would be out of the stone fortress and in Edinburgh tonight, she planned to try Argyll's room again before the halls filled with the rest of the guests scheduled to arrive. Before that, she would force herself to dance in the great hall with anyone who might have the plans for the imminent attack on her brothers, so she needed this fresh air to bolster her courage.

She didn't want to contend with the men who felt they had the right to put their hands on her wherever they pleased, Campbell being one of them. But he seemed to be the one closest to Argyll and would be the one most likely aware of Argyll's plans, so she had to put up with his pawing for now.

This spying business wasn't for her. But if it meant saving her family, she would stay in this filthy city and see her plans through. It was a shame she couldn't confide in Malcolm. But he was hot tempered, and she couldn't rely on him to not do something that might jeopardize his life sooner. Lachlan would know what to do, but he wasn't here.

That left Alan.

He could help, but he was cavorting with Covenanters. She had an excuse for being around them. The Macnab laird, whose clan she'd been residing with, had become sympathetic to the Covenanter cause, even hosting some of them on occasion. It was how she'd grown to know Hamish, as he frequently visited the laird. But how could Alan associate with them?

After all the time he'd spent with the Camerons, he must know they wished her brothers harm.

What had happened between her family and Alan in her absence? The man she knew wouldn't betray her brothers, but there it was: she no longer knew *Alan Mackenzie*. When he'd introduced himself earlier, he'd aligned himself with his birth family instead of her clan.

Alan would never do anything to harm Lachlan, but what if he had grown sympathetic to their cause? He had been returning with Hamish earlier, and if her guess was correct, they had been coming from the Kirk. Could he have converted? In her absence the last few years, she'd done her best to forget him, and as much as she wanted to trust him, she couldn't.

Passing by the stables, she reminisced on what it was about Alan that had drawn her to him in her youth. He'd always been bonny, but that wasn't the reason; it was that he used to visit her as she tended to the horses and made her feel as if she could be more than a simple lass meant for all the repetitive tasks of day to day castle life.

They would talk about what she was reading, and he made up stories better than any of those she'd found in the binding of a book. She'd been able to listen to him, fascinated for hours. Alan had also been the only one to encourage her interest in animals, even helping her evade music lessons when her tutor came looking for her. He'd understood her, or at least she'd thought he had.

She strolled down and away from the castle, alone and unaware of anything around her. As she did, her thoughts turned to the last time she'd seen Alan.

She'd been seventeen, and he'd been nearly a grown man. There was a celebration of the birth of the stable master Wallace's first grandson taking place at the keep. The great hall of Kentillie had been bursting with people drinking and singing and shoving into each other. It had been too much for her, so she'd escaped to one of her favorite places, the stables. No one was there that night.

She was talking to one of the horses that had become jittery with the uncommon quiet of the night when a figure walked in through the door and strolled past the stalls. Alan.

Her heart raced with the excitement that coursed through her veins anytime she found herself in his presence. Earlier in the day, she'd had a conversation with her friend Donella about her feelings. Donella told her it was time to let Alan know how she felt, and she agreed.

"Good night," she said to the horse, giving it a soft pet on the muzzle then turning to leave the stall. This was her chance because lately, Alan was always with either Lachlan or Malcolm.

When she emerged from the stall in front of him, he gave her a small smile, but his shoulders sagged and no joy reached his eyes. Actually, he didn't really even look at her. He was off somewhere else as he skirted around her and kept going.

She'd never seen him look so sad, and her heart ached to reach out to him. His hands shook. It was hard to make out in the low light of the stables, but there appeared to be blood dripping down his knuckles.

Taking a few quick steps to catch him, she reached out for his arm. He flinched and drew back to strike as if he was expecting the devil, but he stilled when he realized it was her.

She pulled his hand up to inspect it. It was blood. She tenderly touched it. "What happened?"

"'Twas just a brawl. 'Twill be all right." He tried to pull away and keep walking, but she held him.

"I-I have been wanting to tell ye something." Her voice caught as she tripped on the words that would lay her soul naked before him.

"Can it wait, brat?" She should have kenned then, should have stopped, should have run, but she had been young and foolish.

"Nae, Alan, I've waited too long." Her thundering heart wouldn't let her back down now.

Reaching with her free hand, she rested it on his cheek. He shuddered and closed his eyes, seeming to lean in to her touch. Taking the caress of his soft flesh in her palm as encouragement, as a sign that he welcomed her affections, she pressed on.

Her eyes stung and threatened to run over, even at the memory now. She thought she had moved on, believed her heart safe, but even these last couple years with the Macnabs had not relieved the pressure. It had been hidden beneath the surface waiting to bubble up and seize her again.

The rest of that fateful night played through her head. There, in the middle of her sanctuary, her gaze had met his, and she thought they held desire. But now Kirstie knew she had been too inexperienced to comprehend what she had seen. "I love ye, Alan." Her confession was shaky, because it had come from the too-tall girl with no figure and no confidence. His breath seemed to hitch, but he said nothing. She moved closer and rose up on her tiptoes to place a gentle kiss on his lips. They both stilled.

His arms wound around her and crushed her to his muscled chest. His lips were moving over hers, and she did her best to match the caress. His tongue jutted out and delved between her lips.

Gasping in surprise, she quickly recovered. He was honey and male and everything she had ever wanted. Letting her own tongue duel with his, she thought he groaned, and his grasp around her waist tightened.

The moment was gone just as quickly. Withdrawing, he grabbed both of her shoulders while holding her stiffly at arm's length. His fingers dug sharply into her skin. "This cannae ever happen again."

Her body closed in on itself as his words slapped her, causing a numb tingling to erupt somewhere deep inside, and if he'd not been holding her, she was certain she would have fallen. Her tongue was frozen, her breath lost or stolen.

"Kirstie, do ye understand?"

She didn't, but she nodded anyway, not really knowing what she was agreeing to.

"I could never do this to Lachlan. He's the closest thing I have to family, my brother. Ye are like a sister to me."

Her body started to vibrate as chills extended from her chest to her fingertips. He had rejected her. Not only that, he thought of her as nothing more than family.

If a heart could crack, hers was bleeding and leaking out into every cavity of her body. She was like the cook's cat the time an overzealous dog bounded toward it, unmoving and waiting for the impact, for the rest of her world to end.

And then it happened. Letting go, he turned and, without another sound, stalked away. Numbly, she watched as his long lean legs carried him and her dreams out through the back door of the stable. She stumbled back to the stall she'd been in with the lonely horse. Collapsing into the straw in the corner, she curled up into a ball and let the pain drown her in darkness.

The next day, she had been able to convince her mother

and Lachlan that she should go to Blair's for an extended visit. Receiving a request the week previously from her cousin begging for her to come for a visit and help tend some ill horses, she jumped at the chance to flee her humiliation.

Then, every time Lachlan and her mother would come to see her, she found a way to stay when they insisted she return. She was pretty certain at this point that her oldest brother had guessed why she was reluctant to return. Each time Alan's name was mentioned, she either left the room or changed the subject.

She'd not been able to keep the truth from her mother because she had the uncanny ability to read anyone. She and Blair were the only two people who knew of her secret shame.

Her life had meaning again, and she didn't need that infuriating Highlander. The Macnab stables had been in disarray when she'd made it to their lands, unhealthily dirty stalls and dingy, putrid water the previous caregivers didn't refresh near enough, equipment not cleaned, and the beasts treated poorly. Only losing a couple of the ill horses that had been too far gone upon her arrival, she had saved the rest and convinced the Macnab laird to let her take over as their stable master.

Those horses were her life now, and she couldn't see herself anywhere else, despite the knowledge she would have to find a husband once Blair married. She didn't want to be near a man who didn't want her, especially one with gray eyes the color of tumultuous Highland skies before the heavens unleashed a summer storm.

Kirstie continued to explore, coming to an old abbey whose outbuildings lay peacefully moldering in the late afternoon sun. They were deserted, but not eerie, just sad. It had been such a beautiful place, but the walls had crumbled and left a shell of what it had once been.

This temple had been built to hold the hearts of its

Catholic worshipers, just like she had set herself up to be the keeper of Alan's heart, the protector of his soul, and the person he would come home to at night. She was just like this forsaken place. Despite the distance she had put between Alan and her, there had been no way to outrun the desolation that had been left by his rejection.

She'd heard stones of the cloisters had been ripped down and were used to add onto the castle high on the hill. The roof of the nave was still intact and the beautiful arched windows and doors inspired awe, but it felt like a cold, empty tomb. Had Alan found someone else and given that lucky lass the pieces of his heart, the ones she had so desperately wanted?

Her feet felt heavy as she climbed the hill back to the castle. Dread filled every step as she planned out the evening ahead, determined to make progress on her quest.

· · ·

Sending Blair ahead with a story that she would skip the meal tonight due to women's problems, Kirstie bided her time until Malcolm's guards outside her door disappeared. 'Twas for the best, because the main course might be a better time to sneak into the Earl of Argyll's room.

Slinking toward the other side of the castle, she stuck to the shadows and did her best to avoid being seen. She had brought several different tools to try this time, determined that damn lock would open for her. Standing in the darkened hall yet again, her hands shook and her heart beat so fast she could feel it in her ears.

The hairpins proved to be too weak, bending as she fidgeted with them in the small hole. The wooden knitting needle she'd found in one of the antechambers rewarded her with a solid click on the first try. Finally breathing, she stood to check the hall before turning the knob and backing silently into the room.

This was one of the larger chambers, and despite the earlier warmth of the sunny day, peat blazed in the fireplace to keep the evening chill from the room. It supplied ample light but did nothing to sate the fear that kept her eyes darting around the deep shadows of the stone corners. Slinking over to the desk, her fingers trembled as she rifled through the papers scattered on the smooth wooden surface.

Maps detailing different areas of the Highlands and letters about commissioning men to fight for the Covenanters, names she didn't recognize, blurred as she strained to focus in on any imminent threat, and it wasn't long before she found her eyes watering at the lines of the letters and intricate details on the maps. Rifling through the drawers, she discovered the rest of the documents all had to do with crops and cattle.

Resisting the urge to throw all the documents into the fire just to thwart any undiscoverable evil plans they contained, she pushed back from the desk, deciding it was best not to alert the Covenanters to someone searching their rooms. Letting out a frustrated breath, she scanned the surroundings; it dawned on her that she should have guessed there would be nothing incriminating in his room. The earl was a cautious man. This had all been a huge waste of time.

The lock clicked in the door, and she inhaled sharply. Kirstie fell to her knees and rolled under the desk. She focused on controlling her breath. One little sound could get her discovered. What was the penalty for breaking into the Earl of Argyll's room? Surely, she would be put in prison, and she couldn't save her brothers from the dungeon.

She didn't hear another sound, but the fire exposed a large shadow that could only be a man. It moved toward the desk, and a hand clasped onto her arm, dragging her out from under the wooden structure.

"What do ye think ye are doing?"

Fear almost turned to annoyance when she realized the voice was Alan's.

He didn't give her time to answer as he yanked her across the room and to the other side of the chamber in an instant. Opening the door, he peeked out into the hall. He must have liked their chances, because he dragged her from the room and shut the door. Thankful she was tall and didn't have to strain to keep up, they'd taken three large strides in the direction of Malcolm's room when the sound of boots marched down the hall.

Alan's arm still latched onto her like an eagle that had captured its prey. He stopped and spun her around, backing her harshly to the wall. She inhaled sharply at the impact. He stood over her with his arms on the walls beside her head in a fierce protective stance. Trembling, her hands locked onto Alan's sides. His warmth was reassuring, but the tempo of his steady heartbeat thrummed into her fingertips. The rhythm of her own faltered at his close proximity.

"Hell, they're going to see ye." His gaze darted from the sound and back to her.

As the clacking cadence of the approaching threat neared, she spared a glance down the hall to see how close the man was, but Alan's position blocked her view. When she glanced back, something had shifted in his eyes, and her inhalation of air lodged in her throat, the bodice of her gown becoming tight and restrictive as her chest swelled.

In the scant light of the hall, she imagined his eyes had darkened and dilated. Was it fear or hunger she saw there? Maybe both. Shuddering, her lips parted to let in the air that refused to reach her lungs.

She froze as his hands came down to clasp both of her cheeks, again seeming to hide her face from the newcomer. One thumb traced her lips as his breathing became heavy. She, on the other hand, couldn't breathe as his head dipped closer.

Damn, he was going to kiss her.

Her body heated and her chin tilted up, lips parted to give him easy access. No, he was going to destroy her. But right now she didn't care. Exhilaration rushed through her as she realized she was going to let him do what he wanted. Awareness and desire claimed her as his head dipped, and it became too late to protest as his lips covered hers.

She had kissed other men since her first kiss with him, so this time she thought she would be prepared when his tongue swept into her mouth. Yes, she had had other kisses, but none of them had made her come undone the way his did. None made her forget the world around her like his caress.

Surrendering, she gave everything to him. All the years of pent-up longing and frustration manifested in such stark need that her body took control and left her logical side reeling at how easy she succumbed to his touch. Her hands slid higher to curl around thick arms and grabbed on, pulling him closer. His tongue tangled and played with hers, and she thought she would explode with the feelings that were ignited deep in her chest.

Everything disappeared except him and this embrace. He groaned into her mouth, and her fingers skimmed up to his neck to thread their way to thick tresses that slid through her hands like French silk. They tightened in the shoulder length tendrils at the base of his neck as she slanted her head to the side to give him better access.

Alan leaned into her, crushing her between the solid wall of his chest and the stone behind her. It didn't hurt, it was real and warm, and it felt right. As they continued to kiss, her body became heated and needy, an ache growing in her, and she knew this kiss wouldn't be enough.

"Take her to a room." Some deep male voice jested from behind as she became aware of the boots as they continued past them and down the hall.

Alan froze, hands unmoving on her cheeks, pulled back and rested his head on hers as he continued to shield her from the view of the passing man.

No, screamed a voice deep inside her head, *no, no, no, please don't stop.*

A click sounded and then a soft thud of a door closing.

Kirstie fought to control her breath as Alan stayed still, face near enough she could smell sage on his ragged breath. Pressed so close, she could feel his heart pounding. It was a rhythm that called to the deepest part of her and spoke to feeling long buried. The thumping beat played the notes she had yearned for but not found until now. His head nuzzled into hers, and he spoke softly into her ear, "Are ye trying to get yerself killed?"

Her body was still reeling from the passion he had awoken in her. All she could do was shake her head.

His voice became hoarse and raw. "Dinnae ever let me catch ye doing something so foolish again. Ye willnae be able to sit for a year."

Anger had seeped into his words, and the pleasure she'd felt was replaced by a bone-numbing chill. He straightened and retreated. Now, her limbs were cold as well. More boots clambered down the hall, but she didn't look. Her eyes were fixated on the flames she saw dancing in Alan's eyes. For a moment, she dared to think they were filled with need for her, but then they flickered and all she saw was irritation.

Her wobbly limbs were difficult to peel from the wall, but she forced herself to move because she didn't have to listen to him. Sticking her nose up in the air, she attempted to move gracefully toward the stairs.

"Kirstie." He grabbed her wrist, pulling her toward Malcolm's door. Even that touch set sparks ablaze on her skin, and she wanted to cry from the sheer frustration of it.

After inserting a key into the lock, he pushed in the door, drawing her in behind him and shutting it with a soft clunk. "Ye have no business playing games with Argyll. What did ye think ye were doing?" Fury was evident in the soft hiss of his whispered words, and her gaze drifted down to avoid his penetrating eyes.

"Kirstie, what are ye doing up here?" Malcolm asked from a corner of the room. She gulped, thankful he'd made his presence known before she'd been forced to make up some unbelievable lie and annoy Alan further.

"I need an escort to the hall. Blair is already there without me." She avoided Alan's eyes and tried to pull free from his grip, but his fingers didn't budge.

"Aye, of course. I am on my way there right now," her brother said.

Alan said, "I just caught Kirstie breaking into Argyll's room. Dinnae let her out of yer sight tonight." Something passed between them in some shared code she wasn't privy to.

Releasing her, he stalked over and whispered something to Malcolm. Why would the two be keeping secrets?

Malcolm said something inaudible, then both gazes shot in her direction. "What were ye thinking, Kirstie?"

'Twas thinking I would save yer life, she thought, but she held her tongue.

"Ye shouldnae be seen here." She was about to protest when she saw Malcolm's brows rise as he gazed at Alan, not her.

Alan nodded and turned. Opening the door, he peered out as if checking to make sure the hall was abandoned then retreated without another word.

"Why can he no' be seen here?" She turned her gaze to her younger brother and tried to forget the tingling sensation still humming on her swollen lips.

The kiss had meant nothing to him, and he had shredded her heart again, interrupting her quest for answers in the process. Well, maybe he had actually helped her, because she wasn't sure if the man who had spoken to them in the hall went into the earl's room or another. She had been so wrapped up in how Alan's embrace had felt like home and mist on a hot day that she hadn't cared.

"Dinnae worry with that," Malcolm answered. "'Tis best if Alan doesnae appear to take sides during these negotiations."

They *were* keeping secrets.

Her brother broke into her thoughts. "Ye have some explaining to do. Mayhap I should send ye back home to let Lachlan deal with ye." Shaking his head, he started for the door, opening it and nodding for her to exit. She stopped as he turned to lock the door, then he proceeded down the hall without her.

She wanted to leave, but then she remembered why she couldn't.

The day she had first arrived at Edinburgh with Blair and John, she had lingered in the stables to brush down Poseidon. It had become a ritual for both of them after a long ride.

Deep male whispers carried from just a few steps away. The men nearby hadn't known she was there.

"The Cameron laird is not traveling with them."

She cocked her head to better hear. Were they speaking about Lachlan?

"He sent his brother in his stead."

"We cannae take the Cameron clan with either alive." The voice sounded familiar, but with the hushed tones, she couldn't make it out. Heart racing, she shifted to make sure Poseidon's body kept her hidden.

"Ye will have to be the one to tell Argyll. Mayhap he will have someone send for the Lochiel."

Kirstie bit her lip and ducked down as they mentioned her oldest brother's title. These were the men plotting the death of her brothers.

. . .

Alan adjusted his painfully hard cock as he bounded down the steps. He groaned and shook his head to dislodge his treacherous thoughts. It didn't work. She tasted just as he'd remembered, honey and spice, and she'd melted into him with those curves and long legs.

He could still feel where her breasts had been crushed to his chest. Ugh, he wanted to scream in frustration. *Hell.* If she were any other lass, if she had another name, if she wasn't Lachlan's sister, he would have claimed her.

It all came down to honor and betrayal and things you just did not do. If Lachlan were here now, maybe he would find the courage to beg for her. But the only thing he had ever learned worth any value from his father was that you did not betray your brother.

He wanted Kirstie so badly he could taste her, but two things stood in the way. He couldn't be a husband to her. What if his father's brand of madness affected him? It was a risk he wasn't willing to take, and she deserved so much better. Her love and devotion were worth more than what he could offer. Not only that, he couldn't betray the one man whose loyalty and approval he valued over everything or the one woman who made him want to forget he wasn't worth her affections.

As he snuck down the hall to avoid being seen near Malcolm's room, he reminded himself that the safety of his brother and sister came first, aye—*Kirstie was like a sister, sister, sister*, he repeated to himself. As he entered the stairwell, he told himself the impulse to kiss her had been to protect her from the man coming toward them, but he was having trouble believing that had been his only reason.

It had been necessary; no one needed to know she had been there. And it had worked. The man had no idea who they were, but touching her had reawakened that longing he'd pushed away after the first time she'd kissed him. The timing had been so wrong on that night, too.

The events of that long ago evening were still etched in his head like the initials of scorned lovers on an old oak.

It had seemed as if the entire Cameron clan had been crowded into Kentillie to celebrate. That didn't bother him. What did was the inebriated state of several of the clan and the pressure to join them in drinking the whisky and ale.

Having the urge to escape, he fled the crowded hall in favor of the cool night air. A squeak caught his attention, and he glanced over to the side of the building to see a large Cameron man had pinned Arabella to a wall and she was screaming at him. Arabella was a manipulative wench, but no man should lay a hand on a woman when she didn't wish it.

Rushing to her defense, he put a hand on the beefy man's shoulder. "Leave her be, Angus."

The red-faced, sweaty lout turned, and a wave of liquor-soaked breath spewed on him. "Go away," the man slurred. "'Tis none of yer concern."

"Aye, 'tis if the lady does no' seek yer attentions."

Angus's arms fell, and the lass stole from behind him to run into the castle. The lout grabbed Alan's arm and then swung with the other. Alan ducked to the side, and the blow just skimmed his chin.

Memories of the beatings he'd endured by his father's hand assailed him, but unlike in his youth, he fought back. Everything blurred, and before he knew what was happening, Angus lay whimpering on the ground with a battered face. Disgusted with what spirits did to a man, and that he'd lost his temper and resorted to violence, his legs carried him toward the stables.

His hands shook with rage at his family's curse and that he'd let the anger consume him. He'd had no control, and the correlation between his father and he had never been so prominent. He was a monster.

Kirstie was there, and she kissed him. He liked it. But when he opened his eyes, he saw blood covering his bruised knuckles and remembered who she was and what he was. He would never be good enough for her, and Lachlan would kill him if he touched her and didn't wed her.

Releasing Kirstie, he swung away and walked out to the loch to be alone. Within the next week, she was gone. He'd always known it was for the best, but every time he walked by the stables, he still caught his gaze drifting through the windows to look for her.

Trusting Malcolm would watch out for her, Alan continued out through a side door instead of waiting for the pair to appear in the great hall. She must know something of the plot against the Royalist lairds or she wouldn't have been snooping in Argyll's rooms. He'd tried to retrieve her as soon as he'd seen her slip into the earl's room, but people kept appearing, and he couldn't be seen going in, either. He'd gotten to her, probably saved her life, but it had taken longer than he'd wanted.

If he weren't trying to avoid being seen with Malcolm, he'd talk to him about sending Kirstie to Kentillie now. But he had to keep up the ruse that he and the Camerons were no longer friends. It was the only way the Covenanters would let him into their inner circle.

For now, he was off to The Full Cask to pretend to be someone he wasn't while that silly Hamish Menzies put his hands on Kirstie. He might have to start a brawl with someone. More points for him if the man was a known Royalist so he could impress the Covenanters. John Macnab had better stay away from him tonight.

Several hours later, he walked back into the hall to find Kirstie dancing with Hamish and Malcolm nowhere in sight. He had thought she was safe with her brother around, but maybe he didn't grasp the importance of the situation. He couldn't blame Malcolm since he'd lived without a sister to watch over for years. This was Lachlan's fault for letting her have too much freedom.

Kirstie's cheeks were red with exertion. How long had she been dancing? Then he noticed how slow she was moving and how carefully she watched her steps. Hell, she'd been drinking.

Debating whether or not he should grab her and escort her out of the room to scold her for being so careless, he opted for rubbing his head and eyes to tame his temper. She was going to drive him mad. He knew when someone was drinking, their nature was amplified. Another lesson from his father.

She was a sensual woman. Hamish was watching her like a hawk closing in on a mouse. Niall Campbell's eyes were on her as well; so were several other men he didn't know. He had to get her out of here.

Song ending, he prowled over to them and bowed politely. What he really wanted to do was drive his fist into the man's gut, but he needed to remain in his good graces for now. Straightening, he took Kirstie's hand. "May I?" Hoping he didn't come across as uncivil, he gave neither of them the chance to answer as he drew her in and whisked her away.

Kirstie's eye's widened, but she'd had too much to drink to react in time or protest with her usual fervor. He had gathered her close, and they were twirling around to some music he'd never heard and could have done without, but she was safe and she was in his arms. Now that he could breathe again, the anger returned.

"Ye look like ye drank a whole barrel by yerself tonight." He tried to keep the bite he felt out of the comment.

Mornings of waking to find his mother battered and passed out on the floor ate at him. He might not have been big enough to help his mother, but he would never let it happen to Kirstie.

Kirstie's eyes were weary, showing none of the fury he'd expected her to turn his way. "I couldnae handle the crowds." Shrugging as she offered the explanation, he let the words play over in his head.

She'd always stuck to the corners of a room. It was one of the things he had loved about her. She was a solitary soul like he and avoided the celebrations where anyone was drinking. He'd never thought about why and assumed it was because she didn't want to be around the vile liquid. Now, he realized she had her own reasons.

Biting her lip, she looked down, and he'd swear her cheeks were blushing if they weren't already flushed from the dancing and drink.

"Does the close quarters bother ye?" Guilt stabbed at him when he remembered his rush through the crowd last night as he'd dragged her along and then the paler color of her skin as they'd made it outside.

"Aye. I've always felt sick when there are too many people about."

She leaned into him and rested her head on his chest. She was just tall enough for him; their bodies fit. Och, the touch was light and innocent, but it sent a wave of longing coursing through him. She was vulnerable, and some part of him that wanted to be her rock reveled in the soft weight, wanted to pull her closer and say "mine."

He yearned to stay like this, but people were watching as they swished by with the music he could no longer hear.

Somehow, he and Kirstie had stopped moving, and the moment had apparently become too intimate for the bustling dance floor. Reluctantly, he drew back, but not wanting to lose the connection completely, he snaked his arm through hers.

"Let's get ye back to yer room. Where's Blair?"

"John was escorting her and Henry on a walk." She leaned into his side, and her free hand reached over her midsection to clasp onto his arm. The embrace was warm like a hug, and she inhaled deeply then closed her eyes as if she'd been smelling him.

"Who's Henry?"

"Henry Graham. He's the cousin to the Marquess of Montrose."

He knew Henry, and although the man was a staunch Royalist, he was rumored to be quite violent. Another of their kin had been found murdered in the castle this morning, and with the intrigue about, he lamented that Kirstie and her friend seemed to be involved on all political sides.

"And what would they be doing with the Royalist leader's kin? I thought their father supported the Covenanters."

"Aye, but John is different, and I think he's trying to arrange a match between Henry and Blair."

"And she agrees to the plan?" He doubted any of them knew of Henry's reputation.

"Aye. She's infatuated with Henry's good looks." They'd reached the edge of the hall.

"They should be back soon. I can wait here for them."

He didn't trust anyone but a Cameron with Kirstie. "I'll take ye. Do ye have any idea what happened to yer brother?" Scanning the crowd, he spied Malcolm, who had reappeared, his gaze resting on them. He nodded so only Malcolm could see and kept walking them toward the door as he carefully took the least crowded route.

"Aye, 'tis stomach problems. He keeps running in and out."

That explained why he'd not seen Malcolm on the way in.

A figure almost bumped into her, and Alan pulled Kirstie closer to narrowly avoid the man's body colliding into hers. Hell, she felt so good snuggled up close to him. He cursed himself for allowing such a pleasure.

As they cleared the hall and stepped out into the night air, he voiced what had been bothering him all evening.

"What were ye doing in the earl's rooms?"

"I'm so tired. Can we no' talk about this later?"

Her words were starting to slur together. She pulled from his arm and picked up her pace. Deciding not to push, he followed.

Starting up the steps, Kirstie stumbled, and he wrapped both arms around her before she hit the unforgiving stone. Excessive spirits apparently magnified her awkward movements, but the real problem was his body's reaction to holding her in his arms. Everything in him stilled, and a desire to press his lips to hers once more welled from some deep hidden part of him.

"Thank ye." Tilting toward him, she smiled with sleepy eyes, making him envision lazy days falling into bed with her. His heart thudded. She was too close, but he couldn't find the strength to remove his hands from her sides.

Anytime, he burred in his mind but knew he couldn't say it out loud. He couldn't give her hope when there was none. Not that she wanted him now, anyway. Managing to peel his hands from her delicious curves, he set her straight, watching her carefully as she held up her skirts to ascend the rest of the way. "Yer welcome."

When they reached her room, she retrieved her key from a hidden pocket on her gown. It slipped through her fingers, and she swayed as she dipped to retrieve it from the floor.

"How much did ye drink tonight?"

"Nae much. I'm just no' used to strong drink, and it helped me cope with the crush of people."

"But 'tis also no' safe. There are many dangerous men here."

"Well, I'm lucky then to have ye here with me." She giggled.

"And what if I'm one of those dangerous men?"

Something akin to admiration lit in her gaze, and he wanted to be whatever she saw in those sapphire eyes. "Nae, that's no' who ye are." She placed her hand on his chest, and he wanted to take it in his until he realized she might have done it to steady herself.

"Alan Cameron, ye are a hero and ye'll save me like ye did the lad today." She beamed up at him before dropping her hand and twirling around to insert the key in her door.

When Kirstie pushed it in, he was overcome by the moonlight that shown into the room, causing her brunette hair to shimmer like the dark waters of Loch Arkaig. Pulling his gaze away from her, he noticed the chamber was sparse and lacked a fireplace. He hadn't observed that the previous evening, but his gaze had been on something much more interesting. "It must get cool in here at night."

"Aye, it does. Blair and I huddle under the blankets. We warm up nicely when she isnae stealing the covers."

She's one lucky lass. We would make enough heat we wouldnae even need the blankets. Shaking his head of the stray thought, he turned to close the door as Kirstie walked over to a small table and lit a candle.

He had opted to stay at an inn down the hill from the castle. Finding a room at a tavern close to The Full Cask had given him easy access to the Covenanter's meeting spot. The room was smaller than this one, but it had a fireplace, and the innkeeper kept a nice supply of small peat blocks that burned for just long enough to last through the night.

Hoping his accommodations gave credence to the story that he, Malcolm, and the other Camerons weren't on friendly terms, he now wondered if he should have stayed closer to keep a better eye on Kirstie. He'd been following her this evening, or he wouldn't have seen her enter Argyll's room. A chill ran down his spine even now as he thought of what could have happened to her.

Ambling over to the table, he enjoyed the silhouette of her figure. She had wide hips that gently arched into a small waist. His hands itched to feel those curves, but instead, he reached down to pick up a stack of bound papers.

"What's this?"

Her eyes lit. "'Tis a copy of a play Donna brought me from London."

"Ye still read, then?" He flipped up the binding and read aloud, "*A Chaste Maid in Cheapside*." Puzzling over the strange title, he lifted his gaze to meet her sparkling stare as she took the bundle from him and hugged it to her chest. He'd never been jealous of a book before, but hell, he wished to again be worthy of the affection she'd held for him when she was younger.

"'Tis by Thomas Middleton. His plays are supposed to be wonderful."

"Sounds as if 'tis 'bout some boring wench. I am questioning yer tastes. What happened to the more exciting books I used to catch ye reading up on the turret?" Fond memories of her hair blowing in the wind as her sweet voice carried to his ears came rushing back with nostalgia.

"If I remember correctly, ye found me every time I went to read." Her gaze became glassy, and he couldn't tell if she was reminiscing affectionately or if it was sadness reflected in the blue depths.

Smiling inside, he recalled that she would sneak up to

the turrets at the west end of Kentillie. He followed her every time. He'd been enthralled by the stories she read, and her voice had always been comforting. On occasion, he'd even fallen asleep with his head in her lap as she sat on the stones propped against the wall.

"I will admit that I liked yer stories, but this one?"

Her gaze returned to his, eyes alight as she straightened her shoulders at the challenge. "I havenae read it yet, but 'tis supposed to be good. Shall I read the first scene to prove it?"

"Aye."

He'd always felt at ease with her and taken comfort in her routines. She was predictable—at least she had been before she started cavorting with the enemy. He'd never thought about why her habits had meant so much to him growing up in the Cameron house, but then he remembered the days and years before he'd come to live with them and knew exactly why.

He should leave, but the strength to turn around and walk out the door eluded him.

"Aye, prove to me this story is fit for my ears." Easing down onto the edge of the bed, he patted the thick blankets for her to join him.

Sitting, Kirstie unfolded the first page and started to read. He was taken back in time. He didn't realize how much he had missed this and how soothing it had been. He could listen to her all night. Wanting to do just that, he let his mind stray to stretching out on her bed and falling asleep with her voice filling his ears, knowing she would be there when he woke. Shaking the image free, he grudgingly admitted that as much as he enjoyed this, she deserved better.

As she read, he fantasized about laying her back and making love to her slowly and then falling asleep with her nestled in his arms, her soft curls splayed across his chest. It was an indulgence he couldn't afford.

The reading ended too soon. "What did ye think?"

"Not too bad, but 'twill need to hear more. I dinnae want to rush to a conclusion."

She stood, set the book down, then ran her fingers over the binding as if it were a treasured artifact. "Another time. I'm tired."

Her hips swayed as she walked across the room and stopped in front of another small table. "Ye must be happy Skye is back," she called over her shoulder.

Smiling at the mention of his cousin, he relaxed and leaned back onto the soft bed, resting on his elbows. She turned to him and stretched her neck from side to side.

"Aye, 'tis good. I'm still no' convinced that at some point I willnae have to take off Brodic's head."

Kirstie unpinned her hair and ran her fingers into her scalp to massage where it had been pulled back. Mesmerized, his gaze lingered as she dropped the pins on the table and waves of deep chestnut curls cascaded down to brush her cheeks. He was tempted to reach out and run his own hands through the thick mass, but she seemed oblivious to her effect on him.

He tore his gaze away before he acted on the impulse, because that would surely drive him mad or cause him to lose control.

"'Tis time I get back." He stood and took a step toward the door.

Turning back, his breath caught, gaze landing on her dress as the lavender silk slid down her shoulders before she shimmied her hips to guide it over her waist and then off entirely. He groaned internally as his cock came to life. She was going to drive him mad. She wore an undergarment, but the material was thin, and it didn't cover much. Mouth watering, he had to swallow.

"What are ye doing?"

"Going to bed."

She flung her dress over a chair, slipped out of her shoes, then leaned down to wrestle her stockings free. His mouth went dry. As she leaned down, her shift bunched in the front and gave an enticing glimpse of the tops of her well-proportioned breasts.

"Ye shouldnae be doing that with me in here." He tilted his head to the ceiling, but his treacherous eyes lowered back to take in whatever they could. His heart pounded as he tried to fight the urge to touch every inch of her.

"Why, seems if any man had to be in here, 'tis perfect, 'tis ye."

"What gives ye that idea?"

She narrowed her eyes on him and swayed slightly. "Ye are the only one who isanae trying to get in here to see me undress."

So she wasn't completely unaware of her charms. She had at least four men that he knew of vying for her attention, and the thought of them seeing her like this angered him. None of them were worthy. Hell, he wasn't.

She moved past him to draw back the covers and slide under them.

When she looked back up at him, there was a sadness that had not been there before. Her shoulders were pulled in, and she looked smaller. "What's wrong with me?"

What was she talking about? "There isnae a thing wrong with ye."

"Then why do ye no' want me?"

Her assumption nearly broke his heart, but he couldn't tell her the truth. It wasn't her; she was perfect. She was everything he knew he could never have; she was Kirstie, the girl who had haunted his dreams for years.

He knelt down beside the bed to be at her eye level. "It isnae ye, kitten. Ye couldnae be more right." He couldn't resist pushing back the silky curl that had fallen over her cheek.

"If ye think ye are protecting me, ye are wrong." She burrowed into the bed, and her head tilted into the hand that had lingered at her temple. "The me without ye is more vulnerable than the me with ye by my side."

They were sweet words, but she didn't know what she was saying in her defenseless, drunken state. She didn't know why she was better without him.

He picked up several curls that were draped across her neck and brought them to his nose. She smelled of fresh air after a storm. He wanted to soak in the scent of her so he would never forget.

If he weren't so tainted, maybe he could ask Lachlan for permission to marry her, but he had felt the rage inside, had even felt it tonight as he'd seen her dance with Hamish. He was like his father, and she wasn't safe around him.

He started to reply but her eyes were closed. He gently placed her hair on the pillow and got up to walk out. He cursed when he looked at the door. If he left, he couldn't bolt it. He returned to the bed.

"Kirstie." No answer. He tried again, softly shaking her shoulder. "Kirstie." She still didn't wake.

Pulling the chair to the side of the bed so he could watch her, he settled in. It wasn't long before Blair showed, but in that time, he had come to a conclusion. He had to keep his distance, because everything about Kirstie tempted him. He was too close to giving in to the urge he had to hold her and never let her go. But it was a selfishness he couldn't afford. That's how his mother had died.

Chapter Five

Waking to an odd pressure, Kirstie turned to see Blair laying on her unbraided hair. Confusion set in, and her head started to pound before she remembered Alan had walked her back, but she didn't remember him leaving. Och, maybe the pain in her temples was from the drink and not her friend.

"Blair." Kirstie pushed at her shoulder.

"What?"

"Ye are on my hair."

"Ugh," she groaned and lifted long enough for Kirstie to pull free before she fell back to the bed.

She ignored the fogginess and pushed through. "How was yer walk with Henry?"

"Ugh, let me sleep." Her friend rolled over, giving her a nice view of the lass's blonde hair and backside.

"Damn, Blair, wake up. I'm dying to ken what happened." Rolling over to face her, Blair sighed. A sly teasing smile appeared, and her eyes lit even through their sleepy haze.

"He kissed me."

"Well, how was it?" Forgetting her aches, a flush of

excitement had her cheeks lifting with the corners of her lips. She was happy for her friend, even if she had reservations about Henry, who acted like a pompous arse.

"Pleasant." Blair sat up and stretched.

"Well, will ye marry him?" She stepped over to the wardrobe and pulled out a dark green gown Blair had insisted she bring. The color did look good on her, but it made her long for the greens of the open fields she would not be seeing anywhere near this blasted castle.

"He hasnae asked yet." When she glanced over her shoulder, Blair's full lips pouted back at her.

"Do ye think he will?"

Her friend stood, finally looking awake, and rushed over to retrieve a dress, a sage color that complimented her pale skin and light eyes. "I dinnae ken. We were only able to steal a moment alone, and we didnae have time to discuss it. John says Father willnae approve, but John does."

Although Kirstie lived on Macnab land, she hardly saw the Macnab laird and never discussed politics with him. Thinking on why The Macnab might not approve, she remembered that although Blair's brother John held the belief that the people of Scotland should be able to choose whatever religion they wanted, her father was a staunch Covenanter. "'Tis because he is Montrose's cousin and a firm Royalist?"

She almost asked the other question on her mind. *'Tis because he is so arrogant?*

"Aye."

"Will Montrose be here for the meeting?" She pulled the dark gown over her head just as Blair did the same with the sage one.

"Nae. John says Montrose and Argyll cannae stand to be in the same room together." Blair went to work fastening the matching ribbons.

"Henry will marry ye, and then what am I to do?" Of course Henry wanted Blair on his arm. Every man wanted the petite blonde lass. "I'll be all alone, and what if yer father decides I cannae stay and have to go back to Kentillie?" Her voice sounded sad, but buried deep, she could feel excitement bubbling up at the possibility of going home. She turned so that her friend could help her with her own ribbons and to hide the little thrill that might show on her face.

"Ye should. Alan was watching ye when I came into the room last night."

"I am no more than an obligation to him. I undressed in front of him last night, and he didnae say a word or look the slight bit interested."

"Ye dinnae see it, but I swear that man is as crazy about ye as ye have been over him. Ye just have to find out why he is holding back." Blair grabbed the brush from the little table and ran it through her hair.

"I ken what it is. He sees me as a sister. I cannae go back, because at least in the Macnab stables I feel important."

"Nae, that isnae brotherly concern I see in his eyes."

"What do ye think I should do? If he doesnae want me, I'll stay on yer father's lands or find a husband who will let me take care of his horses." She contemplated a million other things that would be better for her than Alan Mackenzie.

"Ye should make him jealous. Then ye'll believe me."

"How am I going to do that?" After running the brush through her hair, she set it back on the table.

"I think ye already are, and ye will not have to worry about it if ye keep cavorting with those Covenanters."

"Ye ken what I'm doing."

"Aye, but Alan doesnae," Blair protested.

Well, he had an idea after catching her in Argyll's room last night. "And he doesnnae need to ken it or he'll tell Malcolm."

"Tonight, wear the blue dress. That will get his attention."

"I cannae wear that. I told ye 'twas too tight in my chest."

"'Tis perfect." A devilish grin teased at Blair's lips.

"I can barely breathe, and 'tis indecent." Stepping back over to the wardrobe, she pulled open the doors and ran her fingers down the silky blue material.

"Do ye want his attention?"

"Aye, but—"

"Do ye want the others to confide in ye?" Well, it was important she gain the confidences of whoever may be out to get to her family.

She swallowed, knowing the argument was lost.

"Then ye must wear the dress."

Tightening her lips together, she pouted, knowing she couldn't deny the dress would bring a lot of attention her way.

Blair smiled. "Let's go eat. I'm famished."

. . .

After breaking their fast, with Finlay as their guide, Kirstie and Blair strolled the streets of Edinburgh, taking in the early morning sun. The bustling city was pinned in by walls built many years ago to protect the residents from English invasion. The stone barriers, green with moss where they remained shaded, hadn't been successful and now seemed more for controlling goods traversing into and out of the city than any threats of invasion.

Marveling at the tall buildings that sometimes eclipsed the height of Kentillie, the Cameron castle and stronghold, she imagined the claustrophobic feeling of being stuck on one of the higher floors of the structures. The homes were so close together that some of them were even touching, leaving room for windows only on the fronts and backs of the facades. Although her breath refused to fill her lungs as merchants and the townspeople crowded and hurried around, it was still better than the stifling environment of the castle.

Malcolm had been busy and could not accompany them but had reluctantly relented and let them go as long as Finlay came along. She agreed, determined she was not going to spend all day stuck in that fortress on the hill, especially now that the other guests were arriving.

"Is that Alan?" Blair cut into her thoughts.

"Where?" Squinting, she followed her friend's gaze.

"Just outside that tavern."

It was Alan. He was putting something in some wench's hands. Too far away to see what it was, she concluded it was probably something innocent, but there was no mistaking the woman's hand going to Alan's shoulder. It lingered there, and then her finger trailed down his arm slowly in a seductive way.

Kirstie's heart stopped, or at least it felt as if it had. A strange dizziness, or was it numbness, washed over her as her breaths came too fast. She made sure the head covering she had worn today was in place, then she strolled a little too fast farther down the street. She couldn't let him see how she had been affected by the thought of him with another woman.

Blair continued to stare at Alan while Finlay struggled with whom to keep an eye on, finally muttering something to her friend Kirstie couldn't hear. Blair stood her ground when their chaperone kept his watchful gaze on everything as he moved to her side. Their chaperone kept his watchful gaze on everything as he moved.

Finlay, who had been silently brooding the entire walk, chose now to speak up. "I'm sure 'tis no' what it seems."

Damn, she'd given too much away and now the man knew how she was affected by her brother's best friend. She studied a port in the town wall, anything to seem uninterested, but her reaction had told the truth.

Finlay, suddenly talkative, continued, "Alan has never

paid for a woman."

Oh, that makes me feel so much better.

Meeting his eyes, she asked, "Does everyone ken?" She would have blushed if her face wasn't already flushed with anger and a renewed sense of determination that she would not let Alan back into her heart.

"Nae, I just ken what it looks like to want something ye cannae have." His gaze drifted longingly to Blair, who was still watching Alan with her hands on her hips and tapping her foot. Kirstie looked back to Finlay.

"Why does he no' want me?" She wanted to cry, but she wasn't going to let Finlay see her shed tears over that horse's ass.

"I dinnae ken why some people dinnae see what's right in front of them."

Kirstie wasn't sure if he was talking about Alan or Blair. It was really a shame Blair was infatuated with Henry, because Finlay was a good man and he obviously cared for her. If they married and she went back to Kentillie, she wouldn't lose her friend. But she would have to be near Alan, and she would lose her position in the stables, again being reduced to a nuisance, decimating what sense of self-worth she'd accumulated during her time with the Macnabs.

"He didnae look at her as anything other than a woman selling bread in the market."

Kirstie cringed at what was supposed to be a reassuring comment. "Let's move on. I dinnae want him to see us." She started walking without them.

The clouds darkened as they crested the top of the hill, and the sky opened up. By the time they got to the castle, she was wet, cold, and ready to escape to a quiet corner to lament over Alan and attempt to come up with a plan to save her brothers and find a suitable husband.

Hamish was at the door to meet her when they walked in.

He wore a pale yellow jacket that stood out against the gray stones of the castle. He was dry, while she must look like a drowned rat. Her hair clung to her face, but despite the chill, she had welcomed the rain. It had cleansed the courtyard of the scores of people.

"I was worried you left without telling me. I couldn't find Blair or John either." He took her cool hand, the warmth of his instantly reminding her of the stifling nature of the castle, and she regretted pushing to get back so quickly after seeing Alan.

"I wouldnae leave without saying goodbye. I think I will stay as long as Malcolm does. I dinnae see him enough."

"Yes, that's right, your brother. Now how is it that he and Alan Mackenzie are no longer friends? I thought all of you were raised together."

"I cannae tell ye what happened between them. I havenae asked. I've been away so long." And she didn't want to add that she'd purposely avoided the subject of Alan with her brothers, but now she saw she would need to change that, because the family that she knew stuck together. Something about the whole situation was off.

He let go, and she brought her hands to her elbows, making a protective circle and warding off the chill bumps that were threatening to erupt on her arms.

"I was hoping to escort you on a walk today." He raised his hands palm up and looked to the sky.

"Sounds lovely, but I'm afraid we have missed our opportunity. Maybe we could tomorrow morning."

"She will need an escort," Finlay interjected as he stepped up beside them.

"Nonsense. Hamish is a good friend of the Macnabs. I have kenned him for quite some time. Finlay, have ye ever met him?"

"I have now," Finlay snapped, and she noticed he'd positioned himself between Blair and Hamish. "I have heard ye are a radical Covenanter." Her guess was that he would pull her away if he felt he could, too.

Her mouth fell open at the animosity she'd not thought him capable of. "Finlay," she protested, but then she remembered Finlay had another life. She knew little of it, other than his father, who was English, was a close friend to King Charles.

"No, Kirstie, it is right for a Cameron to be wary with everything going on." Hamish put a reassuring hand on her shoulder, and Finlay looked like he would knock it off. Slowly removing it, he ran his tongue over his teeth as he studied her brother's man.

"'Tis all right," Blair said, reaching out to touch Finlay's arm. The gesture soothed him, but only slightly.

"I may not be the same religion, but I do not believe force is the way to God. You have nothing to fear from me." Hamish gave a gentle smile, but Finlay's scrutiny shifted between the two of them, obviously not believing a word.

"I believe the lasses need to get some dry clothes on." Holding onto Blair with one hand, Finlay grabbed Kirstie's arm with the other and pulled them in the direction of their room.

"Will I see you at dinner tonight?" Hamish called out as she looked over her shoulder and gave him a quick smile she hoped conveyed her embarrassment over being dragged off like a child.

"Aye. I will be there."

Hours later, when they were leaving the room for dinner, the rain had stopped but the dank smell of the castle persisted.

"How do I look?" Blair twirled, and her pink skirts swished around.

"Ye are so bonny. Ye make the dress look nice."

"I am growing fond of the clothing." She had to admit that the shapely curves of the gowns were more flattering to a woman's figure than the folds of a plaid they were accustomed to wearing, but they weren't as comfortable.

"I admit if yer father had no' insisted on the dresses during the visit, I probably never would have put one on, but they arneae so bad."

"I think they are wonderful." Blair sashayed from side to side as her hands gripped the rustling material.

"Even this one would be nice if it were no' so tight in the chest." Running her fingers up the side of her ribs, Kirstie wondered how she was going to breathe tonight.

"Ah, but that's the best part of it. Ye will have them all spilling their secrets tonight."

Aye, if she didnae spill from the confines of the tight material that threatened to cut off her circulation. "I hope so." She was growing tired of Niall's wandering hands and Hamish's nonstop chatter.

"Did ye tell Malcolm what ye heard?"

"Nae, but I will soon. Whatever the plot, at least I ken 'tis no' supposed to take place until after the meeting. We still have two days, but Royalists are already turning up dead, so I must act swiftly." She twirled at the ribbons that held locks of hair from her temples to the middle of the back of her head in a plain but stylish look as she contemplated how she would discover something that would help put an end to the scheme against her family.

"Mayhap ye could just get Malcolm to leave as soon as the gathering is done."

"I dinnae think 'tis likely, since the assembly will be in the afternoon. He may want me to leave with him, too."

"What will ye do?"

"If 'tis the only way to get him to leave, I will go. I dinnae think I could travel with Alan, though." The less time she spent around the pompous man, the better.

"I dinnae think that was money he was giving the tavern

wench. It looked like 'twas a message he was having sent to someone."

"Doesnnae matter. I am done pining for a man who doesnae want me. Tonight, I will flirt with the Covenanters, and then when all this business is over, I'll start looking for a husband." It just had to be one that met her long list of criteria, but she knew even now, the only man for her didn't want her.

"I think Alan will surprise ye. And are ye sure ye are ready to look for a husband?"

"Aye. If ye are going to wed, Henry, 'twill no' be long before I will need to leave yer father's home."

"John would never turn ye out." Blair looped an arm through hers as they stepped toward the door, to be met by Dougal, ready to escort them to dinner.

"I ken he wouldnae, but I wouldnae feel comfortable without ye there, especially considering yer father's views and my religion," she continued, knowing their guard wouldn't understand what they were discussing.

The door clicked shut behind them, and she moved to lock it then hide the key in a cleverly sewn pocket in the folds of her skirts. Walking down the hall, she steeled her nerve and peeked down once more to make sure her breasts weren't spilling from the gown. It was time to go pry a few secrets out of some Covenanters.

· · ·

Rushing into the great hall, Alan cursed to notice the room was already filling. There would be no easy way to find the Covenanters he needed to make inroads with before the meal started. Malcolm stood not too far from the main entrance, flanked by Finlay and Dougal. Upon seeing him, Lachlan's younger brother pointed down with two fingers on his right hand, the signal that the Camerons had received the message he'd had the tavern owner's niece deliver.

The lass had returned and reported that Malcolm read it in front of her then tossed it into a fire to burn the evidence. The missive had let them know that a group of Macphersons and MacDonalds had been attacked on their way to Edinburgh. The Royalist Resistance, a rebel group fighting against the Covenanters, had swooped in to help, but not before the Macpherson laird's eldest son had been killed. The group would no longer be making their way to the city and were returning to Macpherson lands. The letter also told Malcolm that Kirstie was up to something other than just flirting with the enemy.

Maybe Malcolm would keep an eye on her or, better yet, send her home, leaving him to concentrate on his job.

How was he to mingle with the Campbell and Menzie men if he was constantly distracted by her presence?

Discovering who was behind the plot to eliminate the lairds of the Royalist-supporting clans had to be his top priority because if the bastards eluded him here, next time they might not be forewarned of an attack. If they'd known of the extent of the threat before they'd left Kentillie, Lachlan never would have let Malcolm come. As it is, he'd probably go into a rage when he learned that his sister is in the thick of it.

As he scanned the crowd around Malcolm to assure himself that his friend's brother was in no danger, he noticed Malcolm's eyes widen. Turning, his jaw dropped as Kirstie and Blair strolled into the room. Kirstie was wearing, *oh hell*, what was she wearing?

Each time he saw her, he seemed to see more of her. The cut on this dress was low and squared; the curves of her breasts were like ripe melons peeking from behind an elaborately woven blue frame. He swallowed.

Before he had a chance to react and close the short

distance between them, Niall Campbell had found her. Niall was a drop taller than Kirstie, and the way he stood it appeared the man was glued to her chest instead of looking into her blue eyes. She seemed to notice, and she smiled.

Knowing she had no intentions of seducing a known Covenanter, he was convinced now that somehow, she had discovered there was more to this week's events than a simple meeting and was putting herself in danger in order to get the details. It was the only reason she could be toying with this man.

His chest tightened. She deserved someone to love and care for her, but by God, he was not going to let that man be an enemy of the Cameron clan.

Stewing as Niall escorted Kirstie to the table and sat next to her, he had to push away the flush of anger that had assailed him. Before Alan could make it to the table, she was surrounded. Hamish was on her other side with the radical clergyman Robert Baillie next to him. Argyll and his men had also moved in with a couple of ladies he didn't know. There was no way to get close to her without offending one of the men he needed to trust him.

Hamish passed Kirstie a platter, and his hand stayed on hers a little too long for comfort. Niall noticed, and his eyes narrowed. Pouring her some wine, the Campbell man offered her the cup to steal her attention from Hamish. It was like watching two grown men play tug-a-war with a steak they both wanted to sink their teeth into.

Kirstie wasn't oblivious to their affections, smiling and flirting with both men. She was even able to send glances to Argyll that made Alan want to hurry her from the room and bend her over his knee. The Earl of Argyll wasn't a man to trifle with. That lass had been too long without a firm hand to guide her through behaving like a lady should.

He found a table that afforded him a good view of the scene playing out in front of him. Resting her chin on the back of her hand, elbow on table, Kirstie smiled at Niall as he rambled on about something. She looked quite alluring.

Hamish said something that caught her attention on the other side. Turning to him, she said something that made him laugh. Niall peered at Hamish, and from where Alan was sitting, he could just make out the anger burning in the Campbell man's eyes. Seeming unaware of the currents roiling between the two men, Kirstie twirled a ringlet with one finger.

Skirts swished beside him. His eyes never left Kirstie and the men he would have to kill if they made one wrong move. Maybe it would only be one by the time they took care of each other.

"Ye are the most stubborn, lack-witted man in all of Scotland," a high, soft voice accused.

Turning, he was surprised to see Blair had taken the seat beside him. "What makes ye say that?"

"Ye are going to lose her. She is going to have to marry soon, and if ye dinnae do something, ye will both be on the losing side of that arrangement."

He shouldn't have been affected by those words, but they somehow cut. He leaned back in his seat and crossed his arms, cutting his glance back to the object of his frustration. "She should have done so already."

"What do ye think of the two men vying for attention now?" His gaze drifted back to the small blonde, who pierced him with an indignant challenge.

She didn't need to hear what he thought of those men in particular. Her pretty little ears would probably ache with the curses he would use to describe them.

"They arennae worthy even to speak with her." His stare returned to Niall and Hamish as a burning clawed at his chest.

"The first intelligent words I've heard ye say. Are ye going to do something about it?" Her palm landed on the table, surprising him and causing the trencher set out in front of him to wobble with the force.

"I amnae good enough, either." His gaze shifted down to his folded arms.

"Why do ye no' let her decide that? What if she thinks ye are? 'Tis going to be yer own fault when someone undeserving gets her."

He remained silent.

"She will be miserable, and I will blame ye." The wench folded her arms and dared him to challenge her. She was a good friend to have. "Ye ken she gave up her home because 'twas too hard for her to be around ye."

His gaze cut back toward Kirstie, mostly because he didn't want Blair to see the guilt that must show in his eyes.

"And she may believe yer lies about brotherly feelings, but I see the truth. 'Twill tear ye apart when she chooses someone else."

Hell, did she ever stop?

"Hamish is determined to have her, and yer going to stand back and let that happen."

He slammed his fist onto the table and cut his gaze back to Blair.

"'Tis no' my place to stop it," he gritted out through clenched teeth.

"Aye, 'twould that be because ye are nothing like a brother to her?" She pinned him with steely determination then, dismissing him, turned away and began speaking to her brother.

Returning his gaze to the smiling lass who dominated the attention of those at her table, he felt his heart plunge as Blair's words gnawed their way into his thoughts. Kirstie's dark chestnut hair had been pinned back in a fashion he'd never seen on her, but rebellious strands broke free at her temple and framed her rosy cheeks.

He glanced at the opposite end of the room to see why

Malcolm wasn't doing anything to protect his sister, but he was engrossed in a conversation with a priest, of all people. He didn't know what that was about, but he'd tear into Malcolm about watching out for her as soon as it was safe to get him another message.

His scrutiny moved to Kirstie. Her neck was long and slender. It arched enticingly as she sat with her shoulders back and head held high. Licking his lips, he imagined the tilt of her neck and noises she would make if he kissed her there.

Niall stared at her neck, too, as she glanced at Hamish to laugh at something he'd said. A haze of anger clouded Alan's eyes, and he started to stand to remove her from the man's marauding gaze.

"Sit." The order came from Blair. "Ye have no right. 'Tis yer own fault she is over there with them and no' ye. Do ye think that is a real smile she wears on her face?"

He hadn't thought about it, but now that Blair had brought it up… Kirstie's smile was normally subtler; the one she wore now did appear forced.

The rest of the meal was just as painful, but at some point, Malcolm did appear at Kirstie's side, draping a plaid across her shoulders and covering her then whispering something in her ear. The Covenanters tensed with Malcolm's arrival, and Kirstie's behavior changed. She must have realized that Malcolm being at her side put him in danger, and she was more reserved the rest of the meal.

When Alan wasn't bearing the brunt of Blair's tongue, the most annoying lass in Scotland, the lass on his other side talked about baking, needlework, and trivial stuff until he thought his ears would bleed. It dawned on him the only lass who could keep him entertained was Kirstie, with her knowledge of how to care for animals and the stories she would read. He never felt bored in her presence.

When dinner was done, he tried to make his way toward

Kirstie, but she was dancing with Niall before he could get to her. He should just leave; he needed to get to the pub to see if he could discover more of the plot, but Lachlan would never forgive him if he let something happen to Kirstie or to Malcolm.

Hell, he'd never forgive himself.

As he fumed on the side of the crowd, Hamish came up to talk to him. "Are you ready for the meeting?"

"Aye, 'tis the reason I am here."

"It is good that at least you made it to represent the Mackenzies. We will need your help to persuade the Camerons it is in their best interest to follow the Covenant."

"Think 'twill be a hard thing to do. They willnae listen to me."

"It must have been tough living there with them. At least you got to look on that every day." Alan stiffened as he noticed whom Hamish was talking about. Although Kirstie had kept the plaid draped over her shoulders, her bonny face was flushed, and she outshone all the women present.

"The Camerons abandoned me. I am glad I ken who my real family is now." He tried to steer the conversation to something more useful.

"Yes, ye will have to tell me more of this rift between ye, but still, I plan to have Kirstie as my wife."

He somehow had to convince this fool he didn't have a chance with Kirstie. "I dinnae think she will convert."

"I think she will be biddable when the time comes. I will wed her. She has an accepting heart."

Alan balled his hands at his side and fought the urge to punch Hamish. "She has a mind of her own."

"I think she will come around. You have." The calm confidence in the steady voice and the man's piercing, unblinking eyes sent a chill through his backbone, even as he noticed how the room had turned hot like the kitchens at Kentillie on a summer day. Thinking of Kirstie's aversion to crowds, his gaze strayed back toward the dance floor to evaluate her condition.

"Aye." Was all he could say as he tore his gaze from Kirstie to focus on Hamish and ignore the despair threatening his senses.

"I do not like the way Niall looks at her." Hamish ran a tongue over white teeth.

"I dinnae, either. Despite my differences with her brothers, I still see her as a sister."

Hoping the man beside him didn't see the reflex, he felt his jaw tick as Kirstie urged Niall's hand back to her waist. The bastard was again trying to touch her in places that only a lover would dare.

"There. She has put him in his place."

Alan didn't see that; Campbell still looked at her as if she were the dessert at the end of a long meal, one he was more than willing to wait for.

The music was ending, and Hamish hurried out and took Kirstie's hand. Oh hell, he had to watch another man with greedy hands all over her.

The lass who had been seated next to him appeared at his side. "Will ye dance with me? I dinnae ken many people here."

"Aye." He reached out and took her clammy hand. It would be rude to turn her down, and it gave him the opportunity to get closer to Kirstie. The lass's incessant talking was back, and she went on and on even when he didn't respond.

Alan didn't take his eyes off of Kirstie as she and Hamish moved around the floor. At least the man was respectful with his hands, but the possessiveness in his gaze probably reflected what was in his own.

When the music ended, he left the chattering lass with a brief "Thank ye for the dance," and hastened toward Kirstie.

Taking her hands, he started to spin her but slowed a bit when he noticed she nearly tripped over the hem of her gown. He was so frustrated at that point that the first words from his mouth were clipped and angry. "Why are ye toying with those men?"

She tried to pull free, but he kept his hold. "'Tis none of yer concern."

"Aye. It is."

"I hear ye going about introducing yerself as a Mackenzie. Why are ye acting as if Malcolm doesenae exist?" A fierce protective spark lit in her eyes, one which told him despite her absence from Kentillie, family was above everything with her. Hell, he admired her, her loyalty, her compassion to animals in need. Even if he couldn't have her, she had to come home.

"'Tis no' what ye think."

"Then enlighten me."

"Nae, I cannae do that."

"Then ye have no reason to be angry with me."

He wasn't just angry, he was furious, and she'd tried to evade his question. "I amnae angry. What are ye doing with Covenanters?"

"I will tell ye when ye explain to me what kind of game ye and Malcolm are playing."

She tilted her chin up and pulled her shoulders back.

Guiding them toward the edge of the crowd, Alan took her arm to draw her into a secluded alcove to talk privately. He hoped her admirers weren't watching, but this conversation couldn't take place where just anyone might hear.

"Tell me what the hell ye think ye are doing." His words came out harsher than he intended.

"What do ye mean?" She shrank into the corner as he shielded her from view.

Glancing around to make certain no one was near, he lowered his voice. "Breaking into Argyll's room, associating with all these Covenanters. Making these men think they have a chance with ye. Take yer pick and start explaining."

"I dinnae owe ye an explanation." She pouted.

"Aye, I believe ye do." He took her chin and lifted until her eyes met his. "If I had not found ye in Argyll's room, ye could be dead or worse right now." Glancing around to ensure they were still alone, he shuddered as he thought about what could have happened. "Ye are into something ye shouldnae be, and ye are going to tell me what it is."

"I willnae." She fisted her hands on her hips.

"Aye, ye will, or I will haul ye and Malcolm home tonight."

She peeked around him to make sure no one could hear them. "Someone is trying to kill my brothers." Her lip quivered.

"How would ye ken that? I want to kill them almost every day." It was a poor attempt at trying to lighten the mood. He didn't know how to react to the frightened lass who stared back at him. She was easier to manage angry.

"I was in the stables, and I overheard some men talking about it." She gulped and bit her lip. He heard laughter and pivoted again to reassure himself no one could hear their conversation.

"So ye decided the best thing to do was break into the earl's room? Have ye gone daft? Why did ye no' talk to me?"

"Because I dinnae want to spend time with ye." That stung. At least she was cautious enough to lean in and whisper, "And ye have only been with Covenanters since ye arrived. How do I ken ye are not part of it?" Her cheeks reddened, and she poked him in the chest.

She sounded confused and hurt when she continued, "I want to think ye wouldnae harm them, but I feel as if I dinnae ken yer heart anymore."

"'Tis crazy, kitten, ye think I would do something to yer brothers." Still looming over her, his fury abating, he gently clasped his fingers around the hand that had been assaulting him. She pulled back as if burned.

"Nae, but yer up to something."

"Why did ye no' tell Malcolm what ye overheard?" He leaned closer; she smelled earthy but floral at the same time.

"Because I was afraid he would do something foolish."

"Anything he would have done couldnae have been worse than what ye attempted." He wanted to pull her in and hold her, just to know she was safe. "Ye are lucky ye are no' dead." He was dangerously close to her ear now, and his breathing had become heavy.

"Please, leave me be," she whispered. Her blue eyes were full of longing, fear, and unshed tears.

Some primitive part of him reacted to the luscious scent of her and the husky way her voice trembled. His hand went to her waist, and she shivered at his touch. Eyes fluttering for a moment, she bit her lip. She was beautiful, and he wanted to sink into her and give in to the emotions welling up, the ones he had worked so hard to hide.

She must have seen his reservations, because she shook her head. "Ye arenae my brother, and ye arenae anything more to me. Stay away from me. I dinnae wish to see ye."

She pushed away from him, and emerging from their private alcove, she ran for the door.

Hell, that could have gone a little bit better. Och, he doubted Finlay or Dougal saw her leave, and she wasn't safe out there on her own. Worse, she might not be safe with him. He followed but walked slow because he knew where she was going and he wanted to give her time to calm down. Hell, he needed time to simmer, too.

As he reached the entrance to the stable, Kirstie's scream penetrated the cool night air, and his blood froze.

Chapter Six

As Alan bolted for the entrance, fear snaked its way around his heart and constricted painfully.

"Nae, stop." Kirstie's voice was pitched an octave higher than normal, like the time she'd run for help after her father had fallen from his horse lifeless, a sound he'd hoped to never hear again.

Frantically running down the aisle of stalls, the only thing he saw were horses stabled for the evening with heads tilted toward the sounds of a struggle coming from farther in. Deep male laughter taunted, "Did ye no' come down here looking for yer stallion?"

"She's a bonny one, Ceardach. I want her first," a second voice came, this one slow and slurred.

"Get yer hands off me."

The long row of stalls became a blur as he focused on the sounds of the voices.

"Ah, ye bitch," the deeper voice spoke again.

The crack of flesh hitting soft skin was followed by a gasp and whimper. The sound had been branded in his head as a child and could never be removed.

"Dinnae mess up her face." The slurred response confirmed his suspicions.

Almost there. A soft thud sounded, followed by Kirstie's sharp intake of breath. Helplessness washed over him, a feeling that had plagued him through his childhood years.

"That's right, lass, stay down there, cause that's where ye belong," said the thick, beefy voice.

"Nae, I get her first, Willy. Ye watch the door. She willnae fight ye when I'm done with her."

Alan rounded on the stall at the end. Kirstie was on her knees bent over, holding her stomach. He tensed as the sight of her injured hit him like a horse at full speed, so blinding that his gaze narrowed in to the threats before they could strike again. There were two men standing over her with smug smiles plastered on their faces. The bigger one started to unbelt his plaid.

"I believe I heard the lass say she wasnae interested." Alan tried to look calm and uninterested as he leaned against the side of the entrance, arms folded, hiding the fists that trembled as fear and fury ignited in his chest.

"Go away. 'Tis no' yer concern," the larger one said as he stopped unfastening his belt and took a step toward Alan. The wiry man, he assumed Willy, didn't move.

"Aye, 'tis when two men are forcing themselves on an unwilling lass." The rage he kept buried inside sprung to life, ready to unleash itself on these cowards.

"Ye should leave now. I willnae show mercy on ye."

"Like ye have for the lass doubled over in the corner. Where is her mercy? I dinnae think ye have any in ye." His words were becoming more clipped, and his voice shook with the pent-up energy surging to the surface.

Ceardach, the man who seemed to be the leader, advanced, and Alan rose up to meet him, blocking the exit.

"The only way ye will leave is on yer knees begging for the lass's forgiveness."

The man grunted and charged, knocking him in the chest; they both went flying with the momentum. He turned during the fall and was able to land on his side instead of under the beast.

A moment of remembered fear assailed him as the smell of the brute reached his nostrils. A potent mix of sweat, ale, and whisky permeated from his pores. The man had probably drunk enough to make a horse sick. It made him dangerous because in his current state, consequences wouldn't mean a thing to the arse. Alan had seen it enough with his own father.

Jumping to his feet just before the other man, Alan moved into a braced stance ready for attack, something he'd not known as a wee lad.

The drunken brute swung and missed then swung again in rapid succession. As Ceardach's second blow connected with the side of his arm and slid off, Alan ignored the sting. Taking a step back, he struck and planted his fist squarely on the drunken man's jaw.

The brute staggered but recovered quickly, pinning him with the fury of someone convinced of his own self-worth.

Standing tall, Alan straightened his shoulders as he waited for the next attack.

"Ye can still walk away if ye leave now," Ceardach spit out.

"And leave the lass to endure yer bad breath and unwanted attention." He was not going to let this abuser of women leave standing upright. They were out in the passage between stalls now, but the image of Kirstie on her knees was still fresh in his mind. No man would ever raise a hand to her again.

The drunk stepped closer, but Alan stood his ground. "Ye will regret that. Mayhap I will let ye watch before I kill ye."

Rage rose in his chest and threatened to overwhelm him.

Taking advantage of his distraction, the brute swung, a hard hand landing on Alan's jaw.

The sting bringing him back from the horrid image, he threw a punch of his own. Bone crushed beneath his fist as the man's nose collapsed, and a strangled sound came from deep in Ceardach's throat. When he pulled back, blood was streaming down the arse's face.

His arms were grabbed from behind, and he realized he'd forgotten about the smaller man, Willy. Already having dismissed the willowy man as a non-threat, he kept his focus on the raging beast in front of him. Ceardach, too drunk to feel the injury to his nose, wiped the blood from his face and ranted, "Ye will pay fer that."

Stepping forward, he spit at Alan before the arse planted a fist in his side. Oh hell, a crack followed by a stab of pain meant the brute had done some serious damage.

An unfamiliar thwack sounded, and Willy's hands were wrenched away, jerking to the side. With Ceardach's attention focused on whatever had happened to his partner, Alan spared a glance at the man behind him.

"Ye bitch." Willy stumbled then charged at Kirstie, who was holding a large metal object.

She shrieked and threw the shovel at him, but Alan didn't see the rest because another blow landed on his side and he almost fell over. Turning, he pummeled the man just under his jaw, and the brute's head flew back as he stumbled and blinked.

Alan didn't wait to see the man fall, instead bolting toward Willy, who held Kirstie up against his body by her hair. "Dinnae come any closer."

This man was scared. If the brute had Kirstie, Alan would listen, but this man just wanted to get out of here with his friend.

Alan stepped forward, and Willy pulled harder. Kirstie's head was forced up, and she beat at the man with one hand while she cradled her other arm at her chest.

"Alan, behind ye," she yelled.

Pivoting just in time to miss the next blow, he straightened. The evil smirk on the man's face terrified him more than anything else he could have done, and Alan realized instantly what had pleased him.

"Ye ken the lass, then." The man rubbed his hands together then wiped at the blood that was still dripping from his nose. "Willy, bring her."

Fury burst behind his eyes, burning like an angry blaze of a roaring fire in the pitch black of night. That brute would not put his filthy hands on Kirstie again.

Flying through the small space between them, he knocked Ceardach to the ground with such force a whiff of alcohol-soaked breath was pushed from the man's lungs into Alan's face. He wanted to gag.

It only fueled the flames. The years he had stood by helpless as his father beat and raped his mother exploded to the surface. Unleashing a storm of punches, he stood and drove his boot into the arse's side as the man tried to evade the assault. Alcohol apparently no longer keeping the pain at bay, Ceardach curled into a ball.

Alan jabbed again, and the man moaned and tried to roll away. He kicked two more times, the anger taking over as his body tensed and the coil that had tightened around his chest spilled over. Everything else blurred.

"Alan."

He heard his name but kept going.

"Alan!" It was Kirstie. She had managed to break free from the wiry man's hold. He was hunched over as if she'd managed to get a direct hit on the man's groin. Not only that, he glanced toward Ceardach, who lay motionless on the ground whimpering.

Willy's gaze darted back and forth between his fallen friend and Alan. Alan took another step closer, but the man moved behind Kirstie, pushing hard into her back and propelling her forward. She landed straight on Alan's chest.

After catching her, he looked up to see Willy was halfway to the exit. He could give chase, but that would mean leaving Kirstie alone with the piece of shite on the ground. That wasn't going to happen.

Kirstie's hand rose, gently caressing his cheek. It was so tender that he turned into the soft touch. Glancing down, he caught sight of undercurrents of worry and relief swirling in the blue depths of her gaze. "Are ye all right?"

"Aye, I'm fine. What about ye?" She still cradled her other hand. He brought his up to touch it but was afraid of hurting her so he stopped short.

"'Tis just a sprain, I think. The big one bent it back."

"Are ye hurt anywhere else?"

"Nae, I'll be fine. What about ye?"

"'Tis nothing. Let's get ye out of here and get someone to take care of that arse before he wakes up."

. . .

Wincing inside and trying her hardest not to flinch, Kirstie turned her focus to the nearby wall to study a portrait of a portly man, the same doctor who was wrapping a bandage around her wrist. Although she'd wanted to shut herself in her room and pretend the night had not happened at all, Alan had insisted they come to see the physician after the guards had dragged away the barely breathing, tree-sized attacker that he had taken down.

The guards had directed them down into the city to see

this particular physician, but he'd only confirmed what she already knew—it was a sprain. The doctor gave her some kind of medicine for the pain, and she took a spoon of it right away because it did hurt.

"Ye should have him look at yer side," Kirstie said. She'd seen him grimace a couple of times when he thought she wasn't looking.

"Nae, 'tis fine."

"Please. Ye made me. Now 'tis yer turn."

Giving in, her savior sat as the physician fumbled around a bit and declared his ribs bruised, giving Alan the same medicine, but he refused to take it. By the time they were done, she could barely keep her eyes open.

Glancing up the stairwell on their way out, her gaze was caught by several more portraits lining the stairwell up to what she assumed to be a private residence above stairs. She wasn't sure how much Alan had paid him, but she was certain his fee would be exorbitant if he was able to afford such luxuries.

Shivering as they stepped out into the cool late night air, she stumbled.

Alan said, "I'll send word to Blair. My tavern is close. Ye can stay there tonight."

She froze.

He was probably relieved not to have to escort her up the long hill to the castle with the pain in his side. He looked as exhausted as she felt, so she ignored that silly childish part of her that at one time had wanted him to ask her to stay with him.

The medicine had made her so tired she could crawl into a bed of old rushes and fall asleep right now. "Aye, that will do."

Shrugging as a mixture of excitement and trepidation threatened to shock her out of her exhaustive state, she squashed the feelings down and let the bone weary tiredness reign.

"I dinnae think I can make it all the way back up there tonight." She didn't want him to try, because she was certain his injury was worse than he was letting on.

"I remember ye used to fall asleep under the big tree out in front of Kentillie when ye were supposed to be doing yer chores." His words brought back fond memories of warm summer days and childhood innocence.

"I loved that spot. It was my favorite. Ye and Lachlan would always tell on me." Strolling down the street, she held her hurt arm close to her chest as she let Alan lead the way.

"Aye, we only did that a couple of times and usually 'twas because ye had done something to get Lachlan in trouble."

"'Twas because ye two always left Malcolm and me out. Ye were forever hiding from us."

She stopped to look in the window of a bakery that still had a light burning in the background. She'd been so busy with Hamish and Niall that she'd barely eaten dinner. The fruit tart in the window looked dry, but her mouth still watered.

"I saw ye protect that boy playing in the great hall." Drawing her gaze from the window, she glanced at Alan and saw a man of honor and generosity before her, not the lad who had teased her as a child. She felt a new appreciation for the person he had become, and although she'd been able to grow as a caregiver to animals, she'd missed seeing his transition the years she had been gone.

"They were just lads having fun." He shrugged casually, not realizing that when he'd turned, the lads had gazed up at him as if he were a conquering hero. She was glad she had seen their admiration, and she wondered if that's how she looked upon him now.

Her gaze returned to the bakery window, hoping he

didn't see. "Aye, but no' many adults would have defended them the way ye did. I admire that ye are always looking out for others."

And he'd been looking out for her tonight as well. She didn't want to think about what could have happened had he not been there. It didn't matter if he viewed her as a friend or a sister, he had been there. She liked that he was dependable.

And despite the childhood feelings, which threatened to erupt, she was proud of the man he was now. Some lass would be lucky enough to catch his heart one day, and if it couldn't be her, maybe she should keep an eye out to make sure the woman was worthy of him.

When her gaze returned to his, she saw something there that made her want to lean into him, and it frightened her. Turning away, she continued walking, not quite sure where to go but certain she couldn't stand with his eyes focused on her like that and not delude herself into thinking that more emotion reflected back to her than sibling affection.

"Aye, and I fear tonight nothing will wake me. That medicine is strong."

Weak from the tonic and the night's events, she drifted into him, and he wound his arm around her waist as they walked the dark street. She felt warm, safe, and all too comfortable in his strong embrace. Despite her fatigue, she wanted to remain in the moment, but they arrived at the tavern too soon.

"Ye'll stay in my room tonight. I dinnae trust this place." Clinging to her, he pulled her up the stairs as his gaze darted in every direction. He may have been looking for threats, but the streets and the tavern were deserted at this late hour. She saw no one. The hall was dark and smelled of stale ale, smoke, and urine. She held her breath as Alan unlocked the door at the end of the hall.

"Och," she said as he stood back, holding the door for her

to enter. The door clicked shut behind him, and he pivoted to bolt it. "Why are ye no' staying with Malcolm? This place is filthy."

Turning back to her, he avoided her gaze, but it wouldn't have mattered—she couldn't see in the darkness of the room. He fumbled around as he lit a candle. "Finlay and Dougal are there. He has enough company."

Something in the response caught her attention. She'd been away a long time, but she couldn't imagine that things had changed so much at home that Malcolm wouldn't have wanted Alan there with him. She was too tired to start a debate over it, so she let it go, telling herself she would bring it up again tomorrow. Something was going on between the men, but they hadn't let her in on the secret.

"Thank ye," Kirstie said as the events of the evening played back in her mind.

"What for?" Alan responded as the flame took, and he turned around.

"Saving me. I dinnae ken what would have happened if ye hadnae come along." Rubbing at her injured wrist, she cringed as an image of the large man's lust-filled eyes invaded her head.

"Just promise me ye willnae wander around by yerself here. This isnae Kentillie. There are too many men here who dinnae have any morals." Sitting in a chair, he removed his boots.

"I thought ye were going to kill that man tonight." She bit her lip while he removed his sporran and tossed it on the table then leaned down, his broad shoulders drawing her attention as he pulled off his boots.

"He reminded me of my father." Alan's eyes narrowed, and an unreadable cloud appeared, hinting at a storm that brewed in their depths.

"I never kenned him." Pacing, she tried to picture the

man.

"Be glad ye didnae. He was a drunk and a monster." He unbelted his plaid and stood.

"Is that why ye dinnae drink?" she asked.

"Aye, I dinnae want to become him. He was most dangerous to those he was supposed to love."

After pulling off the plaid, he draped it over the back of the chair. Alan was only wearing a shirt now, and she wondered how he could be so unaffected by her presence. The room suddenly seemed too warm, despite the cool breeze blowing in from the open window.

"That would never be you," she said.

He looked away, but not before she saw a deep sadness cloud his gray eyes. "He beat us."

A piece of her broke inside. No one had ever told her; it was like her family to shield him from those harsh memories. How had she not known? A child should never have to endure violence, especially at the hands of the ones who were supposed to love them the most.

Emotion simmered, hidden beneath the surface, but the words were delivered in a deadpan, dismissive tone. Alan took a step toward her. "Turn around." When he made a waving motion with his hand, she obeyed because she didn't want him to see the despair in her eyes. If she'd known when they were children, would she have been able to help him?

"I didnae ken he was like that."

Risking a glance behind her, she was rewarded with a view of his dilated gaze fixed on her neck as he took her hair and draped it over her opposite shoulder. His fingers skimmed across her back, and she felt her gown loosen. Odd, she thought once the restrictive garment was off, she would be able to breathe better, but it seemed now that each inhale was sharper and didn't fully reach her lungs.

"Aye, yer parents and Lachlan were the only ones who

kenned what happened." His fingers stilled, but he didn't back away.

Twirling to face him, she held the gown tight at her chest. If she let go and dropped her arms, it would fall free. "And they didnae stop it."

Exhausted, she moved toward the chair and let her dress glide down her arms, careful not to jostle her injured wrist with the material. Stepping out without looking back to him, she placed it next to his plaid. Last night, it hadn't bothered her to undress in front of him, but something had shifted, and the way he'd looked at her tonight reminded her not of a brother, but of a man who wanted something more. Her shift still kept her covered, but she felt naked and exposed and thankful only one small candle was lit, because it hid the blush stinging her face.

"They didnae ken the truth until 'twas too late." His gaze was off in a distant memory, and he took no notice of her. The flush receded.

"What happened?"

"My father came home from drinking like usual. That night, he started beating me because I left something on the floor and he stepped on it."

Kirstie stepped closer and put her hand on his arm.

"Mother pulled him off, and he started in on her. 'Twas always in her stomach or side. Somewhere people couldnae see. That's what they were doing to ye tonight."

Voice drifting off, strong arms encircled her waist and drew her into his solid chest, so close she could feel his heart beating. He nuzzled into her, and her heart shattered into a million pieces at the pain and vulnerability he'd laid bare for her to see.

Continuing to talk into her shoulder, he held on tight. "He hit my mother too hard that night. She didn't get back up. I tried to wake her, but I couldn't. He threw the peat from the fireplace all over the house to hide what he had done. He burned the house down with us still inside and left."

Tears rolled down her face as she thought about the scared little boy who had witnessed his mother's murder at the hands of a man he should have been able to trust.

"How old were ye?"

"Eleven summers."

"Ye were just a babe. Is that when ye came to live with us?"

"Aye, yer parents took me in."

She'd never loved her family more, knowing now they had taken him in and protected him.

"Did ye ever see him again?" She ran her fingers through his thick hair and cradled him to her chest. Pain ripped through her to realize what he had endured and how he had kept it hidden from everyone. From her. Her heart bled for him.

"Nae. He's dead. Drank himself to death one night. Yer parents went to see the body to confirm it was him." Alan's detached tone sent a chill down her spine, but she didn't blame him; the lack of emotion was probably a way he'd learned to cope.

"I'm so sorry ye had to go through that. I cannae fathom how a father…" She couldn't even say it.

"'Tis a madness. My father had it, the man who attacked ye tonight has it, and—" He choked on whatever he was about to say and released her, retreating to put distance between them.

"Ye should have told me." Suddenly cold, she crossed her arms to stave the chill.

"Ye were a wee thing, and then, I only wanted to forget it." He moved to peer out the window into the dark night.

"Ye ken 'tis no' yer fault." Taking a few steps closer, she came to his side. He nodded but didn't turn to face her. "Yer a fighter, a survivor, and ye were just a child. 'Twas nothing ye could do."

"Enough." Shaking his head, he declared an end to the conversation, shutting her out. Inching in front of him, she reached up with her uninjured hand and caressed his cheek.

He drew her in and held her. Not knowing his intent, she did not sink into him and offer everything like she had on the night of their first kiss when he'd turned her away. His proximity and the confusion in her chest tore her apart, but he needed to be held. Whether the embrace came from a sister or a lover, she would be what he needed.

Her sides burned and her blood heated at the feel of his touch even through her shift. And a longing to be closer to him beat at her, so she attempted to squash it.

But her traitorous heart yelled at her, *Just for tonight, let him love me.*

She would give anything if he for once forgot who she was and looked at her as if she were a woman. She wouldn't care what tomorrow brought if he would just lie to her tonight and tell her she was everything. It would be a lie, but she didn't care; she would welcome the pain tomorrow for just a few moments of this aching need in her being returned.

Giving in and melting into his embrace, she put her hands on his hips, careful not to touch where he'd been hurt. She was sure the world went on somewhere around them, but time had stopped while he held her. It was as if he were a lover. Her heart pounded a rhythm deeper and stronger than any she'd ever known, and she thought it might explode.

Inhaling, she took in the warm, salty, male scent that beckoned her to tilt her head to his. To ask for his lips to touch hers and to beg for him to love her. He looked into her eyes, and desire flashed in his gray depths. It gave her hope. The intensity made her knees weak.

His lips parted and started the descent toward hers, then

he winced and folded toward his hurt side. His arms fell from her, and she shivered as she lost the warmth of his body.

"Are ye okay?"

"Aye," he said, but his gaze revealed the pain even as he tried to hide it. He nodded toward the bed. "Get some sleep."

Too tired to argue, she climbed in and slid to the side by the wall. He followed.

"Sleep well," he said.

"Ye too."

He leaned over and kissed her on the forehead just as a brother would do. Alan turned to lie on his back as far away from her on the bed as he could get. She wanted to fight sleep and enjoy just being beside him, but at the same time, she wanted to cry and scream at fate for the cruelty of the night.

For just a moment, she had dared to believe he could think of her as a woman. She had been wrong. She lay there and fought back the despair. She was on the verge of breaking in two, but thankfully the darkness claimed her.

Chapter Seven

Kirstie woke to Alan's fingers dancing across the sensitive, exposed flesh of her arm. The simple gesture elicited thousands of sparks, erupting on her skin and leaving a trail of sensations tingling in the wake. She wanted more. It was surprising how aroused she was just from the featherlight movements of an innocent motion probably meant only to wake her.

Opening her eyes, she was enthralled by Alan studying his finger as it explored her flesh. He looked at her, and his lips curled up into a lazy grin. She didn't want to move, didn't want to break the spell. This, yes, this is what she'd always wanted, to wake beside his smiling face.

His eyes were hooded and still full of sleep, but she was able to make out a raw longing that she'd never seen. A hint that maybe there was something for her hidden in the recesses of his soul. If there was, what was holding him back?

She wanted to reach for him and give him everything she was; her entire being was his for the asking. But last time she had put her heart into his hands and kissed him, he had squashed it along with her dreams. She was no longer a naive child, she was a grown woman, and she would do what she had to in order to protect what dignity she did have left. She wasn't going to give him the opportunity to do it again.

Last night, between the fear of the attack and the drug from the physician, she'd been weak, letting herself fall into the old pattern. But no, she was different now. Och, she had to possess more self-discipline. That meant she needed to put distance between them.

"Ye are so bonny when ye sleep," he drawled in a sated, sleepy voice that sent shivers down her spine and threatened her resolve.

She felt color rise to her face. "Ye are a nice sight to wake to as well." Her own voice sounded deeper and husky. She barely recognized it, and why did her chest feel so tight?

"I'm going to do something I shouldnae." His eyes slowly roamed from her face down to her thighs and then back up again. An unnamed intensity she glimpsed in his stare excited her, causing her pulse to race with fevered urgency as her vow of self-control dissolved.

"What will ye do?" She could barely get the words out, and when the throaty reply did come, her head spun with a deep awareness of him as a man. It was so strong she thought she would melt. Her heart beat erratically, and she was having a hard time controlling her breathing.

"I'm going to kiss ye."

The words sent shockwaves of awareness and need vibrating through her so intense that some part of her was already screaming his name, and even though the logical part of her told her to flee, she couldn't move.

His gaze never strayed from her as she focused only on him. The rest of the room blurred, and desire surged deep in her core. Licking his lip, he continued to watch her, a sweet torment that left her hot and needy and lost to everything else.

When she thought she wouldn't be able to breathe again, his head slowly dipped toward hers. He paused just before her lips as if he were either going to change his mind or he was savoring the moment before knowing he was about to have the one and only thing he had ever desired. At least, that was what she felt.

She wanted so desperately to inch forward and make the connection, but her heart had some sense of self-preservation left. She remained still and waited. He smelled of warm covers and sleep and a woodsy male scent that beckoned and tempted her to make that final move.

Her gaze drifted from his mouth to his eyes that were so close she could make out dark blue flecks in their gray depths. She would have looked away if she could have, because whatever burned there was so hot it almost scorched her with a brand that would most likely never go away.

He groaned softly, and magic happened. His lips were on hers, and her whole body trembled at the desire that flooded through her. There was no part of her that she retained control of and that didn't cry out to move closer to him, to cling, to become one with him.

The velvet soft touch deepened as his mouth widened to take in more of her lips. He did it again and then a small kiss, then his tongue delved into her mouth and found hers. She moved hers to match his, to dance and to tease and revel in the pleasure the caress elicited in her. Chest tightening, her breasts became engorged, and the thin material of her shift tightened around them.

His tongue left hers, and her hands rose to grasp his hips, ignoring the pain in her wrist but making sure he didn't go anywhere. She faintly heard a husky, satisfied chuckle escape from his throat. His teeth nipped at her bottom lip and tugged gently. Her body arched into his and begged for whatever was next.

His hand slid up her thigh and took her shift with it. It rested on her ass and left a burning trail of need, igniting a flame so hot inside her that she thought she would burst.

He nipped again, and her hips pushed into him, needing whatever he had that would put out this all-consuming ache threatening to eat her alive.

"Alan," she gasped.

His hand rose under the material and grasped her breast. The pressure of his large calloused hand on her sensitive skin drove her mad. Then his fingers pinched the apex of her mound. She saw small explosions behind her eyes as sparks of need assailed her.

A light knock sounded at the door, and Alan froze. She gulped and thought, *No, no, no, go away. Dinnae stop.* But the knock came again, this time a little louder.

"Alan. Kirstie."

Her mother.

Alan's face went white, and he looked as if he'd just been caught committing a crime. Retreating, he pulled away so fast that her soul went with him. Her heart shattered like glass all over again. All it had taken was one unforgettable kiss.

"Just a minute." He stood and moved to the chair to collect his plaid and hastily belt it on.

Not capable of movement, she fought the sting in her eyes. She felt like a bucket of cold water had just been thrown on her. Her perfect moment was already gone.

Alan's face was hard stone when he turned to her. "This was a mistake." He shook his head. "I willnae let it happen again."

"Alan, is Kirstie in there with ye?" Eslpeth's voice filtered in through the door, but as much as she loved and missed her mother, her query had not penetrated the hazy fog of pain that had clouded the room. Sitting up, she pulled the covers to her chest like a shield against Alan's hurtful words replaying over and over again in her head.

Mistake. Mistake. Mistake.

"Give me a moment, please." He finished dressing and pulled on his boots.

Alan unlatched the door, and it flew in. A small, determined woman pushed him aside to get to her.

"Are ye hurt?"

Kirstie shook her head no but thought, *Yes, yes, it hurts more than words can say.* She was glad she hadn't voiced it when her mother continued, "We heard about the attack. How's yer arm?"

Oh, she'd forgotten about that. Her mother reached out to take her hand and hold it up. It was still wrapped in a cloth bandage. "'Twill be fine. I barely feel it."

Elspeth turned. "Alan, are ye hurt?"

"Nae, I am all right." Kirstie peeked around her mother to see Alan stood by the door with arms folded to block the view of whoever else was there.

"I need to go. Ye cannae be seen with me," Alan said as he turned and disappeared through the door, shutting it behind him.

Elspeth released the grip on her and leaned back. "Have ye two finally come to yer senses?"

She felt her face crumble. "He doesnae want me."

It was safe to talk to her mother. Other than Blair, Elspeth was the only one she'd ever told of her affection for Alan.

"Did he tell ye that?" Elspeth quirked her brow.

"Nae, but he might as well have." She pouted and glanced down at the bed.

"Ye are wrong. I'm amnae sure why he is holding back. He cares for ye deeply." Her mother took her hands and held them.

"How would ye ken? I've no' been home for ye to see him

with me."

"I ken how his eyes light and his ears tilt in when we mention yer name. 'Tis like a pup waiting for a piece of meat he kens yer about to drop from the table."

"Yeah, so he can chew me up, swallow, and wait for the next." She wiped at her eyes with the blanket.

"Ye ken what I mean."

"Well, I am done with him. 'Tis time I moved on and stopped running." She broke free of her mother's soothing hands and crawled from the bed to dress.

"Aye, I agree. 'Tis time for ye to come home. I tried no' to get involved and let ye two work it out, but that may no' have been the best course." Her mother gave a firm nod.

"I have pined after him since I was a child. I am nae longer a little girl. I will make my own happiness instead of waiting for him to come to me." She pulled the dress up around her and tucked the shift under the material.

"Ye ken if I tell yer brother I found ye in a compromising position with Alan, he would ask him to make ye his wife."

"Nae, we only kissed. Dinnae do that, because he would resent me. Besides, Alan has been treated like my brother for years and is considered an appropriate chaperone by all the Camerons."

Her mother nodded, and she knew her wishes would be followed.

After the gown was fastened, Kirstie touched her lips. Her body still tingled with the desire he'd awoken inside her. She didn't regret the kiss; it had been magical, and it had been real.

She remembered Alan's burning eyes as they looked at her with such need she'd wanted to dissolve into him. Those eyes hadn't lied. He did want her.

For the first time, she admitted her mother was right. There was something there and he was fighting it. If she continued to be easily attainable, he'd never get close again. It was time to show him what he would miss if he let her go. And if he truly didn't want her, so be it. She would find someone else and move on. She was done living on a dream that would never come true.

Kirstie turned back to Elspeth. "How is Maggie? Did she have the babe?"

"Aye. He is such a bonny wee thing."

"A boy." Kirstie's eyes lit. "Did they name him?"

"They named him William."

Kirstie's eyes watered. "Och, 'tis a fine, strong name." She draped one of Alan's extra plaids over her shoulders, and she and her mother headed for the door.

Once outside, Dougal interrupted their conversation. "Hurry, we cannae be seen here. It puts us all at risk."

She did as instructed, but when she could find one of her brothers, they had some explaining to do—why were they and Alan acting as if they hated one another?

· · ·

Alan had put himself in an impossible situation. That kiss this morning had pushed him over the edge. The wall he'd built to protect himself and Kirstie had crumbled as easily as the wooden blocks children played with. He'd been such a fool to think he could touch her and not want more.

Now Elspeth and Lachlan knew she had spent the night with him. Would they forgive him if they knew nothing had happened? Well, almost nothing had happened.

The temptation had been too great, but last night only proved that he couldn't be with her. He'd lost all control and nearly beaten the arse in the stables to death. He was a monster, and Kirstie wasn't safe with him. If the pain in his side hadn't reminded him, he might have gone too far last night. He'd almost kissed her then, and there wouldn't have been anyone to stop them.

Hell. He might not have been able to stop just now if Elspeth hadn't knocked on that door. His hand still trembled as he remembered the slight curve of Kirstie's waist and her soft skin. Her reaction to his touch had lit a fire in him no woman before had ever been able to produce.

He had tried so hard not to follow in his father's footsteps, but here he was, falling for the one lass who was forbidden. He ran his hand through his hair. Och, he was such a fool. He might have just lost what meant most to him, the only real family he'd ever had.

Brushing by Dougal in the hall, he whispered, "Get them back to the castle and then meet me at the safe place."

The Camerons shouldn't be seen anywhere near him. He'd taken a risk bringing Kirstie here last night, but he'd been cautious, sneaking her into the inn. Having them all here this morning was perilous, but at least it was early and most would still be in bed.

Continuing on without waiting for a reply, he descended the stairs. Relieved to see no one about, he collected his horse and took off for a tavern two villages away. It was a secluded town, well off the path most would take on a traditional route into the city and far enough from Edinburgh that it could serve as a place for emergency meetings.

A couple hours later, Alan spied Dougal, as the Cameron man stepped through the door of the tavern and made his way to the private dining alcove in the back of the main room. Pulling the thin curtain closed, the man left a small opening to watch for the arrival of any new patrons. "They came in last night," he answered before Alan could ask.

"Lachlan?" He looked directly into Dougal's eyes, thinking if he showed courage he would eventually feel it, but as he sat there waiting for the Cameron man's answer, he dreaded the fall of the knife that would sever the brotherly bonds he'd built over the years.

"Aye," Dougal said.

Alan dropped his head into his palms while his elbows dug into the table. He swallowed. His hands slid to his temple, and he stared at the table. Any appearance of calm had disappeared. "Is he angry?"

"He didnae look too pleased when he got yer message. If he had known where ye were last night, I'm sure he would have come."

"Why did he no' come now?" Facade back in place, he looked up.

"He had matters to discuss with Malcolm, and Elspeth said she would retrieve Kirstie." There was a lot of information Malcolm had to pass on to Lachlan.

"Nothing happened." Alan shook his head.

Dougal snorted. "Do ye think that will matter to him?"

He started to offer excuses for why he hadn't made sure Kirstie made it back to her room last night, but it didn't matter what he said. He had crossed a line, and no excuse would be good enough. Despite the ache in his ribs, he should have slept on the floor outside the room. Then he wouldn't have to deal with Lachlan or this unwanted ache that told him Kirstie should be his.

Lachlan would never force them to wed, and if the man couldn't see into his heart, he would probably blow off the whole incident as Alan doing the right thing and protecting his sister. But he suspected Lachlan knew of the hidden desire for Kirstie he held buried deep inside. It was probably why he had never asked him to accompany the family to visit her.

"I cannae believe Lachlan left Maggie," he said.

Dougal glanced around to ensure no one else had entered the tavern and could overhear, but he still leaned in to whisper. "They received yer note two days after Maggie had her babe, and she insisted they come to get Malcolm out of danger. She said she and the babe would be all right until they were back."

"Ye have to tell Lachlan I caught Kirstie sneaking into Argyll's room. He and Malcolm will have to keep a closer eye on her. She must ken something of the plot, but I havenae had a chance to find out what she kens."

Dougal's eyes widened. "I'll tell him. He's already told Finlay and me to keep her in our sights after what happened last night."

"We need to watch her closely. Her proximity to the Covenanters is unnerving, but I also think she's learned something of the plot and is looking to gather information from them."

"Lachlan kens that until the Macnabs take a side, he needs to bring Kirstie home to Kentillie, but he cannae risk alienating them until they've chosen. So, he's not going to keep them from her while we're here in Edinburgh."

Lachlan was always levelheaded, but he didn't know how deep Kirstie had dug herself in. "Why does he no send her and Malcolm home now?"

"He might. Who kens what he'll do when he finds out everything that's going on, but until then, 'twill be up to ye to keep Kirstie safe when she's around them."

Oh hell, he couldn't spend all that time near Kirstie. He didn't know if he could be near her anymore without thinking of how she tasted, how she made him feel, and how she filled a void in his life that he hadn't even known was there.

Dougal stood to leave, but Alan grabbed his arm. "Tell him to send her home. She isnae safe here." *But even worse, she isnae safe with me.*

Chapter Eight

"Marry me, Kirstie Cameron."

Kirstie was well aware her eyes must be the size of saucers. They had been strolling along on what had turned into a beautiful sunny morning in a small garden near the castle when Hamish dropped down on one knee.

She couldn't speak, and the moment dragged on, an awkward silence between them, until he finally rose back to standing.

A flash of anger lit his eyes, but it just as quickly disappeared. She shivered but at the same time wondered if she had imagined it.

"I-I need time. This is so sudden, Hamish."

"Do you think Friday night will give you time? I must leave after the meeting." His words were clipped but calm. She'd never heard him angry and didn't suspect he ever lost his temper.

His grip on her fingers was tight, and she wanted to protest and tell him to let go. But she bit back the pain, because she'd just broken his heart. Of course, he would react oddly. A broken heart could do strange things to a person.

"Aye, 'twill do. Why do ye want to marry me? I amnae Presbyterian."

He released her hands. She shook them gently, hoping the numb feeling would disappear. "You have a kind heart, and you would be a good companion and mother."

They strolled back down the path toward the castle.

Spending most of her time with horses, she'd never thought about children. She tried to imagine what a babe of their union might look like. Hamish was not an unattractive man, he had striking hazel eyes, but when the vision of a little boy popped into her head, she saw familiar smoky gray eyes staring back at her. *Oh stop*, she told herself and pushed the image away.

"Would I be able to visit Kentillie and my brothers?" The Menzies land was close by.

He was silent for a moment. "We can visit Kentillie as often as you would like."

That made his offer worth considering. She did need a husband. Blair would be married soon, and she had already decided if the Macnabs wouldn't let her stay to care for the stables, she needed to move on with her life, and this morning, her mother had insisted she needed to start considering a man for a husband.

Not wanting to dwell on the unpleasant task of planning her future, she changed the subject. "Are ye optimistic for the meeting tomorrow?"

"Not especially. I have spoken with several of the Royalist leaders, and none of them seem willing to accept the Covenant. It is worth a try. I honestly believe that it would be the best for Scotland and for the souls of all its men and women."

She would have to press him further on the religion question before accepting his proposal. She wasn't willing to change her views, and she wanted her children to share her own. Maybe he would be open-minded to accepting that they could be different and still have a good relationship, but would he also be willing to let her work in his clan's stables?

"And if the meeting doesn't go well, our wedding might bring some kind of peace between our clans."

"I will think on it." She bit her lip.

A Covenanter wouldn't be her first choice for a husband. But if their union could somehow help bring peace to some of the fighting factions, it might be worth the sacrifice. Heaven knew Alan didn't want her, and she did need to marry. Hamish was easy to get along with. She would consider it.

Blair caught them just as they entered the castle courtyard. "Hello, Hamish." She beamed at him and turned her radiant smile to Kirstie. "I need to speak to ye. Sorry, Hamish, I need her now," Blair called over her shoulder as she pulled Kirstie down a pathway and toward the great hall.

"He didnae look happy with me." Blair laughed. "But I couldnae wait. Henry asked me to marry him, and I said yes."

"Oh, Blair, 'tis wonderful." She wrapped her arms around her friend. She still had reservations about the bonny Henry, but Blair was so in love with him that she had to be happy for her.

"When?"

"I still have to talk to Father and John, but Henry said not to say anything to them until all this business here was over. He didn't want it to overshadow our news. We will wed in the fall." Blair squealed and jumped up and down.

Blair's enthusiasm was contagious, so when a deep male voice came up from behind and said, "May I escort ye ladies to the meal?" they happily went with Niall to the great hall.

"Is yer cousin optimistic about the meeting?" she asked Niall once they were seated. She wasn't sure how to break through the walls, but it was time to start fishing for information.

"Aye. The Earl of Argyll is a born leader and is confident everyone will come around to see what is best for Scotland."

Eager to see Lachlan, she scanned the gathered guests to see if her brothers were present; her gaze was pulled to the door as Alan entered the hall, freezing when he found her. She dismissed him and turned to the man at her side to try to find answers.

"And what will happen if they dinnae? Will he let them go about their lives?"

She tilted her head in toward Niall's to see his gaze riveted on her. She'd worn a demure gown of lilac today, and although it didn't reveal the top of her cleavage, it was still a flattering cut and shade for her coloring.

"Nae, something will have to happen. A divided Scotland cannae defend herself." Niall's stare dipped, and his eyes dilated.

"I am hoping for the best outcome."

Kirstie kept her eyes on Niall and studiously avoided Alan. She found the exercise difficult; she so wanted to know what he was doing and if he was watching. When the meal was over, Niall took her hand and headed out to the courtyard as she cradled her hurt wrist to her belly, thankful the pain was not bad enough that she needed another dose of the medicine. The sun was high in the sky, but clouds were sailing by and the light faded in and out.

The Earl of Argyll stood on the opposite side of the space. The earl's eyes caught Niall's and motioned him over. His stern visage indicated he had something of importance to relay.

"Excuse me. I must speak with my cousin. Will ye wait right here for me?"

"Aye. But dinnae keep me waiting too long."

As she watched him leave, she realized she'd been looking

in the wrong Campbell's room. Niall appeared to have garnered the trust of his cousin's inner circle. With the added guests now roaming the halls, there was no way she was going to get caught sneaking into someone's rooms again, so she resigned herself to spending the evening dining and dancing with Niall to see if she could get more information from him.

A hand clenched onto her upper arm, and she twirled to come face to face with Alan. His expression was dark and dangerous.

"What are ye doing with him?" He was angry.

"Niall? He's a friend." Straightening her shoulders, she met his gaze straight on and pushed his hand away.

"He is dangerous." Through clenched teeth, moving in so only she could hear, he mouthed, "Ye are aware he is Argyll's cousin?"

"Aye." Although doing her best to look innocent, she knew it was no use with him, but she wouldn't give him the satisfaction of being repentant. Especially knowing all she was to him was a mistake.

"Of course ye are. Ye are trying to get information. Do ye no' ken how treacherous that man is?" Grabbing her by the arm again, he started to guide her back toward the castle.

"He is completely civil to me." She dug in her heels, but he still managed to inch her forward.

Thankfully, the courtyard was nearly empty, and no one was close enough to see or hear what was truly going on between them.

"'Twould appear he wants to be more than civil with ye."

"'Tis none of yer business." She stuck her chin up in the air and did her best to look defiant and out of reach.

His eyes darkened. "Yer safety is my concern."

"Get yer hands off my sister, Mackenzie." A voice boomed from halfway across the courtyard.

Alan froze, panic flashing in his eyes at the voice of her

older brother, their laird. She wanted to ease the worry, but Lachlan was upon them. Alan was spun around and lost his grip on her. She stumbled then turned to see her brother stood behind Alan with his fists clenched, looking as if he were about to rip Alan to shreds.

"Do ye ken what she's doing?" Alan asked. Kirstie barely heard his muffled words.

"Nae, but I do ken ye are acting as if she belongs to ye, and ye have never once asked what I think of the match." Despite Alan's hushed tone, her older brother's voice reverberated through the air, and every eye turned their way.

Her brows knit together. Lachlan loved Alan and would be thrilled if they were to marry. It had been she who urged Lachlan to not let Alan visit her, while he had tried to convince her to come home and talk things out, but she'd refused. Why would he have a change of heart?

Kirstie jumped between them. "What are ye doing, Lachlan?"

"Back up, Kirstie," Lachlan clipped out, but before she could respond, arms were around her waist, dragging her back. She looked over her shoulder to see Malcolm. Shaking his head at her, he held on while she watched helplessly. Lachlan attacked.

He swung at Alan, hitting him square in the jaw.

Kirstie started to struggled. "Malcolm, stop him."

"It has to be done," Malcolm whispered in her ear.

"Nae." Desperate to stop the carnage as Lachlan lunged again, she fought to free herself.

"It has to appear as if he isnnae one of us."

"Does he ken what ye are doing?" Balling her fists and ignoring the pain in her wrist, she wanted to beat her brothers for what they were doing to Alan.

"Nae, but we'll send word when he leaves. Argyll is watching, and 'twill keep Alan safe if they believe his story."

She stopped struggling and wondered what the hell he was talking about. She'd known something wasn't right, but she'd been too busy avoiding Alan to ask questions about their strange behavior.

Alan's face and shoulders had dropped. She had never seen him look so dejected. His hands were clenched, but he didn't strike back. Lachlan started in again but threw no more punches. "Stay away from Kirstie. She'll never be yers. Ye arenae good enough for her."

All color left Alan's face. He glanced at her, and she thought she saw her heartbreak mirrored in his eyes. His gaze left hers, and he nodded to Lachlan.

"I never want to see ye again, Mackenzie. If ye ever step foot on Cameron lands, ye will have to pray for mercy."

Kirstie noticed the silence for the first time. The courtyard had filled with curious onlookers, and every eye was focused on them. Niall and Argyll were on one side studying the scene as Hamish and some other men were farther away, intent on the altercation.

"Ye should have warned him, Malcolm," her voice cracked. She was shaking, she was so angry at her brothers. How could they have done this without letting Alan know what they were up to? Why did they need the earl to believe Alan's story? What was Alan trying to do?

Turning, he walked toward the stables.

"Let me go," she pleaded with Malcolm as a tear ran down her cheek.

"I cannae let ye go after him."

Lachlan strode up and growled at her, "Dinnae follow him, Kirstie. That is an order."

As Malcolm eased his grip, she flew at Lachlan, beating at his chest, ignoring the sharp needles in her injured arm. "Did ye see how yer words hurt him?" Alan wasn't acting. Something had broken inside of him.

Lachlan's arms circled around her and hugged her tight, pinning her in a secure embrace as he twisted, shielding her from view of the others and walking her to a more secluded area. "It has to be this way."

It felt as if she'd had the air knocked out of her; she could barely breathe, could barely talk, barely stand. "Ye just destroyed him. Ye are his whole world."

Out of the view of the others in the courtyard, Eslpeth and Blair hurried up. "Come Kirstie, let's get ye inside. The rain will be here soon."

Lachlan eased his grip as Blair took her hand, and they walked toward the door.

"Mother, I canne let him think Lachlan hates him because of me."

"I ken that, but first we have to talk." Meeting her mother's gaze, she realized Elspeth was holding back the tears of a woman who had just seen one of her children injured. She grieved for Alan as well.

The walk through the castle back to her chamber was a short distance, but each step felt like a long journey. As they reached the bottom of the stairs, her mother turned to Dougal and Blair, the only people who still followed them. Lachlan, Malcolm, and Finlay had disappeared without an explanation. "Can ye two go to the kitchens and find some wine and cheese to bring up, please?"

Her heart ached, and she shook uncontrollably. Once back in her room, she eased into a chair and waited.

Her mother said, "I ken Blair is yer friend, but ye cannae say a word of this to her, and I think they didnae tell ye because of yer ties to the Macnab family. Because of yer association with Blair's family, ye have been accepted by the Covenanters."

"What?" She straightened; she never kept secrets from Blair.

"Alan is trying to infiltrate a group of Covenanters who are set on killing the lairds who dinnae sign the League and Covenant."

"Why would Lachlan let him do something so dangerous?"

"Alan came up with the plan. And it seems to be working. He's been meeting with them at a tavern in the evenings."

"If they found out, they would kill him." A tremor rent through her body, causing the hair on her arms to rise.

"'Tis why Lachlan acted as he did. 'Twas to protect Alan."

She could see why they had to truly appear estranged, but what she had seen in Alan's stance and eyes was a man who truly thought himself unworthy. If Alan had just been putting on a show, he would have thrown a punch of his own.

She may very well be the only friend he had right now. There was no reason Alan had to think he was completely deserted—she could converse with him without it looking suspicious. Damn, she was so mad at her family, she could pretend there was a wedge between them.

A knock sounded, and her mother whispered, "Ye cannae tell her a thing."

"Aye. I'll keep quiet." She would do anything to keep Alan safe, but he had to know he wasn't alone.

A short while later, she'd convinced the group to leave her in the room to sulk as they made their way to the great hall for the mid-day meal. After they left, she quickly donned an inconspicuous traveling gown then draped a plaid over her face and shoulders to hide her identity.

Sneaking through the bustling kitchens, she made her way outside into the storm, which was pummeling the grounds, then through the gate to walk down into the city. Taking Poseidon was too risky. She couldn't be recognized, so she made her way in the deluge to a bakery across the street from Alan's inn and waited inside to make sure she wasn't followed and no one was watching the inn. Very few people moved about in the storm, and those who did were only watching where they were going and not the world around them.

When she felt it was safe, she snuck across the street and found the innkeeper cleaning tables in the empty dining area. The man raised an eyebrow, so despite knowing the way to Alan's room she had to say something or risk looking suspicious. "I'm looking for a Mackenzie," she said as she kept her face hidden beneath the plaid. Pressure invaded her chest as she used the name of his birth clan, but the last thing she would do was risk calling him a Cameron.

"Second door on the right." The man pointed up the stairs, and she nodded.

Knocking, she buried her face deeper in the plaid, scanning the empty hall, and then held her breath as she waited for a reply that didn't come. She wondered if he was out.

She knocked once more.

The door swung in, and Alan peeked out into the hall, his sword by his side. "What do ye want?"

She showed him her face.

"What are ye doing here?" Clasping onto her arm, he pulled her into the room as he stuck his head out farther, likely checking to either see if the inn's usual inhabitants were outside or if she'd been followed by Lachlan.

Satisfied the hall was empty and no immediate threat loomed around the corner, he retreated back into the room and bolted the door.

Before he could say anything, she blurted out, "He didnae mean it."

Alan's gaze was sad. She reached out to touch him. He backed as if he'd been burned. Shaking his head, he moved farther away from her. "Ye shouldnae be here."

"'Twas a show. Lachlan didnae mean it."

He shook his head at her. "Go back to the castle."

"Nae, I willnae."

He scanned the room as if he were looking for a way out or looking for something to strangle her with.

"He did it because Argyll was there. He did it to convince them ye were enemies."

"Even so, he was right."

"Right about what?" She prayed he wouldn't call her a mistake again.

"I amnae good for ye."

Blinking, she tried to make sense of what he was saying.

"'Tis no' true." She moved toward him and reached out to touch his arm.

He groaned. "What are ye trying to do to me?"

"Make ye see the truth."

"Kirstie"—he caught her hand—"we shouldnae be alone." His tone was pleading. It didn't sound like anger; it reverberated of restraint and conflicted emotions. She wanted him to know he wasn't alone, that no matter what she would always be here for him. He had put his very being in jeopardy for her family, his honor and loyalty beckoned her to open one more time. To lay herself bare before him. Deep down, she knew her heart had always belonged to him.

Luckily, she'd worn one of her simpler dresses; it was more like a jacket that fastened in the front over skirts. Before he'd had time to object, she was peeling it off. "I'm so cold. Can ye start a fire?"

She shivered, and Alan's gaze softened, his regard angling toward the window as the rain pelted it with steady thumps and the *whoosh* of a strong wind breezed by, rocking the tree branches outside the panes.

"Ye will leave when it eases." Apparently mollified, he gave her his back and went to work at the hearth.

While he was occupied, she slipped the shift over her

head and pulled off her stockings to hang with the rest of her clothes, drying on a small chair. Alan had an extra plaid folded neatly on a table. She wrapped it around herself then went to sit next to him on the floor as the flames roared to life.

As he saw her undergarments spread out over the chair, shock registered. Looking to her huddled on the floor, next to him in only a woolen blanket, he finally spoke. "Are ye trying to get me killed?"

. . .

Alan couldn't believe Kirstie would be so bold. "Lachlan willnae be pleased to find ye naked in my room."

Staring at the dancing flames, he kept his eyes averted, thankful the storm outside had intensified, drowning out the sound of his beating heart and darkening the chamber.

He rested his elbows on his knees and planted his head in his hands. He'd never felt so defeated.

Her gentle voice broke into his misery. "Ye are wrong. He would be happy for us. Do ye really no' feel anything for me?"

"Doesnae matter what I feel." He risked a glance in her direction. The ongoing war between his head and his heart was splitting him apart inside. He wanted to reach out and touch her, to feel that soft skin and slide the plaid down her shoulder.

"It does to me." When his gaze did meet hers, the sadness in her eyes called to him. His heart ached at the pleading in her voice. She shivered.

"We cannae be together." He had to tear his gaze away from her or he would move closer. He rose and gathered another piece of peat to put on the fire. Out of the corner of his eye, he noticed her pull the plaid tighter around her chest as she made herself smaller.

"Why?" she persisted.

He stared at the flames a moment before turning toward her. "Because I cannae marry ye." A familiar crushing ache in his chest rose up as he finally voiced what he'd held back for years.

She stood and inched toward him. "I deserve an explanation."

He couldn't hide it any longer. She was right; he owed her the truth.

They were just a breath away from each other. She reached up and took his cheek to gently turn his face to hers. "What's wrong with me?" Her voice quavered as her hand fell from his face.

Gulping, he met her gaze directly. "Oh, kitten, 'tis no' ye. I didnae tell ye why my father became a drunk."

She shook her head.

"He betrayed his brother and was forced to leave the clan."

"What did he do?" Her blue gaze remained on him, listening intently as they stood, face-to-face in front of the fire.

"He stole my mother from his brother." Closing his eyes, his mind conjured up an image not of his father, but his friend, Lachlan. The man and the symbol of the family that meant more to him than anything else in all of Scotland.

"What yer father did nae longer matters. Ye are a Cameron now. What Lachlan said today was a lie to make others believe ye were at odds."

"It doesnae matter. He will hate me if I take ye to my bed and then dinnae marry ye."

"Why can ye no' marry me?"

"Because I cannae risk hurting ye."

"I still dinnae understand." She tilted her head as confusion danced in the blue depths of her eyes before understanding took hold, and then what looked like anger rose up.

Disgust churned in his gut, but he continued. "I told ye what my father did. I have the same rage in me. What if I hit ye? I could never live with myself."

Her mouth fell open, disbelief etched on her features before they turned fierce and determined. "'Tis no' ye."

"My uncle had beat her. That's why she left with my father. My grandfather beat his wife, too. So ye see, I cannae marry ye. I wouldnae be able to live with myself if I ever hurt ye."

"As many times as we have fought, have ye ever wanted to raise a hand to me?"

"Nae, but that doesnae—"

Placing her hand over his lips, she cut him off. Piercing his eyes with blinding trust as she removed her hand, she spoke as if she had complete faith in him. "I ken who ye are. Ye are a good man."

Could she be right? He had never had the urge to strike a lass, but doubts lingered. He couldn't risk it, so he closed his eyes and turned away.

"Look at me, Alan Cameron," she ordered. His gaze returned to hers. "'Twas a cycle with yer family. Ye arenae longer one of them. Ye were raised in a loving home by the Camerons."

In her eyes shone a conviction and innocent trust he longed to believe. She held more faith in his nature than he had ever dared to accept as truth.

He thought back to growing up with the Camerons and the loving relationship Elspeth and Robert had. He'd never seen the man raise a hand to her. And when Lachlan's betrothed had betrayed his brother, although he'd claimed to want to kill her, he had not harmed the wench.

"It may be, but I cannae risk hurting ye."

Slipping her arm once again from beneath the plaid she held around her, she took his hand. "I ken ye better than ye ken yerself. 'Tis no' who ye are."

"I want to believe it, but what of my family?"

"The Camerons are yer family." She stepped so close he could feel the warmth of her through the blanket and his clothes. The scent of fresh rain clung to her dark curls, and she smelled of new beginnings and hope. Maybe she was right. He had been able to stop before he'd killed that man last night, and as angry as he'd been with her over her attempt to pry in the Earl of Argyll's room, he'd never once thought of raising a hand to her.

His heart pounded. Her eyes dilated, and his breath caught at the need he saw in them, calling for him to take what he'd always wanted.

"'Tis my risk as much as yers."

She released his hand, stepped back, and dropped the plaid to the ground. Kirstie stood before him naked, and every part of his body froze, well, except the part that started growing painfully hard.

Her lilting voice and tempting body reminded him of the story she'd read him of Sirens and the destruction they left in their path, luring him into troubled waters with promises of what could be. It was too late to turn back; he was already ensnared. Truthfully, he had been since the moment she kissed him that long ago evening in the stable. He wanted to believe.

"Alan." She stood bare before him with the firelight glowing on her skin. The nipples of her full breasts were erect and called to him. "I want ye. Please."

Those words were his downfall. He took a step toward her and felt his breath become shallow as his body tightened all over. She reached out and took his belt. He couldn't move as she unfastened it and dropped it to the ground. Her hands rose up to his chest and seared him even through his shirt as she pushed the plaid from his shoulders, and it fell with a soft *whoosh* to the floor.

"Kiss me." She pleaded in a throaty purr that sent shivers of need racing through him. His body thrummed as his blood heated and desire pumped through his veins.

His shaking hands found her curves and pulled her into him. Head tilting down toward hers, he took her lips. She quivered, and her arms wrapped around his waist, cocooning him to her fevered flesh. His body sank into hers as his tongue plunged into her mouth to tangle and dance with hers.

She made a little mewling noise that made him want to push faster and harder, but he'd wanted this for so long, he tamped it down. He wanted to savor every second that he touched and tasted her.

One hand skimmed down her soft skin to her hip and drew her tighter to him. Moaning into his mouth, she shuddered, and her limbs became pliant. Her response to his touch set his blood on fire. The pressure building in his cock was heavy and urgent.

His other hand slid up her back, and when his fingers reached her head, they spread into her hair, clasping the base of her neck to hold her to him and prolong the kiss. Each second with her in his arms was a miracle.

His lips left hers, and his mouth went to her ear. The words were throaty and thick with need. "If we do this, kitten, cannae be undone. If we dinnae stop now, I willnae be able to."

He wanted this, but there was still some coherent part of him that knew if he tasted her, everything would change. He wouldn't be able to let another have her. Once she was his, he would never be able to give her up.

His gaze met hers. The heat he saw in her blue eyes took his breath away and called to the deepest part of his primitive male being. She was his woman, and it was time he stopped fighting and acknowledged it.

"Aye, dinnae stop. I want ye so much, I can barely breathe."

He dipped his mouth to the curve of her neck. He'd wanted to put his mouth there for so long and savor the tender flesh. She tilted to give him better access, and his lips closed on the sensitive skin while her fingers dug into his side and beckoned his body to move closer into hers. She tasted of the rain and cool nights under a warm blanket, the Highlands, and everything comforting and real.

Nipping at her soft skin, he was rewarded when she shivered and arched into him. The hand still on her hip slid down and cupped her firm, sweet ass, angling the juncture of her legs toward his hard erection. He ground against her and thrilled at the friction between their bodies. She was slick with her desire for him. Kissing her neck again, he bit down and sucked.

"Alan." The husky words were ripped from her mouth as she threw her head back. His pulse raced as the need he'd kept leashed for years intensified at her raspy plea.

He yanked himself away from her. She was dazed and beautiful, her lips swollen from his kiss, her curves waiting to be held again. And her hair, slightly wet, cascaded to her breasts and shoulders as if it, too, could not get enough of the feel of her skin.

"Here," he instructed as he moved her to the side and spread her discarded blanket on the ground. He was still wearing his boots, so he quickly kicked them to the door. After pulling the shirt over his head, he threw it to the side, heedless of where it landed.

Her eyes were wide as she took in the sight of his erect cock. She trembled, and he remembered she'd never done this before; he would have to be gentle and go slow. The thought brought a smile to his face because that was just right. He didn't want this to ever end.

Taking her, he drew her into his arms again, kissing her until the fear he'd seen in her eyes vanished. He hoped she was as hot and needy as he was. His hands urged her toward the floor and onto the blankets.

The bed was just a few feet away, but here, in front of the firelight, he would be able to see her face clearly. He would see the pleasure wash over her as he thrust in and out. He wanted to always remember this moment.

Kirstie inhaled with surprise as he scooped her up in his arms. He'd held her like this once before. That time, she'd screamed and kicked as he threw her into the loch on a playful dare. This time, she gazed up with eyes that looked into his soul and pierced the part of his heart he'd kept locked away. She melted into him, and he took a moment to savor the feel of her.

This is real.

He sank down on one knee to lay her gently on the blanket, inhaling as he took in the beauty of her before him with the radiant warmth from the fire illuminating her skin. His side still hurt from the blow to his ribs, but he ignored it and nestled beside her.

Braced on one elbow, he trailed a hand across her taut belly. She lay on her back, watching him with a spark of hesitance.

"'Tis yer last chance to come to yer senses, lass," he said as the hand on her midsection rose and grasped her breast, stroking his thumb over her pert nipple. The reluctance in her eyes was replaced with a heated stare that beckoned for him to touch more, taste more.

His fingers pinched, and she answered by arching into his touch. Her head flew back and her mouth dropped open on a gasp. Turned to look at him once more with hooded, sultry eyes. Words seemed to be stuck on her tongue as she moved into him again.

"If ye stop, I will go mad," she purred. His kitten wanted him as much as he needed her. He couldn't help the satisfied smile that curved his lips.

His mouth dropped to the breast in his hand, and he kissed the mound tenderly then licked at the peak. His tongue tangled back and forth over the sensitive tip as she writhed beside him. He sucked the whole tip into his mouth, hard and long. She was panting when he released it.

Hand drifting down her flat belly to her curly woman's hair, he ran his fingers through the thick patch in circles, massaging the skin beneath and enjoying the feel as the silky strands slid around him.

He plunged deeper and was met with a welcoming wetness. She was slick and soft. As he ran a finger up and down her folds, his mouth continued to work at her breast. When his finger slid across her tender clit, he felt her hands clench the blankets as she cried out.

His cock throbbed as the need to claim her became overwhelming. Shifting, he was on top of her, pushing her legs apart with his knee. There was no resistance as she willingly opened to him.

He sank down, and the engorged tip of his shaft touched her scalding hot center. Leaning over her with one arm, he took his cock in his other hand and rubbed it up and down her wet passage entrance. With each flick, he soaked up more of her juices. She spasmed beneath him as he rubbed against the sensitive nub at the top of her waiting passage.

His gaze returned to hers, and he watched her, taking in the desire she so easily wore on her face. Her tongue darted out to wet her lips as sapphire orbs silently pleaded for him to sate the ache that matched his own.

He slowly slid into her and only paused for a moment

when her barrier stopped the invasion. Pushing harder, he broke through to her warm, tight center. Her arms left the blankets and grasped his ribs.

The desire in her eyes lessened, but only slightly.

"'Twill be all right. The rest will feel good," he rasped out as he fought to keep his hips from moving on their own.

She nodded, and he shifted forward to dip his lips to hers. She opened to him, and his tongue swirled inside and took with it any trepidation the breaking of her maidenhead had awoken. Kirstie shimmied, urging him to keep going, and he rose to see her eyes had once again dilated.

Pulling back, he plunged into her again. He was rewarded with a soft feminine sigh. He did it again, and her hips rose up to meet his advance. Her head turned from side to side as he thrust again and again.

She cried out below him with fevered gasps as he drove harder, her body arching and bowing beneath him. She glowed in the firelight as her eyes rolled up and the waves of pleasure took her under. He continued to plunge as she spiraled out of control.

Kirstie was starting to catch her breath when he came undone. The spasms in her tight sheath clenched around his swollen cock until he was convulsing above her. His body quaked with each tremor until his seed spilled out and filled her womb.

Leaning down on an elbow, he stayed inside her, not yet willing to let go of the connection between them. Kirstie's hand traced the muscles on his chest and weaved in and out of his hair. She licked her lips and looked up at him.

"Why have ye waited so long to do that to me?"

He couldn't help the smile that he felt all the way to his toes. He'd never dared to dream he would one day have Kirstie naked by his side.

As he studied her, he knew, he would never raise a hand

to her. She meant too much to him. He was nothing like his birth family. Her needs and wants would always come before his so that he could keep that heart rendering happiness on her face. Caressing her cheek, he kissed her one more time before he reluctantly slid from her body.

Leaning on an elbow beside her, he ran his other fingers up and down her body, from her thigh to shoulder, paying special attention to each curve. Her skin was a golden color that had deepened in the dull light of the room.

The rain continued, but they were warm and sated as the outside world disappeared, oblivious to the tranquil scene locked away in this room. It was like being wrapped in a warm blanket with everything he needed. Her cheeks still had a pink blush, and her lips were swollen. She glowed more beautiful in the firelight than he imagined any of the goddesses from the stories she'd read to him ever could.

A sweet, demure smile turned up the corners of her lips.

"I've never seen ye shy before."

"Dinnae get used to it. 'Twill no' last." Her smile turned into a playful smirk.

"I like this side of ye. I may have to find more ways to make ye blush." She turned a darker pink.

"Did I please ye?"

"Aye. Ye did more than please me."

She'd demolished the walls of his self-control and forever changed their lives. He wasn't ready to tell her that she had made him feel complete, that she was his perfect match and he never wanted to go through another day without her. After ensuring her family was safe, then garnering Lachlan's permission to wed her, he would confess all, but he couldn't utter those words until he had proven himself.

Spilling his seed inside her, he had shared himself in a way with her that he never had before. She could even now be carrying his babe. The thought made him want to take her again to ensure the chances, but he didn't want to push her too far too fast.

Their time in Edinburgh couldn't end soon enough. He wanted to get her out of here and back to Kentillie where they both belonged together. He would have to let Lachlan, Malcolm, and Elspeth know of his intentions, and he would deal with the consequences as they came.

"Ye are certain your brother isnae angry and would welcome a union between us?"

It was a little late now to second-guess. Lingering doubts assailed him as her hand brushed across the sensitive spot on his cheek that would purple from Lachlan's blow before the day was out.

"Aye, they will be happy. They love ye and will be thankful for ye bringing me home."

Her gaze ventured from his face to glance appreciatively at his chest and then farther down. She turned onto her elbow and lowered her hand to graze her fingers along his ribs and down to the hair near his cock. An involuntary shudder ran through him, and he felt himself start to grow again.

Her explorations took her back to his side and ribs. He flinched and stifled a laugh. A devilish smile crossed her lips. "I had forgotten how ticklish ye are."

Kirstie swiped across his sensitive skin again, and he tried to pull back out of her reach as laughter exploded from him. She followed and rolled on top of his chest. His laughter stopped as she sat up and straddled to pin him while she attempted to tickle him again. All feeling from his side had moved to his newly erect cock. It was propped up and ready just behind her ass.

"I always loved chasing ye around."

"Aye, and I can tolerate it if ye are going to sit astride me with no' a stitch on."

He was certain his eyes darkened as her wet passage

rubbed against his pubic area. He reached up and took her hands to still her, careful with the wrist that had been injured the evening before. "Ye are trying to drive me mad, kitten."

He pulled one hand behind her back and touched his cock with it. "Feel what ye do to me, lass."

His eyes fluttered back as her long fingers glided up his length. It was not a smart move on his part, because it pushed her breasts out for him to see and the caress of her hand nearly made him lose control.

"Can we? Is it too soon?" The eager gleam in her eyes tempted him, and he grew harder.

"I assure ye we can. But 'twill make ye sore."

"I dinnae mind. 'Twill only give me proof that this day wasnae a dream."

Oh to hell with waiting. He'd waited long enough.

If she had more experience, he'd impale her and thrust into her from below. As much as he wanted her to ride astride him, it would be too much, so he gently rolled her over and took her again, but this time more slowly. Savoring the moment and disregarding the niggling worry that once they left this room, his newfound hope for the future would be ripped away like an unmoored boat in stormy water.

Chapter Nine

Kirstie wouldn't say she was sore, but when she walked, there was a delicious ache that made her aware of her newly acquired state, accompanied by a subtle yearning for more. Alan had the innkeeper bring cheese, bread, and fresh water. He'd also had a basin and some cloths brought to the room. Wetting the soft material, he had leaned down to her private parts and washed away the evidence of their lovemaking. It had been a sensual act in itself.

"Tell me about yer mother," Kirstie said as they sat near the fire, wrapped in blankets.

"I dinnae remember much about her other than her always being angry. I guess it was how she felt about her lot in life." He shrugged.

"I am glad my mother was there for ye, then." She snuggled closer to him and relished the feel of his warm skin against her own.

"I think she was always bitter about being cast out. She missed her family and blamed my father. Maybe it was one of the reasons he drank as much as he did."

"Did ye really think Mother and Lachlan would turn ye out if we were together?"

"No' just for being together, but that I didnae plan to wed ye. I thought I would turn out like my father, and I was no' willing to pull ye into that kind of life."

"Now ye ken that isnae true." She caressed his cheek, determined to get through to him that she was certain he would never raise a hand to her.

"Aye, 'twas just something I had always believed, but ye let me look at it from a new perspective." He placed a gentle kiss on her knuckles, eliciting small tingles of contentment to drift through her stated body.

"Do ye still spend all yer time in the stables?"

She shivered, not from cold—there was plenty of warmth next to him—but from the tenderness of the kiss.

"Aye, taking care of the animals gives me a purpose I never had before."

"Wallace will be happy ye are back." He let go, and she rested one hand on his bare leg.

She smiled as an image of the old stable master from Kentillie appeared in her head, until it dawned on her, if she went back home, she would lose her status in the stables. Wallace was a nice man but old fashioned. He didn't believe in lasses caring for the horses, and as a youth he'd shooed her out of the stalls every chance he had, despite that fact that he had many daughters and should understand a woman should do what called to her heart.

"How are all his daughters?" she asked, pushing away the thought of a life without her horses.

"I am sure they are fine. I dinnae spend so much time there anymore."

She turned her head to the side. "Ye used to be there all the time."

"Aye, 'twas so I could watch ye." He peeked at her

through his lashes.

His admission stunned her. He had never once let on or encouraged her when she was younger. "Nae, ye never noticed me."

"'Twas no' that I thought I had feelings for ye, but I always felt at ease with ye."

She thought back to the days she had cherished, where they had worked side by side, sometimes without a word as they took care of the horses.

"I used to seek ye out by the loch. I always pretended to have something that I needed to wash," she admitted. "Ye always seemed to be there when ye had something to think on."

"My father never went near the water, so it was comforting."

"Should we build a house by the loch or stay in Kentillie Castle?" Kirstie pushed, despite knowing he'd not yet committed to her.

"What if we do both? Build our own private place and keep a room at the castle for when we are there. We can put a cot in the room for Elspeth to watch the babes when we need some time alone." He gave her a wolfish grin and ran a finger up her arm. She trembled as his hand skimmed down her back and rested on her bottom.

"Do ye want children, then?"

"I never let myself think about it before."

"Ye would be a good father."

Visions of Alan with younger kids through the years played back in her head, then the memory from yesterday. She envisioned him hunched down tossing a potato in the air after he'd defended the wee child from some brute who was about to strike him. She'd pretended not to be watching, but it was near impossible to keep her gaze from wandering to him when he was in a room with her.

"I need to start thinking about it, but we havenae gotten our laird's approval yet." His fingers skimmed across her belly.

"How is yer side? Ye seem to be doing okay with it." She had seen a faint bruise there, but he hadn't complained.

"I've had worse."

"'Tis no' what I asked. Does it pain ye?"

"Nae, how is yer wrist?"

"'Tis doing better." She held it up and wiggled her fingers to show him she had removed the bandage. "As long as I dinnae put pressure on it, 'tis fine."

"They havenae been able to find the scrawny one."

"Mayhap he is no' threat without that brute he was with."

"If he stays in Edinburgh, we will find him." Alan's eyes went dark.

They were lazy the rest of the afternoon. It had been a dream come true and she hadn't wanted to go, but now she had to sneak back to the castle before anyone could find her. She also had the business of saving her brothers and keeping Alan safe.

"I need to go." She sighed.

"Aye, ye probably should before Lachlan rushes through that door and unleashes his wrath to teach me a lesson for touching his little sister."

"Ye do believe me that he will be happy for us?"

"Aye, we will work it out." But doubt brewed in his eyes as she pulled her shift back over her head.

It was the same reservation coursing through her veins at the thought of being nothing more than a wife. Could she give up the one thing that had given her life purpose? She would have to if she wanted Alan, and she did, she wanted him with every fiber of her being, but the thought of life without caring for the horses weighed heavy on her.

"I'll see ye back to the castle." He rose and dressed along

with her.

"Ye cannae be seen with me."

"I'll follow from a distance, just to be sure ye arrive."

"See ye tonight," she said as she slipped from the door, already missing him as she replaced the plaid over her head to hide her face. The rain had slackened, but it still kept the streets mostly deserted. The air had cooled, and it chilled her to the bone. By the time she arrived at the fortress on top of the hill, the peace of the afternoon had washed away. Everything that had seemed possible just a few moments ago now seemed out of her reach.

Malcolm paced outside her chamber. "Where have ye been?" he hissed through clenched teeth as she got close enough to hear. The only other person in the hall was Finlay, several doors down, outside her mother's room.

"I went to see Alan." She kept the plaid draped over her head.

"Ye cannae be seen with him."

"Nae, ye are wrong. I can. I have been living with the Macnabs and have as much of a connection to the Covenanters as anyone. Me being seen with him will not be questioned."

"'Tis no' a good idea."

"Aye, 'tis. I can pass information between ye if I need to. He's already been seen with me multiple times this week, so no one will suspect it."

"I'll talk to Lachlan, but I dinnae like it, and dinnae go back to his inn. They could be watching him."

"I was careful."

"Ye cannae be too cautious where these men are concerned."

Nodding, she pushed past him and entered her room, leaving him in the hall. She was still angry with him for not telling her the truth as soon as they had arrived.

After telling Blair she'd spent the afternoon wandering

around looking for Alan, and in the stables with Poseidon, they dressed and made their way down for dinner. She hated the lie but vowed she'd tell her friend the truth as soon as everyone was safe and away from Edinburgh. For now, she had to try one more time to see if the Covenanters would slip up and reveal some hint of their plan at dinner.

• • •

When they arrived at the great hall, both her brothers and Alan were absent. She recognized it as irrational, but a fear came over her that something had happened to them, so she told Blair she would be back shortly and took off in the direction of Malcolm's room.

Malcolm didn't answer, so she moved to return to the hall but had a moment's hesitation when she walked by the chamber she'd seen Niall Campbell come from earlier in the week. Knowing it was too dangerous to search his room, she was about to continue on when Niall strolled around the corner to see her in front of his door. Chills ran down her spine.

"Were ye looking for me, Ms. Cameron?" His gaze pinned her with mistrust. Her head spun to come up with a logical reason for standing outside his door.

"Aye. Nae, no' really."

In the pale candlelit hallway, she could just make out his eyes as they narrowed and darkened. He moved in front of her and placed his hands on the door around her, effectively caging her between the thick wood and his body.

"What are ye doing outside my door?" His voice was harsh and demanding. He wasn't much taller than her, but he loomed over her with a commanding presence that made her want to shrink away.

"I came to see Malcolm, and he wasnae here. I

remembered yer room was next to his, so I decided to see if ye would like to escort me to dinner. I was just leaving when ye didnae answer my knock." Praying her voice didn't tremble, she turned a smile on him.

He stilled and waited for her to go on. Her heart beat a rapid tattoo of fear laced with a healthy dose of self-preservation, so she chose the only option she thought she had left.

"I so enjoyed our dance last night. I thought ye may be interested in more." His mouth curved up in a twisted devilish grin, and his gaze traveled down to her chest.

Och, I've chosen the wrong words.

"More dancing," she corrected quickly and swallowed.

"I would enjoy dancing with ye again."

She tried to maneuver around him, but his arm lowered and braced against the stones to cut off her retreat.

Niall's eyes filled with a dark lust, and one hand drifted to open the door as the other circled around her waist. "Come in, and we can discuss what more I want."

Panic enveloped her. "'Tis no' proper," she started.

"There ye are, Campbell. I was looking for ye." A familiar, warm voice rumbled through the hall. Niall's arms retreated as he took a step back. Alan appeared from nowhere.

Alan's eyes widened. "Kirstie, what are ye doing here? Ye should be down with Blair."

He was a damn good actor, or he honestly didn't anticipate finding her here. She had expected anger from him, not the cool indifference and easy dismissal he heaped on her now.

"I was looking for Malcolm." She took the opportunity to slide from the doorway and farther away from the scoundrel who had just tried to have his way with her.

"Why are ye here?" Niall was able to keep the anger out of his tone, but she saw it in his eyes. He thought Alan had just stolen his chance at getting under her skirts.

Alan had probably just saved her from something horrible. She would make it a point to avoid Niall in the future at all costs. There was no telling what he would do to her if he got her alone.

Alan kept on. If he noticed any undercurrents, he didn't let it show. He continued talking to Niall and ignoring her. "I didnae see ye at the table tonight, so I came up to make sure ye hadn't left for the tavern without me."

Niall's shoulders relaxed. "I just forgot something in my room. I was coming down to dinner right after. Wait here. I'll be right back." He turned the knob and disappeared through the door, shutting it behind him and leaving them alone in the empty hall.

Alan peered at her and whispered, "What did ye think ye were doing?" He grasped her wrist, and she winced. He eased his grip and slid his hand down her arm slowly to inspect it.

She opened her mouth to answer then stopped and looked at him sideways. "Ye followed me." Her lips thinned as anger invaded the relief she'd felt at his presence.

"Aye, I did. And now I forbid ye from going anywhere on yer own. Ye seem incapable of making sane decisions." He guided her farther from the door, glancing around to make certain they were still alone.

She fumed but said nothing.

"I didnae see Malcolm or Lachlan tonight. I was worried." Before she could whisper the rest, the door began to open.

Alan dropped her arm. "I have to pretend as if ye dinnae mean anything to me," he said under his breath before Niall stepped up beside them.

"Now, Ms. Cameron, may I escort ye to the hall?" Niall asked.

The dim light held enough glow that she could see the muscle in Alan's jaw tick and his fists clench at his sides as Niall held out his arm for her to take.

"Aye, ye may. I am quite hungry tonight."

She laced her arm through Niall's, and they started down the hall with Alan trailing behind. The back of her neck burned with the anger she could feel wafting off him.

•••

Alan slammed his cup down on the table a little harder than intended. He'd been forced to sit next to Niall Campbell, while Kirstie was sandwiched between the vile man and Hamish on her other side. Kirstie had pushed Niall's arm from her leg several times already, and if the man touched her again, Alan would be forced to take action. She seemed to be fending off the same type of unwanted attention from Hamish as well.

She had tangled herself up in this web of spiders, and she thought she would get away unscathed. He had to make sure that happened. He had watched her head up to the rooms above stairs but had stayed to the shadows until Niall had looked like a pleased lion ready to pounce on her.

He didn't want to think about what the man would have done to her if he had been able to get her into that room. Niall was known for having a temper and a twisted sense of right and wrong. Clenching his fists under the table, he remembered the fear in Kirstie's eyes and the entitled way Niall had hovered over her. His stomach knotted, and he found himself unable to eat.

To top off dealing with the men pawing at her under the table, Lachlan was watching him from across the room, eyes blazing as hot as the summer sun. If bears were still in Scotland, his laird could have been a descendant of the burly beasts. Lachlan looked like what Alan imagined a bear defending its cub would, ready to lash out with its sharp claws and teeth. He couldn't tell if the anger was directed at him or the two men flanking Kirstie.

Talk of tomorrow's summit filled the evening's conversation. It was a slippery slope for Alan to navigate with both Royalists and Covenanters by his side. He'd kept his eye on Kirstie the whole time but had not been able to make out what she and Hamish had been discussing.

The mood after dinner was somber. It seemed as if the revelry of the week had been an illusion as men and women departed from the hall, as if everyone had decided to head to bed early to prepare their thoughts and arguments for the meeting tomorrow, or maybe the steady rain had just brought down everyone's spirits.

When his table started to disperse, Alan leaned over to Niall and Hamish. "Shall we go to the tavern?"

"Nae. I don't wish to go out in that mess," Hamish answered. "But meet us there tomorrow night when everything is over. I'm sure we will have much to discuss." He was again tracing his teeth with his tongue as some unspoken thoughts flitted around behind his steady, unnerving gaze.

Alan had wanted to walk Kirstie back to her room, but Lachlan and Malcolm motioned for her to join them, and she was off before he was able to speak to her. He was thankful he would no longer have to worry about Niall or Hamish attempting to see her to her bedchamber and feign disinterest in their attention to her. It had been hard enough to make it through dinner pretending he hadn't wanted to cut out the men's eyes for looking at her. He could only hope Lachlan had seen their attentions and was now lecturing Kirstie on being too familiar with the men.

Pushing away thoughts of Kirstie and the coming confrontation with Lachlan, he focused his attentions on what he needed to do next. Right now, he had to think about the plot against the Cameron brothers. Finlay and Dougal were standing in a corner of the room, and he covertly made his way to them.

They stood by an alcove, and he was able to lean into the shadows of the small space. To the rest of the room, it appeared as if Dougal and Finlay were alone.

"Have ye learned anything new?" Alan asked.

"Nae. What about ye?" Dougal countered.

"All I ken is that the threat will come sometime after the summit has concluded." He paused. "They have invited me to meet with them when the talks are done tomorrow. I believe they feel they can trust me."

"Let's hope so." Dougal scratched his nose.

"Where's Henry taking Blair?" Finlay asked. Before they could answer, he started cursing and walked away.

"Ye need to pass along to Lachlan that he, Malcolm, and Kirstie should leave as soon as 'tis over tomorrow."

"I dinnae think he will do it. He has said if other lairds are in danger, 'tis his responsibility to lend them a hand."

"If he is to be so foolish, he should at least get Malcolm and Kirstie out."

"Ye ken with him staying, they willnae leave." Dougal shook his head.

"Then 'twill fall to us to keep them safe." He forked his fingers into his hair, massaging the muscles as he tried to come up with a way to get them out of Edinburgh before something bad could happen.

"Aye."

"Ye stay close to Malcolm, I'll keep an eye on Kirstie, and have Finlay watch out for Lachlan." Releasing his head, he let his hands drop to his side.

"What if I want to take Kirstie?" The words felt like a taunt, although he couldn't see the man's face in his position.

"Nae. 'Tis easier if I do it, since I have access to the Covenanters she's been staying with," Alan said.

"Uh, 'twas right, ye have feelings for the lass. Lachlan

said ye did, but I didnae believe him."

"So Lachlan kens, then. Did he seem angry?"

"I can never tell. I can tell ye he has been a tyrant since we got here."

What if Kirstie was wrong and Lachlan's actions hadn't been an act? *Och*, what had he done? There was no turning back now. Lachlan would either welcome, banish, or kill him.

"Looks like yer new friends are on their way to their rooms tonight."

Alan didn't have to look to know he was talking about Hamish and Niall. "I cannae wait to be back at Kentillie. If I have to listen to one more of Hamish's sermons or watch Kirstie pull Niall's paws off her, I will have to slit their throats."

"Kirstie's scanning the room. I think she wishes to ken where they have gone."

He hoped she was looking for him, but he stayed silent.

"The man who attacked her in the stables was flogged and hung in the square today. From what I hear, 'twas no' a bonny sight."

"Dinnae let it get back to her. She has been affected enough by the filthy cowards."

"'Tis been no sighting of his friend, but Lachlan still has men looking for him and has instructed one of us to stay guard outside the ladies' rooms until we're all back home."

"Good."

"Looks as if Malcom and Lachlan are walking her and Elspeth to their rooms. I dinnae think Blair went the same way. 'Tis why Finlay ran off like he did. He has a tender spot for that bonny friend of Kirstie's."

"I think he will have to wait in line. Henry Macnab was watching her like she already belonged to him."

"I'll get word to ye if I hear anything new. This cannae be over soon enough."

"Be careful."

"Take care of them, Dougal."

Dougal turned and strolled away, while Alan hung in the alcove a little longer. When enough time had passed, he started wandering the halls to see if everyone was where they were supposed to be and if he could overhear something that would make this mission easier.

Sometime later, his appetite had returned, and he found himself leaning against the outside wall in the kitchens, having a small snack and watching the last of the servants cleaning. He was about to leave for the inn, but the food here was much better, so he'd stopped on his way to the stables.

A man inched his way through the door, letting in fresh air and carrying some pans, but he didn't shut the door behind him. Whispered words from a conversation on the other side caught his attention.

"And what is he going to do to the Cameron lass after they're dead?"

Alan froze and stopped chewing.

"It won't be good. 'Tis all I ken."

"Och, there he is, ye better hide." A man darted in the door and bolted through the room as if the devil were chasing him. Alan couldn't see who it was, only noticing shoulder-length, curly blond hair with the build of a boy on the verge of becoming a man.

When he pivoted to peek out the door, whoever the other voice had belonged to was gone. Hell, they could only have been talking about Kirstie. The blood in his veins froze. Lachlan and Malcolm might not be the only ones in danger.

He had to know she was safe. Sneaking up to the hall outside her room, he watched from around a corner as Dougal paced up and down the corridor between her room and Elspeth Cameron's. Finding a metal cup that had been left outside another chamber, he tossed it down the nearest stairwell. When his friend went to investigate the noise, he took off for Kirstie's room.

Finding the door unlocked, he easily slid in before Dougal reappeared. He bolted the door behind him then moved to the bed. Seeing Kirstie safe, he was able to take in air again, but fear still beat in his chest. It seemed odd that Blair was missing, because most of the guests had left the hall. Hopefully, John Macnab was looking out for his sister.

He should leave and go back to the tavern, but his legs wouldn't budge. Her bed looked so enticing, so inviting, and it would take him at least an hour to get back by the time he got to his horse, rode down, and had it settled again for the night. Kneeling, he moved closer to her, and a small sigh escaped from her throat as his finger caressed her cheek.

Considering that her plea for his protection, he set his sword down by the edge of the bed within easy reach, then he rested on the edge of the bed, pulled off his boots, unbelted his plaid, took off his shirt, and discarded them on the floor. There was something reassuring about crawling into bed naked next to her. He slid under the covers and draped his arm around her. She had been lying on her side, so her back was to his chest, with her ass just at cock level. He snuggled in closer to enjoy the warmth of her and quickly fell asleep.

Chapter Ten

Alan woke to delicious tingles on his scalp. When he opened his eyes, Kirstie was there. Her fingers laced through the thick strands of his hair, and a heart-melting smile arched her full lips. Her lazy, hooded eyes were a sight he would be happy to wake to every morning.

His fingers dove into her hair and clasped the back of her head, pulling her close so their lips gently touched. He closed his mouth over hers and deepened the kiss. His tongue delved in and tangled with hers. She was spice and honey and all woman. He wanted more. His hand slid down her shoulders, down her back, and cupped her sweet ass to pull her on top of him.

A knock sounded at the door. "Kirstie, open up. It's me."

He groaned into her mouth.

Kirstie ended the kiss and pulled back. "Hold on, give me a minute," she called to the door. "Ye should put yer clothes on. I cannae leave Blair out there in the hall."

"Come on, 'tis cold out here."

Alan thought 'twas no' much better in here as he threw

back the covers, losing both their warmth and Kirstie's at the same time.

They dressed quickly, and Alan ambled toward the door, hesitant to begin what was sure to be an arduous day. He was going to insist Kirstie join him for breakfast right away. They had a lot to discuss.

Opening the door, his gaze rested on Kirstie's friend. Blair's face was red and puffy. "Are ye okay?" Concern and anger washed over him.

She shook her head and skirted past him as he peeked into the hall to see in the light of the morning. The Cameron men weren't on guard, which made sense because there was only Finlay and Dougal, and they did have to sleep. It was best they didn't know he'd spent the night with their laird's sister before he had a chance to speak with Lachlan.

Kirstie took one look at Blair's disheveled and downtrodden expression and glanced to him. "Can we have a few moments alone?"

"Aye. I'll be back to get ye for breakfast in half an hour."

Alan paced the halls to give the lasses time to discuss whatever calamity had befallen Blair. He would bet his best sword that it had something to do with Henry Graham—surprising, since she had obviously spent the night with him. He'd expected her to come back glowing and happy at finally getting that rogue to commit to marriage.

As he passed the great hall, he saw Hamish in a corner watching the set of steps closest to Kirstie's room. Hamish saw him and motioned for him to come closer. Clapping a hand on his shoulder when Alan walked up, he started, "Are you well rested for the day's events?"

"Aye, I am."

"Sit with me today at the summit. I am sure it will be an interesting meeting."

"'Twill be a good thing if I can report back to my clan

that the Royalists will no longer be a problem." He cringed inside as he told the lie.

"Once we are done, the plan is to head to the tavern to discuss. Join us."

"Aye."

"Have ye seen Kirstie Cameron this morning?"

"Has she no' come down yet?" He deftly avoided answering that one.

"Nae, I need to speak to her. I asked her to be my wife."

His heart seemed to skip a beat, and his fingers shook. "What did she say?"

"She said she would give me an answer tonight after the meeting, but now I fear I will not see her until tomorrow if I don't find her this morning."

Alan was going to make certain Hamish didn't see her this morning. "Are ye no' concerned she is a Royalist?"

"I can remedy that quickly enough." Hamish's twisted smile turned Alan's stomach. Would she actually marry this man? Nae, she was going to marry him after he talked to Lachlan.

"If I see her, 'twill tell her ye are looking for her." Another lie.

"I appreciate that."

"See ye at the summit." Alan walked toward the exit of the castle. He didn't want Hamish to see him take the steps to Kirstie's room, so he came in a side door and took the ones at the other end of the hall.

Cresting the steps, he made sure the hall was empty before rushing toward Kirstie's chamber and knocking lightly. She opened the door, and he snuck in without anyone seeing. "We have some things we need to discuss." He looked over to Blair. "Will ye be all right if I take her for the morning?"

"I dinnae feel well, so I am going to nap anyway."

"All right then, we shall see ye later."

Kirstie drew her in for a hug and whispered something in her ear he didn't hear. Blair nodded and released her. "Dinnae mistreat her." Blair's eyes narrowed on Alan as she ordered. "She deserves to be happy."

"Aye. I will see that she is happy." Did he even know what that meant? Doubts had exploded in his head the moment Hamish had mentioned marrying her. What did Kirstie want? Would she look for it with Hamish if he wasn't able to give it to her?

Alan peeked out into the hall before pulling on Kirstie's hand and guiding her toward the stairs that weren't being watched by her boring Covenanter suitor.

"Where are we going?" She dug in her heels, and he had to tug at her to keep her moving.

"We are going to my place. There are several things we need to discuss and cannae do it here. Cover yer head." He tossed her the plaid he'd picked up in her room.

Skirting the side of the castle, he took off when they hit the yard and saw there was no one about to see them together. He slowed when he realized her legs were shorter than his and she'd be on the ground soon if he didn't gentle the pace.

As he sped across, he thought about Hamish. She couldn't marry him. He was a Covenanter and had to be one of the dullest men he'd ever met. Kirstie had slept with him, and although he had not asked her to marry him, they'd discussed a future. Why had she not told him of Hamish's proposal? Was she actually considering it?

They had reached the stables. After scanning the inside and discovering people were starting to mill about, he spared a glance just to be certain she couldn't be recognized.

She remained silent. "Get on my horse and meet me at the inn. Go slow and I will follow on foot to make sure ye arenae followed." She did as instructed.

"Here's my key. When ye get there, sneak up to my room

and dinnae let anyone see ye." He held his hand out to help her mount his horse then gently patted the beast's rump to get it moving.

He left through the other exit, careful not to follow too closely as he combed their surroundings for any sign of danger or one of the men who was vying for her attention. If he was honest with himself, he was trying to keep her hidden away from the rest of the world.

He watched as she stopped by the stable then walked inside the inn. Despite the people who were milling about, no one looked her way as she kept her face hidden. Pausing at the door to the kitchen, he ordered some breakfast to be delivered to his room. They would need their energy for what he had planned this morning.

• • •

Kirstie paced as a myriad of emotions flooded her.

Her heart broke for Blair—her first time with Henry should have been special. She had known all along that man was a selfish arse.

He had been rough with her; he'd not hit her, but he had not been a gentle lover. Blair said the first time had been painful. She had clutched the sheets and squeezed her eyes shut the whole time praying for it to end, while Kirstie's first with Alan had been heaven, so she knew it was not the act itself.

Henry had woken Blair again this morning and been so rough she had cried through the whole experience. Afterward, he had apparently looked at her with disgust and said, "I had not expected ye to be such a whimpering innocent. Ye will have to get used to it because as my wife, ye will need to keep me pleased."

Aye, Henry Graham was a handsome man, but he was

also an unfeeling arse. How was she going to keep her sweet friend, who was always happy, from wedding that monster and becoming his plaything?

Alan burst into the room and sat at the chair her clothes had hung on only yesterday. He motioned for her to take the other seat. "I've asked the innkeeper to bring us some food."

She nodded. "Good, I'm hungry." She inched over and sat.

"I am worried ye may no' be safe."

Och, she was hoping to have another pleasant morning with him, but this was to be a lecture. "What did ye hear?"

"That someone has plans for ye if yer brothers dinnae survive."

"Who said it? And it willnae matter because I ken ye will keep them safe." A trickle of fear pricked at the back of her neck, but then she remembered she wasn't anyone important. Why would anyone want her? Alan was probably just trying to scare her into avoiding the Covenanters.

"I'm going to do my best, but that means knowing ye are protected. Promise me if I amnae with ye, ye will stay with Dougal and Finlay." A light rapping sounded at the door, and she flinched. "Do ye promise?" he asked.

She nodded, and Alan stood to stalk over to the door. He was lost in thought but still opened the door cautiously, just enough to peek out. He must have been content with what he saw, because he relaxed and pulled it open.

He took a tray from the woman she had seen him with that day in the streets, and a wave of uncertainty hit her, but the lass acted as if they barely knew each other. Had he really slept with her? She couldn't imagine not looking at him without longing every day for the rest of their life, after what they had shared.

The woman caught Kirstie's angry stare and shrank back, her eyes widened, then she scurried away. Closing the door with his elbow, Alan held the tray with both hands and stepped over, setting it on the small table beside them. He bolted back to the door to lock it as she inspected the contents, two plates with a nice selection of oatbread, cheese, bannocks, salmon, and eggs.

She picked up a piece of bread, tore off a small corner, and put it in her mouth. Her stomach protested when she swallowed. She'd never been able to eat when something was bothering her.

After picking up the cup, she sipped the hot tea. A sweet floral fragrance drifted to her nostrils, reminding her of cool autumn days. It was comforting, so she held it with both hands close to her chest and breathed in the earthy scent.

"We must get Lachlan and Malcolm out of here tonight." Picking up the fork, she decided to try a bit of the fish; it was perfectly flaky and moist with a hint of lemon scent and buttery taste.

"They willnae go if the other lairds are at risk." He picked up his cup and took a sip of the tea.

"What can I do to help?"

"They have it well in hand."

"No' from what I can see. They dinnae ken a thing. I can try one more time to get information from Niall."

"Nae, ye will let them and me take it from here." There he was, being her brother again.

"Ye cannae tell me what to do."

"I will."

"'Tis like that time I saved the puppy." She pulled her shoulders back and tilted her chin up.

He looked heavenward then back to her. "Ye should never have gone into that freezing water."

"Ye tried to stop me then, too."

"The currents were strong that day. Ye and the wee mutt could have been swept away in an instant."

"I was a strong swimmer, and Titan would have been gone forever."

"But ye arenae a good spy."

He was right. She despised this spying business.

"If my brothers and ye must risk yerselves to be here, then there has to be a way I can help." She forked another bite of the delicious salmon although her stomach churned into knots as she thought on the threat to her brothers drawing near without real answers as to how to save them.

Suddenly, he had wound his arms around her waist and pulled her flush with his chest. His lips closed on hers, hard and needy. Groaning into her mouth, he delved in as his arm splayed at the base of her spine, keeping her pinned tightly to him. She could feel an ache at the apex of her legs, begging to have him inside her. He tasted of the warm earthy tea they had just finished.

Alan's kiss gentled, and his other hand threaded into the hair at her temples. His tongue still swirled and drove her senses mad as everything around them disappeared. This was all about he and she, man and woman, and the primal need to become one.

His hand slid down and fumbled with the buttons on the back of her gown as he emitted a frustrated sound, and she almost laughed into his mouth. His lips left hers, and he put both hands in her hair, removing the pins that held her headpiece in place. His needy gaze never left her as he tossed it casually to the floor. Then he ran his fingers through the long tresses.

He grabbed her by the shoulders and turned her so that she was facing away from him. Then he took her hair and pulled it to one side, draping it over her shoulder. He unfastened one button then his lips were on her neck. She leaned back into him and sighed as need called to her more urgent than the moon beguiling the tides. She breathed in sharply and fought to control the increase in her pulse.

His lips left her skin, and the warm tingles that had spread through her receded, left only with a cool wetness that craved the return of his mouth. Fingers danced down her back and slid another button through its hole. Her gown loosened, but the tightness in her breasts grew stronger.

"Alan," she whispered. She shuddered.

"I didnae take the time to properly taste ye yesterday. I plan on remedying that today."

His fingers eased another button loose then another, and as he reached into the space where the material had parted, he grasped her waist. Even through her shift, she could feel the warmth of his touch and the roughness of his calluses. The ones he had earned fighting and working alongside her family and for their clan. Somehow, the knowledge they had been earned in that way heated her more than any touch of soft hands ever would.

His fingers brushed up her back. When they reached the top of her shift and his skin touched hers, fire exploded as they worked their sensual magic. He clenched the sleeves of her gown and peeled it down around her shoulders. It fell to the ground, and she shivered, not from the cold, but from the intense heat and desire that had been fanned the moment he'd touched her.

His hands delved under her arms and came around the front to capture both of her breasts. He squeezed, and she arched back into him. His thumb and forefingers pinched her erect nipples, and sensation assailed her. There was a wetness between her legs as she fought the urge to tell him to just take her already.

"Yer breasts are so big I can barely hold them all." She felt her cheeks flush. "I cannae wait to put my mouth on them."

But his hands left her breasts and slid back down. She held her arms slightly in front of her, not quite sure what she should do with them. He skimmed down her curves and landed on her hips. He seized her and clutched her against him as his mouth once again closed on her neck. He sucked, and she tilted her head to give him better access.

The caress was so pleasurable she barely noticed his hands had slid lower. They grasped the sides of her shift and shimmied it up over her thighs. Lips leaving her neck, he rasped, "I want ye to do that when ye ride on top of me."

"What?" she asked, but the question was lost as he pulled the thin material from her shoulders. He twisted her around to face him, and she blushed as a hungry gaze devoured her.

"Dinnae be embarrassed. Ye are the most beautiful lass I've had the pleasure to look upon." His words were kind, but they didn't wash away the flush that had reddened her cheeks. She noticed she wasn't completely naked at all. She'd slipped her shoes off before but left her stockings on. How silly she must look.

She bent down to remove them, but he caught her hands. "I'll do it." She stood, and he backed her to the bed. "Lay back," he instructed.

She sank into the warm, soft bed that smelled of Alan—earthy and woodsy and all male. If he weren't here touching her, she'd turn her head into the pillow and breathe him in. Her legs still hung from the side of the bed. She was about to swing them on when he grasped them. "Nae, stay just like this."

He slowly unrolled one stocking as sensation rocketed from her calf up to her chest, and she clutched at the blankets. He tossed it away, and then the warmness of his mouth was on her ankle.

It tickled, but it also sent waves of vibrations shooting up her leg and directly to the woman's part of her that craved to be touched. Her knees clenched together to put pressure on that spot. He kissed and then slowly let her leg dangle.

He rolled the other stocking down, but this time when he dropped her leg, he inched forward, so that he was kneeling just in front of her. Kirstie rose up on her elbows to see what he was doing and froze at the raw need staring back at her. He smiled at her, a wolfish, *I have you just where I want you* kind of smile that made her insides quake.

"Do ye want to watch me taste ye?"

What, she wanted to ask, but the word was pulled from her as he took her knees and spread her legs wide then slid under her bottom and eased her to the edge of the bed.

As soon as he put his mouth to her inner thigh, she forgot everything. His head moved slowly up her leg, leaving a trail of molten hot heat in its wake. The sweet torture was as intense as it could be until his fingers reached into the curls at the juncture of her sex. She gasped, and her fingers dug into the bed.

He looked up to see her still watching. "Ye are so eager, kitten. 'Tis a beautiful sight and makes me want to thrust my cock inside ye until ye scream for me."

Something about the words sent delicious tremors soaring through her. She almost begged for him to do that now, but his head dipped to her other thigh where he continued to adorn the sensitive flesh with featherlight kisses.

His fingers sunk lower and slid across her sensitive bud that vibrated with need. *Oh heavens, do that again*, she thought, but his finger continued down into her slick folds.

"Ye are so ready for me." The raspy voice sent waves of warmth over her.

His gaze returned to hers, and this time his smile was strained and filled with something she couldn't place. Looking dangerous and on the edge of control, he slipped one finger into her tight sheath, and she nearly cried out. She felt as if she would explode right there. He pumped in and out, in and out, while he kept his gaze locked on hers.

"I am going to taste ye now." His head dipped, and all she could see was his thick dark brown hair in between her legs. The sight sent a primal urge to her core, but she was not prepared when he pulled his finger free and started to lathe at her wetness.

He continued to lick and then suck at the sides of her passage. She hadn't known this was possible, but now that she did, she wanted this all the time. The tip of the tongue tormenting her rose and started a slow deliberate rhythm up and down. Each time it made a pass, she could feel the waves building.

His finger returned to her center and dove in. Her hips moved on their own, seeking farther penetration and more pressure from his mouth. He inserted another finger. It was tight, but he moved them around and the pressure built to a crescendo that threatened to make her fall apart.

And then she did. Waves of unimaginable pleasure washed over her and dragged her under again and again. The electric pulses shook her and rocked her. She threw her head back and fell the rest of the way onto the bed. She gasped for air over and over as the waves continued to claim her.

They finally stilled, and she opened her eyes to see Alan watching her, his fingers still inside her.

"Ye are so bonny like this." His finger slid from her, but his hands didn't move from her body; instead, they skimmed up to her waist and pushed her farther onto the bed. He stood above her, and she noticed he remained fully dressed.

She thought to be embarrassed by her state except that she was sated and boneless and he could do anything right now as long as he promised to do that to her again. She felt the smile curve her lips when his control snapped.

Clothes flew through the air, and he was naked on the bed in almost a heartbeat. His mouth was on hers in a desperate kiss where he took everything he could and she let him. His hand pulled her thigh to the side to make room for him in between her legs.

He pulled his mouth from hers and studied her with heated, intense eyes as he drove his cock inside her. He started pumping, not taking his eyes off hers. It was the most beautiful thing she'd ever seen, him truly wanting and needing her. She reveled in the desire she saw there as he thrust in and out.

He screamed out as his seed spilled into her, filling her and making her his. She wanted to be his, always had and always would.

Wiggling his hips again, he burred, "I could get used to this."

"Me, too."

Laughing, he kissed her then pulled out to settle down in the bed beside her.

"Why did ye no' ever find a lass after I left?"

"I didnae want one."

That was not an acceptable answer. "Did ye no' have feelings for another?"

"Nae, I was done the moment ye kissed me in the stables."

She turned her head toward him. "Ye pushed me away that night."

"I did."

"Why? I have gone this whole time thinking I wasnae good at kissing."

"I still had blood on my fists from beating Angus."

Looking heavenward, she shook her head. "Now that makes complete sense."

"I found him forcing himself on Arabella."

Kirstie's eyes narrowed. She wasn't sure if it was because of what Angus had done or the mention of Arabella herself, the woman who had betrayed her brother. "Why did that matter? Ye did the right thing, if the advances were no' wanted."

"I almost killed him. I had become a madman and couldnae stop. I wanted ye, but I kenned then that ye wouldnae be safe around me. I thought I would turn into my father, and the last thing I wanted was to hurt the one lass that I wanted."

"Ye wanted me?"

"Aye." He drew her to his side.

He lay there quite for a few minutes. "Did ye ever find someone else ye cared for?"

She turned and met his gaze. "Aye."

Alan's expression darkened. "Who?"

"He is a bonny specimen." She said it with the real admiration that she'd always had for him.

Alan leaned up on an elbow and loomed over her. "I need to ken who I should kill for touching ye."

She couldn't hide the wicked smile that spread across her lips. "I am certain he would fight ye for my affections. 'Twould probably trample all over ye."

Alan's jaw started to tick.

She'd taken this far enough. "Poseidon. He has had my heart from the moment I met him."

"Is that no' yer horses name?" His tense jaw slackened slightly.

"Aye, 'tis the only male I have had eyes for since I left Kentillie." She gently pushed at his shoulder.

His muscles relaxed, and his eyes brightened. "Ye wench. Are ye trying to drive me mad?"

"Aye, I want ye mad with jealousy. So much so that ye run away with me and we never come out of hiding." Och, she'd not meant to say that, not meant to give away her true heart.

She slid her fingers over his strong, firm abdomen and found his ribs. Her fingers frolicked across his skin. Alan folded over and laughed uncontrollably. The sound was like bells to her ears. It evoked memories of tickle fights and rolling around in the heather and playing chase on the hills near Kentillie.

She continued to tickle him as he twitched in all directions trying to escape. His hand shot up and caught her wrist and pulled it above her head, then took her injured arm by just above the elbow and gently did the same. He moved on top of her.

He caught his breath, and when his gaze met hers, they were hooded and dark. He wanted her. The hard length of his arousal pressed to her leg.

"Ah, kitten, looks like ye have put yerself in a vulnerable position."

She felt the rise and fall of her breast as he held her arms above her head. She was pinned to the bed beneath him, helpless, no way to wrestle free and completely at his mercy. Somehow, this excited her more than anything he'd done to her.

Her hips rose and sought out the one thing that could sate the sudden craving that had taken over. A fierce yearning grabbed her.

"Mmm, I do like how eager ye are, lass, but I think I should teach ye a lesson for trying to get the upper hand."

She tried to pull her arm free from his, just to reach out and touch him. If she could caress him, he would want to be inside her, and that would make this burning need go away.

"Ah, ye wanted to play, kitten, but ye should ken I am in charge."

Her breasts ached to be held. She was so sensitive all over that she felt on fire. "Please. I call mercy. I want ye inside me."

His lips spread in a wide, satisfied smile. His gaze flared with need as he moved one wrist to meet the other and then held both with one hand. It left his other free to slide down her arm, exciting the sensitized flesh as it slowly teased and dipped lower to change course. It skimmed across her collarbone to her neck then trailed a fine line to her engorged breast.

His heated gaze drank in the desire she couldn't hide. He knew exactly what she wanted, and he was holding back and torturing her with her own clawing need.

He kneaded her flesh, and desire rushed through every part of her being. "Look at me," he commanded, and she couldn't help but obey the only person who could ever make her feel this way.

He pinched her nipple and then held it. Pleasure ignited in the spot and shot down to her legs. She inhaled sharply and arched up into him. She started to pant. "Please." She wiggled her hips into his.

"Please what?"

"Take me. Alan, I need ye. Please."

He thrust his penis inside her. Her tight insides stretched to accommodate his hard, ready staff. She rose off the bed to meet him. His free hand left her breast and slid behind her, grasping her bottom and pulling her up as he seated himself farther inside her.

Her eyes flew back to his, and she saw that he had lost the control he'd wielded so deftly just moments earlier. No sign of the calm, patient man was left. He was all beast and primitive male claiming what was his. His pelvic bone rubbed against her as he thrust and filled her.

Waves of pleasure assailed her as the pressure built and beckoned her beneath the current. She felt her eyes roll as she tried to focus on his intent gaze. Her breath was short and shallow and coming in pants.

His hands left her wrists and rear to grasp the sides of her face. He held her focus on him as the dam inside her broke and overflowed with pulse after pulse of shocks as her release claimed her.

He tensed almost immediately and groaned. She could still feel his seed filling her when his lips crashed down on hers. The kiss was hard and possessive and said everything she felt.

He pulled back, and they watched one another, lost in each other's eyes. She didn't know what to say, how to express the emotions swirling inside, so she just gazed into his soul. It was as if they understood each other and that their world had changed for the better. She felt in that moment that nothing could ever tear them apart again, and the certainty felt good. Surely after this, he would ask her to be his wife and bring her home.

When he finally slid down to her side, she turned, draping her arm around his chest. His fingers made small circles along her shoulder. He didn't say anything, but she couldn't talk, either. After what they had just shared, she was happy just to be in his arms.

Chapter Eleven

Alan trailed his fingers along Kirstie's silky smooth skin as she lay sleeping in his arms. She had always had a special place in his heart, and if anything ever happened to her, his world would crash down around him.

He was already planning their years together, and he hadn't even been able to speak to Lachlan yet. What if his friend really didn't approve? And if his laird had known both his and Kirstie's true feelings, why had he not pushed to bring them together earlier? What if it was because he truly didn't approve of the match? He couldn't betray Lachlan, but neither could he give up Kirstie. It would be a tough conversation to have with the man who was his laird, his brother, and his friend.

He'd been so angry with Kirstie that he could have turned into the devil himself, but he'd never had the urge to lay a hand on her. After years of telling himself he was like his father and their family, he had finally realized he wasn't like his blood kin; he was like the family that raised him. The cycle had been broken. Kirstie would be safe with him.

He looked forward to quiet nights alone with her and whatever bairn they were blessed with. He would make sure their children were brought up like the Camerons had raised him, with love, understanding, kindness, and a good education. In the evenings, he would play with them and Kirstie would read to them until they fell asleep, with him patiently listening until he could take her to bed each night.

The sun rose high in the sky, and he thought about the day ahead. He looked forward to going back to being a Cameron and forgetting this farce, going home with Kirstie and his family to start the life he should have made for them years ago.

He felt confident the Covenanters would tell him the plan tonight. He would get word to his brothers and make certain Kirstie and the other lasses were sequestered in the castle where no harm could come to them. The last thing he needed while protecting her brothers was worrying over her safety in the mix. He wouldn't be able to think clearly if she were in danger.

Reluctantly he shifted, and the light weight of her arm fell from his chest. She was such a heavy sleeper; he admired that, because he woke with every sound. Probably due his nights worrying about his father coming home drunk and angry.

Dipping his head, he kissed her sweet red lips. He stretched back and noticed she still slept but had a smile as if a pleasant dream had claimed her. He looked forward to many mornings of waking her as he slid into her body.

It was time to get to this summit and put on the performance of a lifetime. He would pull it off for his family.

He shook her. "Kirstie, 'tis time to go."

She shook her head with her eyes still closed. "Just a few more minutes."

"Now," he persisted.

She blinked and focused on him then gave a small, pleased smile that went straight to his heart.

"I have to get ye back to the castle and get to the summit. Take this." He held out a holster and dirk he usually kept strapped to his thigh.

Her smile disappeared, but she took the knife. She rubbed her eyes and stretched. "What time is it?"

"Time to get moving. The meeting starts soon."

She sat up slowly. "Och, can we no' just take everyone and leave?"

"I wish we could, kitten, but this has to be done."

She slid from beneath the covers and retrieved her clothes. She turned, and he hardened instantly. Her hair was dishevcled and she was naked, and it was the bonniest sight he'd ever seen.

She reached down, and he was rewarded with a nice view of her backside and long legs leading to that sweet spot he wanted to dive into again. She pulled the shift on, and he inched toward the edge of the bed.

"What will ye do while the meeting is going on?"

"I will probably pace the floor outside the door."

"Mayhap ye should take a ride with Blair and Finlay. 'Twill do ye and them good to get out."

"Ye just want to keep me from spying." After picking up his shirt, she threw it at his chest, but he easily caught it.

"That, too."

"Ye dinnae have to worry. I learned my lesson. I willnae go into any rooms where I dinnae belong."

"If I catch ye spying again, I will waste no time sending ye back to Kentillie."

"I think 'twill do Blair some good to get out."

"Is she all right?"

"I hope so. She does need a friend right now."

"Ye arenae going to tell me what is going on."

"Nae, tis no' my place. What kind of friend would I be if I told ye all her secrets?"

He liked that about her. She was loyal.

"Can ye help me with the buttons?" Taking her long brown curls in hand, he draped them over her shoulder as he helped her fasten the gown.

"'Twas more fun undoing them."

"Ye will get the chance to do it again soon enough."

They finished dressing, and she placed the plaid over her head to once again hide her identity. Once Kirstie left the stable on his horse, she led the way to the fortress on the hill with just enough space ahead of him so he could keep an eye on her the whole way back, but no one would be able to tell they had been together.

At the castle, he found chairs were set on opposing sides of the great hall and a stand had been erected for those who wished to speak. The Covenanters had wanted to have this meeting at Greyfriars Kirk, but the Royalists had only agreed if it took place on neutral ground.

Niall and his cousin, the Earl of Argyll, weren't yet present, so Alan went to Hamish's side and put his facade in place. It was going to be a long day. Between the meeting and Hamish's boring diatribes on religion, the day was sure to be divided between heated arguments and mind-numbing lectures.

Then he remembered he hadn't talked to Kirstie about Hamish. She'd not said a word about the proposal, and he needed to make certain after this meeting, she was kept as far away from him as possible. He'd meant to ask her this morning, but once they'd arrived in his room, they had made love then talked about the past. For a while he'd been lost in her and the rightness of being together. The outside world had barely intruded.

Men with solemn determined demeanors drifted into

the hall while Hamish proselytized on the virtues of the Presbyterian religion. Most of the points were good ones; it was just this forcing of religion on others Alan couldn't abide.

Lachlan and Malcolm strode into the great hall and studiously avoided glancing his way. Good, he avoided theirs, as well. Any tell that he was acting could get him or them killed.

Niall and Argyll entered together and came straight toward Hamish and him. He was surprised they'd not gone directly to Robert Baillie, who moved toward the front to speak. It was a good sign they believed his ruse if Argyll himself was willing to sit with him.

After hours of contentious arguments and name-calling, it was clear no resolution would be met here today. Angry faces and shouts of outrage spilled from the room as men stomped out. Alan's shoulders sank as he realized he would be walking with his enemies to a tavern to plan the death of his best friend.

· · ·

Kirstie tried to cling to thoughts of how perfect the morning with Alan had been, but Blair's unusual silence, Finlay's solemn face, and dread of the coming afternoon filled her with gloom. The meeting had been going on for hours with loud voices occasionally reverberating from the closed room into the hollow halls where they echoed ominously.

She paced outside in the fresh air as heated words like traitor, king, and Parliament escaped through the open windows, but she knew in her heart neither side would give. The Covenanters wanted no less than the acceptance of their religion from the Royalists, who would never give it. The Royalist lairds couldn't ask their clansman to fight for something they didn't believe in.

It had been a beautiful afternoon, but the sun had started to sink and clouds skidded across the sky as if they were trying to outrun a coming storm. The gloomy shadows cast, as the sun ducked behind the white puffs, spread chills down her arm.

Kirstie had been able to convince Blair and Finlay to ride with her in Edinburgh today by saying she wanted a thorough tour of the city before they left. Upon returning to the stables, she took her time brushing out Poseidon. It gave her an opportunity to think while Finlay and Blair waited at the entrance to the stables. She heard Blair laugh for the first time all day. Too bad her friend had not given Finlay a chance before committing herself to such an arse like Henry.

Now, as they sat in the courtyard, Blair picked at imaginary lint on her skirts, and Finlay pretended to look out toward the Firth of Froth but secretly kept stealing glances at Blair. None of them spoke.

Heated murmurs erupted from the hall and spread in all directions. She scanned the crowd and came upon Lachlan and Malcolm first. After jumping up, she ran toward them.

"What happened?" she called before she had even reached them.

"'Twas useless. The Covenanters willnae budge unless we promise to sign the Solemn League and Covenant, and we refuse to side with the English parliament over the king. 'Twill be no peace." Lachlan shook his head. His grim gaze would have told all she needed to know.

"We should leave now." She prayed he would listen to her.

"Ye ken I cannae do that." He turned his anger and frustration on her just as Finlay and Blair joined them.

"'Tis no' safe here." She stood her ground. Anyone else would have shrunk away from his imperious command, but she'd learned long ago to stand up for what she believed. She loved her brother, but in this instance he was wrong.

"That is why Finlay, Dougal, and a couple of the Macnab men will be guarding ye, Mother, and the Macnab lasses at the castle until 'tis time to leave."

"Where is Alan?" She leaned in to whisper.

"He left with the Argyll and his men." Alan had warned her about Argyll, but who was going to protect him if they figured out what he was up to?

"Do ye think he will be safe?" A prickle of unease swirled deep in her gut.

She felt helpless. She cared so deeply for all these men, and they were putting themselves in danger to protect an idea. She respected it but didn't condone it.

"Alan Mackenzie is a traitor," her brother roared.

Blinking at his sudden and misplaced rage, she stumbled back and tried to make sense of his words.

"The moment he set his sights on ye, I disowned him." Lachlan's voice climbed again as chills spread down her back. "Alan is dead to me, and if he ever steps on Cameron lands again, I'll drive my sword through his Covenanter arse."

Her mouth fell open as tears rolled down her cheeks. She knew his words were lies, but they hurt to hear all the same.

"Come, let's eat. Where's Mother?" He wrapped his arm around her shoulder and squeezed tight.

She caught a flash of anger in Finlay's eyes and turned to see Blair's brother John and Henry strolling toward them.

Lachlan looked at Finlay and tilted his head. "Do ye mind finding Mother?"

Finlay shook his head and walked away in the direction of the castle. He looked relieved not to have to watch Henry mistreat Blair.

They strode into the hall while discussing the meeting and took seats to dine, but the words floated over her like the elusive clouds that breezed by overhead. She scanned the crowds for Alan.

Finlay returned with Elspeth and Sara Macnab, who took seats opposite Blair and her. The room was eerily silent for the number of people. The only things that could be heard were hushed whispers and the *clang* and *clank* of utensils.

Roasted meats, buttery breads, and pastries were served along with baked summer vegetables of bright colors, but everything looked gray and unappetizing. The savory scents of rosemary and juicy fowl floating through the air normally would have made her mouth water, but today, the aromatic pungent smell turned her stomach and made her want to run for fresh air, run for Alan. But he and the Covenanters were gone.

She stumbled through the meal, barely aware of the movements of those around her. Even the usual, cheerful demeanors of her mother and Sara were transformed into a strange solemn reflection as they poked at their food, eyes downcast and tongues stilled.

As the group stood to leave, Argyll and Hamish sauntered into the room, but Dougal herded Kirstie away before she could make her way to them to find out where Alan was. Damn, she'd forgotten, Hamish had asked her to marry him and she was supposed to give him an answer tonight. She would tell him no, of course, but her heart ached for him because he seemed to genuinely like her and she hated to hurt his feelings.

He deserved someone of his own religion. She wouldn't have been able to make him happy, anyway. He would see that once she pointed it out.

"Dinnae leave this room," Dougal ordered Blair and her as he pushed open the door to their bedchamber.

She wanted to protest but remained silent. Where was she going to go?

"Bolt the door."

It thudded shut behind him.

Not ten minutes later, there was a knock at the door, and Henry called out, "'Tis me, Blair, open up."

The lass looked at her with wide fear-filled eyes.

"Dinnae go. Tell him I need ye tonight."

Blair nodded as relief flooded her pale skin.

Walking over as her friend stayed immobilized by the window, she lifted the latch. Henry, smelling of redolent ale and smoke, pushed past her and strode in like he owned the room. "Come, Blair. I want ye with me tonight."

"I-I-I—" Blair stuttered. She had never heard her friend stutter.

Breaking in, Kirstie stepped between the two. "Please let her stay with me tonight. I dinnae want to be alone after what happened in the stables. They still havenae found the other man." She feigned as much fear as she could, which wasn't hard because her friend's reaction had her trembling.

Disgust colored his face. "Dougal and Finlay are both in the hall. Ye will be fine." He grabbed Blair's arm and pulled her.

"Please, Henry. Just for tonight."

He continued to drag Blair toward the door, slamming it shut, and was gone without even looking back.

Kirstie hadn't missed the resigned steps Blair took, like she was going to muck out the stables. She would have to seek out John in the morning to see if she could find a way to get the lass out of this situation. Maybe she could have Blair run off with Finlay.

Alone with her thoughts of Alan and the plot against her brothers and Blair with that horrid man, she sulked. She didn't want to face the night alone.

Opening the door, she attempted to follow them, but Dougal stepped in front of her and blocked the way. Finlay was outside her mother's door, and even in the dim light, she could make out the anger etching his taut features as Henry dragged Blair down the stairs.

She turned from Dougal without a word, shut the door, and dropped the latch into place. It clicked and echoed through the quiet room. Kirstie paced as dread clawed at her heart. Even if she knew what she could do tonight to help, her guard wasn't going to let her go anywhere.

Not too long after, she heard voices outside the door. "She is expecting me. We agreed to speak this evening." Hamish was looking for an answer.

"I have instructions that Kirstie isnae to leave the room, and ye are no' permitted in there unless Lachlan himself tells me ye are allowed."

"I just need to speak with her a moment." Hamish's voice had lowered to a tone she'd never heard. He was angry, and she suspected he didn't anger easily.

"Nae, it can wait."

"I shall remember this, Dougal Cameron." The words weren't harsh, but something in them sent a chill down her spine. They sounded like a threat, but even more troubling was the way he'd said *Cameron*. Surely she was wrong; Hamish had been so nice to her.

"Do that Hamish Men-zies." Dougal's own voice was heated and gave a harsh enunciation on Hamish's clan name. He made it sound like a curse.

A moment of silence fell as she envisioned the men staring each other down with fists clenched at sides. She let go of her breath when a clipped *tap, tap, tap* of Hamish's boots retreated down the hall.

Sleep evaded her; she tossed and turned, then got up to look out the window and paced when nothing changed below. At one point, she even peeked out the door, only to be met by Dougal's disapproving stare. She closed the door and went back to her pacing.

She was peeking out the window when she heard a key turn in the lock. Alan entered just as she turned to see who it was. "I didnae think ye would come." Her feet carried her across the room with lightning speed.

"I had to see ye tonight."

She threw her arms around him and held on. His hands spread across her back and drew her in. His shirt was cool from the night's air. It was refreshing to her heated skin.

"Did Dougal let ye in?" But she didn't care how he'd gotten in, didn't even care that somehow he'd found a key to her room, the sight of his disheveled golden hair and his soulful gray eyes gave her comfort that she hadn't felt from the moment the doors had closed on that awful meeting.

"Nae, he doesnae ken I'm here. Finlay must be getting some sleep, and Dougal had to escort some man who'd been drinking downstairs."

"What happened tonight?" she asked. She laid her head on his chest and listened to his heart beat a steady, soothing rhythm; it was comforting and calming, and her racing heart tried to match the beat.

"'Tis no' for ye to worry with." His lips found her temple and placed a featherlight kiss there. He lingered and nestled into her.

Her body shook in his arms as the panic of the last few hours manifested. He had to feel it, too. His cool fingers skimmed up her body and into her hair and soothingly massaged her scalp.

His head left hers, and she turned up to confront him. She had a right to know what was going on, but when she saw his eyes intent on her, her tongue darted out and wet her lips. "Ye have a key?"

"I took the extra last time I was here." He let go of her and walked to the chair, sat, and took his boots off. He stood, his plaid quickly followed as he draped it over the chair, and he climbed into the bed. "Read to me."

Her head tilted.

"Please," he continued and gave her a small, tired smile. He looked exhausted. Her questions could wait for the morning. She picked up her copy of *A Chaste Maid in Cheapside* and thumbed through the pages until she reached the spot where she had stopped.

Alan was asleep moments after she started reading. She blew out the candle and crawled under the covers with him. Wrapping her arm around his chest, she sunk into the warmth of him but still could not fall asleep.

She must have dozed, because she woke when gentle, callused hands skimmed up her leg and across her ribs, then traced back down the way they had come. She sighed and moved into the touch. His fingers felt like magic as they slid up and down her curves.

Her eyes opened to meet Alan's intense gaze, and she melted. The early morning light that had filled the room made them darker than storm clouds just before the fury of a squall. He looked like a hungry wolf as desire swirled around in their depths, and she found herself wanting to go into that storm to sate the beast before her.

"Ye look so bonny in the morning light."

Her lips curved up because she was thinking the same thing about him. "Ye are no' so bad yerself."

His hand stopped on her hip and pulled her flush to his exposed skin. A wave of need cascaded over her as she took in his body's warmth and his heated intentions.

His lip quirked to the side, and he huffed.

"Did I do something wrong?" She tried to withdraw, but his hand still held her to him.

"Aye, something verra wrong." He shook his head slowly as hooded eyes studied her. She blinked. "Ye got in bed with yer shift still on. Now 'tis in my way." His pupils dilated as his gaze roamed her body. His hand lifted the edge and grasped the edge of her shift; she shimmied as he raised it up over her head.

Once the offending material was off, he tossed it to the ground. Gaze returning to her, she shivered under his perusal. A flush washed over her. She didn't think she would ever get used to the way he devoured the sight of her nude.

Alan's hand returned to take hold of her breast and grasp it firmly. He licked his lips then dipped his head to the rounded mound. It felt full and engorged, and when his mouth closed around the nipple, her eyes rolled back, and she arched into him. He sucked and a gasp escaped from her as she gave herself over to his caress, no longer embarrassed by the size of her breasts but thrilled that they made him want to do this to her.

Her hand grasped his side, and when his teeth grazed the sensitive nub at the peak, her fingers dug into him and urged him on. She became bolder and let her hand curve toward his shaft. Her fingers stopped to play in the curls beneath his tight abdomen, and she was rewarded with a moan as he sucked at her breast and angled his body so she could touch him more easily.

She let her hand explore, and it sunk lower to find the base of his penis. It stood tall and erect and ready to claim her. She circled her hand around the width of it and followed the length to the mushroom-shaped tip. The skin was velvet and smooth but hard as granite.

"Mmm. I like that, kitten." The words vibrated and sent need coursing through her. She wasn't sure if it was from the feeling or a primitive response to knowing she had pleased him.

Leaning up on an elbow, she peeked down to study that part of him that completed her and made them one. He moved to her other breast to lather it with attention, which gave her a better view. She wanted to commit every part of him to memory and remember his response as she touched each one.

Her hand slid up and down. He groaned, and his pelvis arched into her touch. A satisfied smile spread across her lips. He tore away from his ministrations to gaze at her. "Ye are going to drive me mad." She did it again. His breathing became labored.

He was losing control, and she liked it, so this time as she slid her hand along his length she studied him intently. His eyes darkened with the intense need she felt.

Suddenly, his hand was on her thigh and spreading her legs apart. He positioned himself above her, and fullness enveloped her as he sank his length deep inside her and stilled. His head tilted back, and he breathed in.

His hips started to rock back and forth slowly. Her hips rose as his pelvic bone massaged the sensitive nub at the apex of her legs.

Now she was the one who lost control. Her hands gripped at the covers as she ground her pelvis against him. He hadn't even fully withdrawn as he thrust back in by wiggling his hips from side to side. She was thrashing madly as she felt the start of a spasm. Her body wanted more, so she continued as he did.

She tore her gaze from the spot where they were joined to see him watching and waiting for her to fall apart. Another spasm shot through her, and her body tensed as she moved in time with him to find that same pressure point.

One of his hands grabbed her bottom and clenched her tighter into his hot flesh. She cried out, "Alan." Then she couldn't breathe, could only watch him as shots of electric fire rocketed through every fiber of her being.

Little earthquakes continued to clench her womb as he changed his rhythm. He withdrew then slammed back into her. She gasped and grabbed his rear as he repeated the movement again. He filled her over and over. His eyes fluttered and his breaths came in short bursts; his speed increased, and his mouth opened on a pant. She watched as pleasure overtook him, and he spilled his seed inside her.

Alan rolled onto his back with her curled in between his chest and arm, her head resting on his shoulder. This was heaven.

In all the years she had dreamed of being with this man, not once had she truly grasped how content she would be in his arms.

She raised her head and looked at him. His lazy, sated grin gave her courage to do something she'd never thought she would have the chance to voice. He crooked his head to the side to stare into her eyes.

"I love ye, Alan."

His arm wound around her and tugged her on top of him. His other hand went to her nape and brought her lips to his. That kiss said everything she needed to know. It was warm, and she was able to feel his soul connect with hers. The rhythm of their hearts beat together, and she knew he felt the same.

He flipped her onto her back beneath him. She'd expected him to return her words, but he didn't, and that was all right, because his eyes sparkled with happiness and mischief and, most of all, the love she felt inside her. Brushing away the small bit of doubt that crept in with his silence, she determined he must feel the same.

His fingers traced her lips then pushed a stray lock of hair out of her face. He dipped his head and kissed her again. When he lay back down beside her, she snuggled back in his arms.

Everything was perfect until a bell rang out, breaking through the quite morning, a shrill reminder of the world out there. Her brothers were out there, and today was the day the Covenanters had planned to kill them.

She sat up and climbed out from under the covers to retrieve her shift from the floor. Looking over her shoulder at him, she blurted, "We have to get my brothers out of here."

He frowned at her as she pulled the material over her head. "They ken what they are doing. All will be well as long as ye, Blair, and yer mothers are seen to a safe location." He put his hands behind his head and continued to rest on the pillows under the deep green blanket. He looked like a god who had just slain a beast and now rested on his laurels.

"Is there no way I can help? Tell me the plan." Her hands fisted on her hips. Was he not taking her seriously?

"Ye have to stay safe for me. Go with Dougal because I willnae be able to think if I am worried ye are in danger." His full lips thinned, and his voice deepened.

"I feel the same way."

"We will all come to the meeting spot, but this has to be done." He sat and threw the covers off. His long, lean legs swung down from the bed, and he twisted to stretch his shoulders from side to side.

"I can help. Just tell me what to do. Ye learned something last night did ye no'?" She inched over to the wardrobe and snatched down the dress she had planned to wear today. It was red; she'd chosen it on purpose, because out of all the gowns she owned, this was the one that made her feel confident and powerful. She needed that feeling today.

She purposely kept her gaze glued to his. She wasn't going to let him get the upper hand on this conversation.

"Nae, ye willnae," he insisted. "Ye dinnae understand. I heard men saying the Covenanters have plans for ye, too. If ye dinnae go with Dougal, I will have to stay and I cannae help yer brothers."

His declaration sent spikes of dread snaking down her

spine.

He stood and stalked over to her. His shoulders were stiff, and he squared them back; if she'd been a smaller woman, it might have been intimidating. He was tall and imposing and an air of authority clung to his naked body. For a moment, she felt weak in the knees, but she wasn't sure if it was from the sight of his hard, lean form or the command in his voice.

"Ye will be leaving for Kentillie this morning." His finger touched her lips before she could protest further. "Ye willnae be safe here, and if we are worried about ye, yer brothers and I willnae be safe either." He retrieved his shirt.

She remained silent as he skirted around behind her and brushed her hair aside to help her fasten the dress. When his nimble fingers were done, he wrapped his arms around her, and she melted into the warmth. They stood there lost in the embrace until a knock sounded at the door.

"Just a moment," he called out over his shoulder. "Promise me ye will go with them."

She nodded, turned, and burrowed into his shoulder, her eyes stinging as her arms squeezed around him to fight the trembling which started from her chest and weaved its way to fingers she couldn't still. She held tight, because if she didn't, she might lose him.

This whole time she'd been focused on the danger to her brothers. Now she acknowledged a truth assailing her with a thousand stabs to a place inside her which protested and threatened to steal her breath.

Alan was going to meet the enemy and face danger from every side.

Her clan and that of the other Royalist lairds were gathering to discuss the outcome of yesterday's meeting and how they would proceed going forward and what options they had to keep their free will while Parliament and the Covenanters continued to push for one religion in Scotland.

This was where the plot against her family would be set in motion. She had faith that although Alan would be with the enemy, the Camerons knew he was still on their side.

What if the other Royalists didn't know he was working with them, and what if the Covenanters discovered his duplicity?

And she realized in that moment, he had sacrificed everything for her family. She'd thought herself in love with him before, but that had been based on childhood longings and friendship. Now, she knew him to be the most honorable of men, willing to sacrifice himself for his beliefs and her clan.

She couldn't bring herself to peel her arms from his waist. What if she never saw him again? A tear streamed down her cheek, and she nestled farther into his embrace, his shirt soaking up the stray moisture.

The knock was louder this time. She flinched. His hold on her loosened, and she wanted to protest.

"I have to go, kitten." The warmth of his body left hers, and large hands clasped onto her arms, angling her to face him. "Now, pack up so ye are ready. I'll see ye soon."

His head dipped and he gave her a kiss on the forehead. It was brief and left her needing more. Alan cut away from her; not looking back, he opened the door and disappeared before she could utter another word.

Blair entered and shut the door. Alan was gone, and she had this gaping hole in her heart. Did he not feel the same? She'd told him she loved him, but he'd not returned the words. Why was doubt creeping in? She knew he cared; it was just when he left, it was as if he were pushing her away. Ignoring the apprehension, she moved toward her bags to pack for the trip home, all the while praying that her brothers and Alan made it back safely.

Chapter Twelve

Leaving Kirstie in her room had been the hardest thing Alan had ever done. Once he'd broken free from their embrace, he'd avoided her gaze, because the crack in her voice had almost done him in, and if ever he needed to keep his wits and strength, it was now. He couldn't afford to let emotion guide his decisions. Not until they were all safe.

She was terrified, and he was leaving her. It had been hard enough to fight back the guilt without meeting her gaze, because there was a real possibility he wouldn't survive the day, and he couldn't face her to assure her that he would be back. He'd apologize later if he had the chance, but for now, he had to ensure the plan was in motion, so he made his way to the house where he'd be joining the Covenanters.

Cameron men hid in plain sight, surrounding the inn named The Red Grouse, the nearby buildings, and deep within the forest. Great pains had been taken to look like locals, with weapons hidden in baskets, barrels, and wagons. There were Grahams, MacLeans, and MacDonalds here as well, along with other clans Alan wasn't as familiar with.

Late in the evening before, after the meeting in the tavern with Niall and his men, Alan had met with Alexander Gordon, the leader of the Royalist Resistance, and they'd devised the plan he saw in place now. It had been too risky for him to be seen with the Camerons, so he'd reached out to one of the most dangerous men in all of Scotland to organize the counterattack. Alex made sure the lairds had advance notice of the threat against them and relayed the layout of the strategy the two had devised to combat the Covenanters' plans of murder. He'd made certain the man would confirm with Dougal that the women be on their way to Kentillie in the morning and out of danger.

When he'd finally broken free from Gordon, he'd run to make sure Kirstie was safe. Relieved the Covenanters had finally trusted him with the plans, and he'd been able to pull together what he thought to be an ingenious campaign, he was bone weary and exhausted. Falling asleep listening to her melodic voice, he dared to relax his guard and dream of a life with her.

Now, he lay in wait as more men arrived at the house from which the Covenanters planned to begin their assault. The Royalists had their prescheduled meeting at the location across the street, and this home had a nice view of the inn where the attack would happen. It had become the Covenanter's base of operations. Last night, they'd told him everything, and now he was here to pretend for the last time he wasn't a Cameron.

• • •

As Dougal came in and knelt in the corner to collect their bags, Kirstie made her escape. Fighting back the tears, she struggled to breathe as she ran through the halls of the castle toward Lachlan's and Malcolm's chamber. She had to tell them one last time to be safe and to make certain Alan came back to her.

As she turned the corner to start up the steps, she stopped suddenly. Hamish descended the steps in front of her. "I've been looking everywhere for you." He weaved his arm through hers as he pivoted and started to lead her up.

"I was expecting to hear an answer from you last night."

Damn, she'd forgotten he'd ask her to marry him. She swallowed. "I am so sorry. After the meeting, my brother sent me back to my room and posted a guard. I couldnae go anywhere." She was stalling, avoiding telling him the truth and breaking his heart, but it was never a good time to impart such news. "Ye are such a sweet man, Hamish, but I think with our religious difference, we just willnae suit."

His grip on her arm tightened just a little. She wasn't sure if he was angry with her or if he was shocked by her response and trying to keep himself upright. "I did make it clear to you that religion wouldn't be a problem between us."

"Ye say that now, but when we have children, I am certain 'twill become a problem. I think ye are a wonderful man, but I think ye need to find someone who shares yer beliefs and will be able to worship at yer side."

"I want you."

They were at the landing now. He continued down the hall toward Lachlan's room. She didn't stop him, because that was her final destination anyway.

"Have ye considered Niall's sister? She would make a good wife. She's verra bonny, and she shares yer beliefs."

"No. That isn't in the plan. I will marry you." She stopped, but he pulled and she stumbled alongside him.

"I am sorry, but I will choose my own husband." She tried to yank free, but his hold remained strong.

Dragging her down the hall and past Lachlan's door, he didn't respond.

"Let go of me, Hamish." His grip tightened to a painful vise as she struggled to yank free.

He still didn't answer as he opened a door with his free hand and pushed her through. Her foot caught on her skirts, and she fell to the floor. The door clicked shut, and she looked up to see him standing above her with a twisted grimace on his lips.

She scrambled to her feet and skirted around the nearest chair to put a barrier between them. "What are ye doing?"

"You have made the wrong decision. I had hoped you would cooperate, but this may be better. I'll have to break you in, but you will learn to obey me."

"Stop this." Fear was replacing the anger she'd felt moments earlier as she realized she didn't know this man at all. Had his kind, cool demeanor been a facade all this time?

"When you are my wife, you will have no choice but to obey." Walking slowly up to the chair, his face turned placid as he again seemed to reverse into the man she'd gotten to know these last few months.

"I willnae marry ye. Did ye no' hear me?" Her grip on the back of the chair tightened as her body tensed.

"You will." His eyes darkened but didn't give away any hint of emotion.

"Ye are starting to scare me."

"Good. You should be afraid."

Chills ran down her spine, and she froze as he yanked the chair from her grasp and tossed it across the room. As she watched it fly through the air, something struck her side where she was still bruised from the attack in the stables.

Pain erupted, and her knees buckled as she crumpled back down to the ground. He stood over her as she shook.

"You will not move if you know what is good for you." He removed strips of cloth from his pocket, and her eyes widened.

Scrambling backward, she jumped to her feet and ran for the door. She tried to call out for help, but he was too quick, pinning her instantly to the stone wall just beside the door. With his body weight pushed into hers, she couldn't scream, couldn't even breathe. He was much stronger than he appeared.

His hand was suddenly on her cheek, and he pushed something into her mouth then grabbed both of her hands and yanked them behind her. He pulled and she had no option but to obey as he guided her down to the floor. She struggled, but it was futile.

When she was flat on the ground, he put a knee into the base of her back and wrenched her hands together. Material dug into her wrists as he wound it around the sensitive flesh several times in different directions. His yanking roughly at the material caused pain to shoot up through her arms as he tied the ends together. He did it so smoothly that it crossed her mind that he'd done it before, like she'd seen men wrestling pigs for sport.

He tugged at the bindings. "That will do." Was that pleasure she heard in his voice? She shivered.

Taking her arm, he wrenched her to her knees and knelt beside her. She tried to spit the cloth out of her mouth, but just as her tongue loosened it, she heard a rip and felt a slight tug as he tore the bottom of her dress.

"Nice," he said, then his arms came around and placed the new strip of fabric over the one she'd not yet dislodged. He pulled it across her mouth and tied it tightly behind her head. Her eyes watered at the ache in her wrists as she struggled.

"You and I are going to have a lot of fun, Kirstie," he sneered in her ear.

There was nothing enjoyable about this, she would have said if she could, so she attempted to hit his head with hers, but he grabbed her hair and jerked her head to the side.

"You will marry me, and when your brothers are gone, I will run your clan and you will convert. I will save my wife. It may appear harsh to you at the moment, but you will thank me for it." His blue eyes were hard and filled with a zealot's religious conviction. He honestly thought he would be helping her, and that was what scared her the most; he couldn't see the wrong in what he was doing through the haze of his Covenanter principles.

Her brothers.

Hamish was in on the plot. Would he murder for his beliefs?

She shook her head in denial. Hamish was too kind and God fearing to be behind that. Oh God, had he been planning this all the times he'd come to visit her at the Macnabs?

No, she didn't know him; he had her tied up on the floor of his room.

He must have taken her looking away for some form of disobedience, because she doubled over as his fist hit the small of her back just below her ribs.

Balling up, she struggled to breathe in through her nose. Her body's natural reaction was to gulp in through her mouth, but no air was getting in that way.

Head spinning, she was pulled to her feet and dragged to the chair still sitting by the hearth. Hamish pushed her down into it and kept one hand clasped around her arm. She felt him stretch for something nearby and then cringed as ropes came around her to bind her to the seat.

Chapter Thirteen

Furniture was pushed to the edges of the common room. Alan fidgeted in the cramped quarters of the house where the Covenanters had chosen to stage their attack. It wasn't a small house, but it was hot and stuffy and almost filled to overflowing with men ready to shed blood for a religious idea. They were no better than the king they railed against.

"What are we waiting on?" a man whose face Alan couldn't see yelled out. "They have been in there long enough."

"Patience." Niall held his hand up, palm out and answered. "We're waiting on"—he was interrupted by a knock at the back door—"that." He strode over to the door and asked, "Who's there?"

A muted reply penetrated through the thick wooden door. "'Tis Neville."

Niall lifted the latch and eased the door in. "Give us the news."

"He sent me to tell ye he's got the lass, and ye can attack as soon as they get started."

Alan's eyes narrowed, and he turned to Niall, who he had mistakenly thought was in charge of this operation. A prickle of unease assailed him as a drop of sweat trailed down the small of his back. "What's he talking about?"

"Hamish. 'Tis the other part of the plan. We didnae tell ye last night because we thought ye still might have some kind of brotherly feelings toward her."

Ice spread through his veins while he fought to remain impassive. The hair on the back of his neck stood up, and chills raced down his spine.

Niall looked back to the boy. "Did she agree to marry him?"

"Nae. He wasnae pleased." Neville, a boy of about fifteen years, shook his head with a despondent air. "'Tis no' a good idea to displease him."

Alan looked back to Niall, who watched him, gauging his reaction as if this was some sort of test. "Tell me about this other plan." He was surprised at how coolly the words rolled from his lips, because he felt anything but calm.

"He's going to wed the Cameron lass and take over the clan." Niall shrugged as if to say, *I tried to talk sense into him, but he wouldnae hear it.*

"But what will he do when she doesnae agree? She willnae convert." Alan could feel his voice rise as the words escaped from his constricted throat.

"Aye, she will." Niall gave a resigned grimace. "Neville, show him what Hamish does when ye question him?"

The boy's eyes drifted down, and his face turned a darker shade of red than his hair. He slowly lifted his shirt, and Alan's heart stopped beating. The lad's pale torso was covered with bruises and burn marks at varying shades of healing.

"'Tis a shame, too. I liked the lass myself."

"Where are they?" Alan was able to manage only after he gulped. He remembered the light bruise on Kirstie's side this morning and how the ones on this boy were magnified tenfold.

"He had it planned all along. Hamish and Argyll, they were both going to leave last night, but Hamish couldn't get to the Cameron lass. She had a guard."

Alan's eyes shifted between Niall and Neville. "Yer certain he has her?" Neville nodded, and Alan's heart sank into the pit of his stomach.

"He's on his way to marry the lass then up to the Cameron lands. He cannae be here and risk looking as if he had a part in the death of the Cameron laird." Niall continued as if uninterested. "Hamish thinks to comfort the people at their loss. Bring them to God his way and take the clan."

Hamish had seemed so normal, boring even. All along, he'd been the one behind the plot. He and Argyll had both fled to deflect any blame if the events of the day didn't turn out as they hoped. Hell, this must have been what he'd almost overheard that night in the kitchen.

Kirstie was in grave danger. She was stubborn and wouldn't give in to his demands, even if it was in her own interests.

The Camerons would be able to handle this group of men. He needed to get to Kirstie before something bad happened. He clenched his fists. If Hamish hurt her, he was a dead man.

"'Tis time," Niall said. Alan stood there looking toward the back door, wishing to escape. "Let's go," came a little more forceful, and Alan moved toward the front since several men had now gathered behind them and blocked his easy exit through the rear of the building.

The men who had been crowded in the house spilled from the door into the street and ran for The Red Grouse on the other side. It was eerily quiet, considering their number.

Up ahead, he could see the first men reach the inn and throw open the door. Several ran in. Alan had taken his time closing the distance. He was only halfway across the street when the procession of men stopped. He knew why. Shouts rang out from inside. "'Tis empty!"

The Red Grouse's owner was a Royalist. That was why the Covenanters had chosen his establishment for the sure slaughter. But the Royalists knew of the plan, and the owner of the tavern had a hidden tunnel beneath the inn that led to his brother's house next door.

All of the Royalist lairds had walked into that inn to make the Covenanters believe they were inside but had sneaked across to the house undetected and prepared to strike. The back door was barricaded and the windows had all been shuttered and locked so the only way in and out was through the front. It was what Argyll's men had counted on, but the tables were turned. Now, a good number of the Covenanters were in the building surrounded by Royalist forces.

Before the men could figure out what had happened, the Royalists came from their hiding places and had the men surrounded. Lachlan came into view and gave a small almost imperceptible nod to Alan. Niall caught it and turned to him with ice in his eyes.

"Ye did this." Drawing a sword, the man held it up between them.

"Aye, I did." Alan unsheathed his own sword but left it at his side.

"Why?"

"I am no Mackenzie." Alan shook his head. "They turned my family out. The Camerons raised me, and I believe everyone should be able to worship the way they want."

Clangs of metal on metal and shouts of angry men filled the air as they circled each other. Lachlan fought a man several feet away, and Niall's gaze shifted briefly to take in the scene. He started to laugh.

The unexpected mirth caught Alan by surprise, and

chills ran down his back.

"Hamish willnae get his way after all. Once he learns the Camerons live, he will kill the wench." Those words knocked the breath from Alan's lungs.

Niall pulled back and swung at Alan. He had been so lost in worry that he almost didn't dodge the blow in time. Pulling up his claymore, he waited for the next strike.

"Hamish said we could trust ye, but I was right. Ye do care for the lass."

"Aye, and if she is harmed, hell will reign down on all of ye." It would not just be him but all the Camerons who would avenge her.

He swung from the side, but Niall deflected the strike and metal clanged, eliciting an ear-piercing screech as the weapons scraped together.

"Ye ken when he tortures and kills her, it will be on ye. He'll have no use for her if her brothers live." Niall swung this time. Metal clanged again.

"I will find them, and if he's touched her, he'll die."

"Ye dinnae even ken where they are," Niall sneered. "How will ye save the bonny lass? Especially when he discovers she's no good to him. She'll be dead before ye get to her."

Alan lunged and missed as Niall swerved to the side. Alan almost lost his footing. *Get it together*, he told himself. If he died, he wouldn't be able to save her.

"Unless he keeps her locked away until his next attempt is successful." Niall smirked at him. "'Tis probably what he will do. He prefers torture to murder."

This time, Alan didn't rush. He pulled the sword flush in front of him and swung down. *Clang.* He withdrew and struck again. *Clang.* Niall took a step back as Alan continued his assault. *Clang.*

"He willnae touch her." Alan's sword came down on

Niall's, and the man's weapon went flying. The force of the jolt knocked Alan's from his grasp, and it slipped to the ground.

They stood face-to-face, evenly matched, Niall close to his size and weight. The Campbell man pulled back and threw the first punch. Alan ducked to the side and missed the impact. He jabbed Niall in the ribs as he came up. The man grunted and winced but wasted no time in throwing the next fist. It landed on his cheek, and he had to shake it off.

Niall lunged at his chest with such force that they both tumbled backward with Niall landing on top. Struggling, Niall got in another punch.

Alan pulled back and then pushed with as much force as he could from his position. It was enough to knock Niall to the side, so he rolled away and jumped up. Niall recovered quickly and withdrew a knife from somewhere.

Niall swiped at him, but he was nimble enough to slide out of the way. Holding his fists in front of him, Niall stabbed at him and missed again. Kicking his foot out, he was able to connect with the man's ankle. Niall roared an indistinguishable sound as he staggered back and struggled to keep his footing.

Behind the haze of pain, anger flashed in Niall's eyes. "I think when I'm done with ye, I'll take a turn at her."

A damn of pent-up fury burst and spilled over as Niall's intent hit him. Some primitive, protective instinct took over. He lunged and knocked the man flat on his back and followed the arse down. He felt a slight twinge in his side but didn't have time to analyze it. After they hit the hard, horse-packed earth of the road, he grabbed Niall's forearm with the knife and drove it over and over into the ground until he dropped the dirk.

"Ye willnae put yer filthy hands on her." Alan's fist connected with the man's face. Niall squirmed beneath him, and the man's other fist connected with his abdomen, but he ignored the pain.

Alan hit again, and Niall's head turned to the side, but his arm came up to Alan's midsection. This time he caught it and noticed Niall had retrieved his knife. They struggled with it, Niall trying to stab Alan, and Alan just trying to aim it away from his body.

Pulling the blade between them, Niall lunged forward with it as Alan fought to twist it down. He pushed as hard as he could away from his own body, and the knife sunk into Niall's belly. It slid in easily, and the man's struggles stopped.

Alan shivered at the blank eyes that seared up at him then he exhaled. He stood but continued to watch the man. The clanks and shouts around him broke in and reminded him that he had other enemies to worry about.

Taking in the carnage around him, he glanced to his left just in time to see Henry's eyes widen as a man ran at him. Blair's betrothed ducked behind Finlay, who faced the oncoming threat with a deft blow low to the man's gut. Finlay peeked around to see Henry cowering behind him and shook his head with disgust.

Three other men took up positions to flank them. Henry pushed Finlay toward two of the men and ran. *The bastard.*

Alan's fists tightened on his sword, and he started toward his friend to help, but Finlay caught his balance and deflected a blow before it crashed down on his skull.

Finlay twirled in a motion that almost looked like a dance, and his sword sliced through the attacker's midsection. Holding out a shaking sword, the second man stepped forward. Finlay eyed the threat and smiled. His friend would have no problem with this one.

Henry, who had turned to run, was met by the third man. Blair's betrothed tried to lift his sword but wasn't in time as one blow from his opponent struck his neck, nearly severing his head. Henry's body collapsed to the ground.

Malcolm appeared to challenge the one who had taken Henry down. Alan relaxed knowing Finlay had a reliable warrior next to him now. Alan glanced at the man at his own feet. Niall hadn't moved. Icy waves of fear assailed him.

How was he going to find Kirstie? He'd just killed the only man who knew where she'd be.

Out of the corner of his eye, Alan spotted Neville cowering behind the corner of a house a little farther down the street. The boy would know where Kirstie was, but he was too far away. He'd have to sneak around and approach him from the back, because he couldn't afford to lose his only connection to Hamish.

After tracking him down, giving him coin for some food, and ensuring the lad's safety if he joined them on Cameron lands, the boy was willing to tell him where Hamish would be staying tonight. Alan gave him extra compensation to wait for Lachlan and Malcolm so that he could guide them to where Alan would be.

Taking off for Kirstie, he prayed he wasn't too late.

• • •

Fighting sleep as it threatened to claim her, Kirstie pushed back the fog as she was rocked along to wherever it was she was being taken. Hamish had put a sack over her head, and men with voices she didn't recognize carried her and put her in the back of some sort of cart in such a way that it was impossible to reach the knife she had hidden under her skirts.

She could hardly breathe, and her hands and arms tingled with a stinging numbness from being bound behind her back. Although she struggled with the bindings for what felt like hours, the only thing her efforts had produced were sensitive wrists where the material had cut into her skin.

The coolness in the air and the darkness in confines of

the scratchy material signaled it was getting late. Earlier, she had been able to make a warm glow through the loosely woven fabric, but now it was more like a tunnel with the light barely reaching her eyes. Her stomach roiled and protested, similar to what she felt when she was in a crowd of people, but she had to fight that, too, because her mouth was still gagged.

Focusing on breathing in and out slowly, she repeated, *My brothers and Alan will find me.* They wouldn't let anything happen to her as long as they were still alive. Her eyes stung with unshed tears at the thought, but her faith in them didn't waver.

The wagon stopped.

"Bring her, but be careful. I do not want her damaged if not necessary." Hamish's voice.

That's a good sign. Mayhap he willnae hit me again.

Arms closed in around her middle. She was hefted up and then folded in half over someone's shoulder. The nausea returned full force as the man's bones pushed into her stomach, and the sack tightened and clung to her head.

Her head was spinning by the time she was right sided then tossed on a lumpy platform. Her wrists were jostled and rubbed on the bindings. She stiffened.

Damn, that hurt.

"Pull it off her," Hamish ordered, and rough hands forced her to her feet then yanked the sack up and over her body. A *whoosh* of air cooled her sweating skin, and she rushed to take a large gulp of fresh air in through her nose.

Hamish took a step toward her and reached out to move the stray curls from her face. She stood still, determined not to show him how his touch curdled her blood. He wore the placid face that had fooled her into believing he was a decent man.

"Turn around." He motioned with his finger.

She obeyed, because what other option did she have?

She'd had a lot of time to consider what to do whenever they got to where they were going. Top of her list was earn his confidence, so she didn't budge when he said, "Stay still."

His hands fumbled at her hair for a moment, and she felt a tightening at the material tied around her mouth. She was rewarded with a slackening in the pressure, but she didn't dare move. Something tugged at her bindings. Her hands were free and immediately fell to her sides, limp and numb.

Hamish grabbed her forearm and moved to her front. Holding her wrist up to her face, he said, "Look what you have done." His tongue ran back and forth over his teeth. She was coming to fear that habit of his.

His other hand removed the gag from her mouth and pulled out the cloth that had been stuffed inside. Her tongue felt thick and dry.

Her hands shook, and she cursed herself for not appearing as calm as she thought she might have been able to. He surely noticed as he inspected the burns from her efforts to escape. He frowned at the red, raw skin.

"Ye didnae have to tie me up." She held her shoulders up and met his eyes.

"You did not appear to want to come without force. If you had just been the good girl you should have been…"

He let go of her arm and traced her cheek with the top of his hand. She pulled back but wished she had remained still, because his eyes took on a feral quality as he pursed his lips. "You will marry me, and one day you will beg for me to touch you."

"I willnae marry ye."

"You will." A sick, satisfied smile slid across his lips. "Your brothers will be dead by now, and no one will come to stop the wedding."

Her heart flipped over at the words as pain assailed her. He could be wrong. He had to be wrong. "Alan will come for me."

Hamish laughed, and chills ran down her spine. "He knew we were to wed. He practically gave me his blessing, and he's one of the men who was going to kill your brothers today. He even led us to them."

Her eyes stung, and she shook her head. "Ye are wrong. He wouldnae do that."

"True. He said you were a sister to him, but he didn't voice any objections to our union." His hand released her arm, and she pulled it into her chest as she held the other gripped in her skirts over the area where the knife was strapped to her thigh. She looked down and bit her lower lip. The only thing that stopped the tears from overflowing was the fear of what Hamish was going to do to her.

"You will convert before we wed tomorrow."

Tamping down her fear, she took in a full breath as rage filled her. "Ye may take everything else from me, but ye willnae take my religion."

Hamish's fist connected with her abdomen, and she doubled over. "You will." As she struggled to catch her breath, she wondered what had happened to her plan to try to appease him.

"We will see the minister in the morning. You will be baptized and take communion." His eyes peered at her. "I don't want to hit my wife, but if you are not obedient, you will be punished."

Managing to stand up straight again, she held her tongue and glanced around. As she did, she noticed three other men in the room with them. They had lingered on the edges and said nothing when he had hit her, so they would be no help.

Her gaze skittered around to see what the best avenue for escape was, but the room had only two doors. The one that must lead outside was guarded by one of Hamish's friends, and the other door was slightly ajar and opened into another room similar to the one they were in. The only window offered a view of high tree branches and a darkening, stormy sky.

"Don't forget that when we get to Cameron lands, I will have access to your mother. If you do not listen, I may have to punish her for not training you to be obedient to your husband."

Fear stabbed at her, and then an even worse thought took shape. Hamish must not know about Lachlan's babe. Was he crazy enough to harm a child? She met his eyes and saw for the first time he was devoid of empathy. He was a religious zealot who cared for no one except himself.

The Camerons would never pledge loyalty to him when they learned what he'd done. He was delusional to the point that reason would not be possible. No matter what happened to her, she would have to keep him away from her people and the baby.

She nodded as if she agreed, because she now understood that nothing but complete control would pacify him. As she appeared to acquiesce, the wheels had started turning in her head. There would be a way out of here, even if it meant denying him in the church tomorrow. He could beat her to death before she let that monster near anyone else in her family or clan.

Three short loud knocks sounded from the door. Hamish started rubbing his tongue across his teeth. "Hold on," he called toward the door but didn't take his eyes off her.

He leaned down, and when he rose, he had the gag in his hand. She started to protest, but his hand was over her mouth before she could make a sound. He quickly reinserted the cloth and wrapped it around her head. She started to fight, but the other men in the room came in front of her, and one man's gaze met hers with worry as he shook his head in warning. It was the first time one had acknowledged her.

Her tormentor held her arms up in front of her with hands together and wrists at her eye level. Hamish looked at the man who had warned her. "Tie her here." He indicated just above her elbows. "I do not want any more marks on her. Take her in the other room and keep her quiet."

The man ushered her through the door that had been left ajar. There was no use in fighting. There were too many of them. The door clicked behind them.

This room was like the one she'd just been in. Faint sounds came from the other room.

"'Twas glad to find ye." Her heart pounded when she recognized Alan's voice. Relief spread through her. He was alive.

"Where's Niall?"

"He didnae survive Lachlan's blade. It was a pleasure to bring the Cameron laird down."

What did he say? Alan wouldnae... Her world imploded as everything around her blurred, her chest caving in and the air spilling from her lungs. *Nae. Alan loved her family. Loved her.* But he'd not said so and hadn't met her gaze when he'd left her this morning. Had he truly had a part in this?

"Well, that is a pity. Were we successful?"

"Aye, we were able to take out each laird who came to the meeting. No one made it out alive."

She broke then. Everything inside her collapsed. She had held out hope that Hamish was wrong, but now, her brothers were dead and Alan had turned into a traitor.

She didn't hear anything after that. She didn't want to breathe, didn't want to believe what she'd heard. Sinking into the nearest chair, tears spilled down her face while she planned how she was going to save her people and Lachlan's babe.

• • •

"I didn't have dinner. Let's go down to the parlor and you can tell me everything."

Hamish clasped a cold, clammy hand on Alan's shoulder. He fought the urge to grab the man's arm, twist it behind his back, and demand to see Kirstie.

When he had entered the room, the first thing he had noticed was she wasn't there. The second was there were too many men in the room to attack.

"Aye, I'm famished." It was the first truth he'd told Hamish since he'd walked into the room.

Hamish motioned to the door, and Alan started toward it, aware he was exposing his back, but if he didn't, it would show he had something to hide and didn't trust the bastard. So, he led them down the stairs, praying they believed his story. Only after they were seated and mugs of ale had been brought to the table did he dare speak again. "What will ye do now that the mission was a success?"

"Kirstie is here. She has agreed to marry me at a kirk in the morning." The confident smile that turned up the corner of Hamish's lips looked real. Gripping his plaid in one hand while he attempted to keep a calm facade, he barely held it together.

Was the boy wrong? If she thought her brothers and he dead, would she have agreed? A serving lass came in and started placing items on the table in front of him, but he didn't pay her any heed. He reached for the mug and took a long gulp, not even noticing what it was until the retched taste of fermented grains filled his mouth and slid down his throat.

He must have been silent for too long, because something sparked in Hamish's eyes, and he continued, "She was in quite the hurry to leave Edinburgh and start a new life."

She loved and trusted him, and he'd not managed to keep her safe.

What had happened to Dougal? Now, she was held

captive by a madman. His heart pounded a rhythm of fear and despair that was so loud his ears throbbed. He would even consider drinking whiskey if it were placed in front of him.

"Did she no' want her mother to attend the service?"

He'd been so focused on the threat to Lachlan and Malcolm that the thought of losing her had never occurred to him. A pain in his chest threatened to suffocate him, so he picked up the ale to take another swallow to wash it away. After the vile liquid ran down his throat, he set the cup back on the table.

"No. She said she couldn't wait until we got back to the Cameron lands."

"Did Kirstie not want to come down for a meal after your journey?" Not wanting to seem overanxious, he leaned back in his seat and let his shoulders relax. He'd looked all about the room upstairs, and there was no indication she'd been there.

"She had a bit of a headache, so I had food sent to her room just before ye arrived."

"How did ye convince her to wed at a kirk? Surely, she would have insisted on a priest." He spooned a helping of vegetable stew into his mouth and pretended it was delicious, but in actuality, he didn't even taste it.

"She has decided to convert and take communion before we wed. Will you join us at the ceremony?"

Alan's spoon paused midair in its descent back to the bowl, a momentary clue he'd picked up, on what Hamish had unknowingly told him. Taking his cup, he raised it in salute, "Aye," he said before pretending to take swig. Hamish was lying. Kirstie had not agreed to marry him, because she would never convert. "What will ye tell her of her brothers?"

"I will wait to tell her until we reach Kentillie. Why bring that sorrow to her on a happy day?"

Alan's mind was racing. Where was she? Hamish must have the rest of his men guarding her.

Standing at the edge of the room was the sturdily built young innkeeper he'd met upon his arrival who watched possessively as the comely serving lass carried in a tray of meats and cheeses then returned with a pitcher to refill their ale. Carefully analyzing the place before entering and having seen no one else about, he came to the assumption that the lass must be the owner's wife.

"Let us pray and thank the Lord for defeating our enemies today." Hamish bowed his head. Alan lowered his but knew better than to take his eyes off the traitorous bastard across from him.

After finishing his prayer, Hamish's eyes gave no hint that anything was amiss, but his tongue darted back and forth over his top teeth as he reached to fill his plate. "How did you know where to find me?"

"The boy, Neville, pointed me in the direction." He didn't add that he'd easily won the boy over and sent him to retrieve Lachlan and the rest of the Cameron men.

"He was only to tell Niall."

"With his last breath, Niall told me to get to ye so ye would ken the outcome."

Hamish took a gulp of his ale.

He didn't touch his cup this time, instead leaning back to give the bastard the false impression that he was at ease with the slimy arse.

"Where did the rest of our men go?"

"They scattered."

"Why?"

"I dinnae ken their reasons. They werenae loyal to me and didnae tell me." He shrugged.

"Did ye no' trust me?"

Hamish chewed slowly, and Alan took another bite while

he waited for a reply. Fighting had always made him hungry, and he'd skipped the noon meal. "I had to be certain. You did live with the Camerons for years."

The lump in his throat made it hard to reply, so he took a big gulp of the vile ale to wash down whatever was preventing his reply. "We had no choice. My father was exiled."

"Which made it difficult to believe you would still feel any loyalties to the Mackenzies."

Alan cursed inside. His tongue had become a little too loose.

Hamish was dangerous, more so than the other Covenanters had been. The man also still had several men with him, two of whom sat just a table away with intent gazes. It was obvious they had been trained to watch everything that went on around them, although they didn't know how to hide what they were doing. He was uncertain how many were still above stairs guarding Kirstie.

"My uncle and grandfather hold me no ill will," he lied smoothly.

"I am glad to hear that. It will be good to have allies to the north and the Campbells to the south."

"Ye will go to Kentillie, then?"

"Yes, I will accompany my bride, and when news comes of her brother's misfortunes, I will soothe the clan."

Alan nodded and popped another piece of meat in his mouth. The innkeeper rushed around the table clearing plates, but he paid the man no heed.

"Will you join me? You would be a great asset since you know the people."

"Aye, I shall return to Kentillie."

Stretching, Hamish said, "You will have to forgive me. I must retire for the evening. I wish to be well rested for the wedding and the journey to the Cameron lands." The conniving bastard spoke with the confidence of a man believing to already own those lands.

"Aye."

"Meet me down here at dawn, and you can accompany us to the kirk." Hamish stood. The minions rose and followed the Covenanter.

Alan stared at the doorway that led to the only staircase and listened intently as the stairs groaned beneath their steps, but they said nothing as they made their way up.

When he finally stood, the room swayed, and he had to throw his arms out to catch himself. The whole place was fuzzy and his emotions had dulled. He blinked. What was wrong with him?

The ale. What had he been thinking? He hadn't. Thoughts of Kirstie with that bastard had been spinning in his head for the last hour as he had sat and drank with the enemy.

He looked down at his calloused hands. He was going to kill the bastard right now. Hamish wouldn't have a chance to put those soft, manicured hands on her curves. She was his. He stalked toward the stairs with murderous intent and stopped suddenly.

Was this what his father felt?

He wanted to beat Hamish until there was nothing left of him. Gulping, he walked back to the table and eased into the chair he'd vacated.

He had been able to stop the rage and sit to clearly think things out. He'd had no desire to take his anger out on Kirstie, only to get her to safety. It was a relief, because doubts had lingered even after their discussion. Now he knew for sure he could handle himself when he'd had too much to drink.

The innkeeper's wife scurried in and started to clear the remainder of the table.

"Do ye have any fresh water?" he asked her.

"Aye." She scooped up the dishes, and for the first time, he noticed the rounding of her belly. He'd been so focused on

Hamish and the other men that he'd missed it.

"I need lots of water and a room. Do ye still have one?"

"Nae. Yer friend and his men have all three. We have a clean stall with fresh blankets in the stable if ye want." She waddled through the door to the kitchens.

Upon first arriving, he'd gone up the stairs and found doors signed with the numbers one, two, and three, and one labeled private. He'd only known to rap on door number two because he'd heard Hamish's voice coming from within.

The woman returned and set a cup on the table in front of him.

"Can ye tell me, lass, how many of my friends are here?"

"Five more came in with the man ye supped with."

Och, so the odds weren't good unless he could separate them. "And was there a woman?"

"Nae. No' that I saw."

"Did my friend have food sent up tonight?"

"Nae, they all came down at different times. Not a friendly lot except for ye."

The hair on the back of his neck stood up. Was Kirstie even here?

Chapter Fourteen

Kirstie determined the sparsely furnished room was similar to the one she'd just been in. Rain battered the windows, and it was dark out, the only light in the room coming from two flickering candles placed on tables at opposite sides of the bed.

She sat in a chair next to a desk that was directly opposite the door to the other room. It was the door she'd been ushered through when Alan had arrived, what she guessed must have been an hour ago. One other door was to her left; it must lead to the hall.

She'd cried until her eyes were dry and she'd almost hyperventilated and lost consciousness with the cloth stuffed in her mouth when she decided it was enough wallowing. She could do that when others weren't depending on her.

Even with her arms tied just below her elbows, if she could get a few minutes unobserved, she would be able to pull up her skirts to get to the dirk, but two of Hamish's men had stayed with her.

Scanning the room for something she could use as a

weapon if she couldn't get to her knife, her gaze caught on the dry, itchy sack she'd been wrapped in on their journey draped over the only other chair in the room. Candlelight flickered from the nearby table as the height of the chair cast shadows dancing ominously on the wall. Determining there was nothing that could help, she turned toward the adjoining door and bided her time, hoping her guards would leave.

As she sat waiting to make a move, her thoughts returned to Alan's words. Pain so fierce it threatened to collapse her chest assailed her with its force.

Her brothers were dead. Had Alan truly had something to do with it? She couldn't fathom it, but he was here and her brothers weren't. If they'd survived, they would have come for her together.

She'd failed them, but she wouldn't fail her nephew or her people. Vowing to do whatever necessary to keep the Covenanters from taking the Cameron clan, she struggled to come up with a plan.

Somehow, she'd have to get a message back to Kentillie in case she didn't make it. They had to know what had happened and to keep little William safe.

Voices came from the adjoining room. "When he returns in the morning, kill him. He was asking too many questions. Make certain the innkeepers don't see it. There can be no evidence that I had anything to do with it."

Flinching at the sudden creak, the door swung in, and her blood turned to ice as Hamish strode toward her. Trying to back away, she'd forgotten she was still in the chair, but he was on her before she could move. His cold, clammy hands clasped her upper arms and dragged her to her feet. Surprising her, he drew her in for a hug then pulled back.

"Your brothers were murdered today."

She wanted to scream, to hit him, to stab him with the knife she couldn't yet get to. Tears flowed anew, and she couldn't stop them. *Och*, she didn't want him to see her vulnerable. His fingers fumbled behind her head, and the gag loosened.

As he pulled the fabric away, he released her from his arms.

Trying to swallow now that the cloth was removed, she discovered it difficult. "May I have a drink, please?" she managed between sobs. Just uttering the words hurt, because her mouth and tongue were dry and thick, and she didn't want to ask this man for anything.

Hamish nodded to the burly man with thinning hair who had stood by the door and eyed her as if she were vermin to be trampled on. The redhead guarding the other door had at least looked at her with some sympathy. Overhearing a conversation between the two earlier, she'd discovered his name was Balloch, and she felt sure if she were left alone with him, she could talk her way free.

The mistrustful guard came back with a small goblet but didn't hand it to her. He passed it to Hamish as if she could only have it once he'd given permission. The arse pinned her with his emotionless eyes before holding it out to her.

She held up her arms. "Can ye no' release me?"

"I believe you are capable of quenching your thirst with the ropes as they are tied. I am afraid you have not yet been brought to heel and may do something irresponsible. I don't want to have to be in a position to punish you again." A shiver ran down her spine at the reminder of his earlier blow.

At her nodding acquiescence, his lips curved up, and he handed her the cup. She wrapped both hands around it and brought it to her parched lips to drink greedily. She'd not had a drink all day, and now she was afraid at any moment, he might take this one away, but he looked pleased at her desperation.

"Your friend Alan is the one who drove his sword

through Lachlan's gut." Her belly contracted at the pain of realizing Alan had been the one to kill her brother. She wouldn't believe it, except Hamish was too arrogant to lie to her and she'd heard it from Alan's own lips. "It doesn't matter, anyway. He'll be dead in the morning. I can't trust a man who would turn on his people as easily as he did. Besides, he knows the truth of my involvement, and if he ever spoke a word to the rest of the Camerons, it would ruin everything."

Shaking her head, she fought back the bile rising in her throat and avoided his gaze.

"I will save the Camerons." He closed the distance between them and put his hand gently on her cheek. She flinched away, and his hazel eyes darkened to a sinister brown. "I will save you."

"I told ye before. I am Catholic and willnae convert. There is nothing ye can do to change my mind."

His hand left her face, and relief had barely registered before his fist collided with her ribs. She doubled over and inhaled sharply as the cup she'd been holding slipped from her grasp and clattered onto the wooden floor. Her eyes watered and her vision blurred, but she inhaled and fought the pain to straighten and meet his gaze. She would never let this man control her.

"Ye bastard." She wanted to retaliate, but her only option was with words, and she was done shrinking into the corner. She had to let him know he would never control her.

"That is no way to talk to your betrothed. You will need to learn humility. I expected better from you."

His cold gaze locked with hers, and she fought back the panic that now assailed her at the emptiness she saw there. What she had once taken for calm peacefulness she now recognized as the sign of an emotionless animal that got pleasure from toying with its prey.

Taking in a couple of deep breaths, she forced her legs to

move. She straightened her spine, tilting her chin in the air.

"Ye will never…"

She doubled over as the solid fist connected with her rib this time. Her eyes watered, and she fought to keep her balance. She wasn't going to give, and the look in his soulless eyes told her he could do this all night. She might be dead by morning, but at least her clan would be safe.

• • •

After getting as much information from the pregnant lass as he could about the upstairs layouts and the men who occupied the rooms, Alan sat at the table drinking sweet cider and studying the main floor and noticed an unlocked window that would give him easy re-entry when he made his move. It had probably only been a few moments, but it felt as if an hour had passed since Hamish had ascended the stairs, a lifetime as each second ticked by, and his concern grew.

Knowing he should analyze the threat carefully, he went outside to circle the tavern in the almost pitch darkness. He ignored the slushy, muddy mess left from horses and the frequent visitors to the inn as he focused on the rooms above stairs. Lightning flashed, and the momentary fear he'd be spotted vanished as quickly as the light. An ominous boom followed that caused a shiver to run down his spine. The pouring rain and time had dulled the unwanted effects of the ale, and all his senses were sharp and on alert.

He had to get to Kirstie tonight while they weren't expecting an attack and before serious harm could come to her. Hell, she could already be hurt. Holding out hope Lachlan and Malcolm might yet reach them, he'd continued to debate what his next step should be, but as his panic over Kirstie's whereabouts grew, he could no longer give them more time.

The owners of the inn had retired. Shortly after they'd gone up, the light from the candle in their room extinguished. Only two other rooms showed signs that anyone stirred— the one he'd been in previously and the one connected to it. Shadows caught his attention in the room adjoining Hamish's. The candle was far enough back in the room that it afforded a glimpse of the people.

Kirstie. He sighed with relief as her silhouette came into view, which took the weight from his chest.

Skirting back around the front of the inn, he tried the door, but it was locked, so he made his way to the large window, easing it open soundlessly. The fit was tight, but he was able to squeeze head first through the open pane. His arm swung wide and bumped into an unlit lamp, which crashed to the floor as he swung his legs in. He jumped to his feet and hurried to the shadows behind the door leading to the stairs.

The groans of the wood planks and stomp of boots descending the steps sounded as one man said, "There shouldnae be anyone down here. The innkeeper and his wife are in bed."

"Mayhap they have a dog," came the second voice.

"There was no mutt in here. I would've seen it. Keep yer dirk ready in case someone found us. I dinnae trust that Mackenzie."

"I'm relieved Hamish said we could end him in the morn'."

So he'd not been able to keep his emotions hidden from Hamish, and they all now knew or at least suspected they couldn't trust him.

With his life and Kirstie's depending on him taking down all six men and getting her out of here, Alan waited until both men had cleared the staircase before he lunged for the one nearest and sunk his dirk into the man's lower back. It slid in and up easily. The man froze then slumped as he pulled the knife out.

The body landed near the bottom steps, making a softer than expected thud, but it was still loud enough to have the other man turning to see what had happened. The hulking shadow growled and then leaped for him, but Alan ducked down and out to the side as the form whizzed by and collided with the closed front door.

He swung around to drive his knife toward the second man's gut just as the brute recovered and turned toward him, but the man caught his hand and fought to keep it away.

An arm wrapped around his neck as yet another man yanked him back toward the stairs. Alan kicked out with both feet to knock the second man to the ground as he grabbed at the vise cutting off his air. When he had a good grip on the third man, he bent and used the momentum to throw the newcomer over his back and into the man he'd just kicked.

Something snapped and a voice he'd not heard before called out, "My arm."

The man who'd come down first said, "Move." He pushed the injured man away, and the sound of scraping metal indicated he'd drawn a sword from its sheath.

Alan had to go in low because he was still cramped in the frame of the door at the base of the steps and didn't have room to draw his own weapon. Driving for the man's leg, he was rewarded when they both fell back and the halberd clanged to the ground.

Wasting no time, Alan drove his knife into the man's side, but the man continued to struggle until Alan was able to twist the blade several times, keeping it buried to the hilt. When the life had drained and the body became still, he looked around for the man with the injured arm to attack, but the coward had disappeared. The front door to the inn was left wide open in the man's retreat, but he didn't have time to give chase. The ruckus they had made surely warned

Hamish they were under attack, so he let the man go and continued up toward the three men who still stood between Kirstie and him.

He paused to see if any more men would come his way, but he heard nothing except the rain and wind that whistled and floated in through the open door behind him. He took each step one at a time, firmly planting his feet on the corners of the platforms to quiet the groans on the old wood.

Reaching the hall, he noticed the glows coming from the slits under the doors labeled one and two. When he crested the top and moved toward the doors, his heart stopped beating at the sound of Kirstie yelling words that trailed off too suddenly through the door of the room he'd seen her in. He wanted to rush in, but there were three men left.

At door three, he put his hand on the knob and gently eased it open. He scanned the small room. No candle lit the room, but lightning flashed, revealing an empty bed. The room was clear, so he turned back into the hall and to the room he'd been in earlier tonight. Thunder boomed and he flinched, thinking he'd missed someone in the room.

Drawing his sword quietly from its sheath, he made his way to door number one and gently eased open the thick wood. Light flooded the hall, and he searched from corner to corner. Hell, Hamish and the other two men were in the room with Kirstie. The door had been left ajar and he saw movement but couldn't tell for certain who it was.

Squaring his shoulders, he took a deep breath and let his eyes adjust to the light as he slid farther into the room to where he couldn't be seen. Luckily, it appeared, the pounding of the rain and the howling wind had drowned the sounds of the confrontation he'd had below.

He was debating if he should wait here for one to come through the door or to take his chances and burst in swinging when he heard Hamish's calm voice. "Let's try this again,

Kirstie. You will marry me in the morning."

Tensing at the sneer he heard in the bastard's voice, his grip on his claymore tightened.

"My answer willnae change. Ye arennae fit to lead a herd of cows, and I will never give ye the Camerons." She sounded breathless but determined.

Her words were followed by a *whoosh* of sound, and she cried out in pain. All rational thought left as he yanked the door open and charged.

Chapter Fifteen

Eyes still watering from Hamish's attack, Kirstie straightened in time to catch a change in the current of energy in the room. It disturbed the stale air that had filled the small space and made her hair stand on end. Blinking, she gasped at the image of the balding man, mouth ajar, staring down at a sword that had pierced his midsection.

Shivers spread through her as she recognized Alan holding the blade at the hilt, but he looked different. His gray eyes were rigid, cold, and at the same time they burned with an intense hardness that would have been frightening if they were aimed at her, but they weren't. They were fixated on Hamish.

Hamish shuddered. It was the first sign of any real emotion she'd ever seen in the arse who had remained passive and distant as he'd beat her when she hadn't bent to his will.

Alan's dark blond hair clung to his head and cheeks, appearing almost chestnut with the sparse lighting of the two sputtering candles at the far corners of the room. As his soaked clothes hugged to his bulging arms, the material highlighted their girth, and he pulled the claymore from the guard and gripped it with both hands in an intimidating pose. Hamish's man fell with a thick thud to the ground, and Alan stepped over the body without a downward glance.

His golden skin glistened as if he'd spent the evening in the rain she'd heard pounding on the roof and windows as she'd prayed for the strength to do the right thing for her clan. This was the fierce warrior who her brother trusted at his side in battle, and despite what he'd done to her, she was thankful he was here now.

"Move, Kirstie," he ordered, but before the words registered, a hand clamped onto her arm and pulled.

"What is this?" the devil with his talons around her asked in his eerie deadpan voice as he drew her closer to his side.

She couldn't lash out at him, because her arms were still bound and she was weak from the lack of nourishment and the beating her body had taken. She had no hope of getting out of Hamish's grasp without distracting Alan.

"Let her go, and I'll think about sparing yer life." Alan's gaze was locked on the man holding her.

"Balloch, get the others." She thought she heard a slight tremor in Hamish's voice.

"Dinnae bother. They cannae help ye."

Until now, she'd kept her gaze focused on her savior, but it shifted to the redheaded man who had earlier seemed to have some sense of compassion. His focus was locked on Alan but skid to Hamish and then back again. Since he was standing so close to the candles, it was hard to see who he'd decided to side with until his hand rose to his side, and she heard the scrape of metal as his sword was unsheathed.

"If ye walk out that door now, ye may avoid their fate." Alan's stare had turned to Balloch, but she was certain he hadn't taken all his attention from Hamish and her. Balloch squared his shoulders then took a step toward Alan. "Ye dinnae have to do this."

"Aye, I have sworn my loyalty." The man slid sideways to cut off Alan's access to Hamish and her, then time stood still as the men assessed each other and awaited the next move.

"Be done with it," Hamish ordered his man from behind her.

A flash of red hair and steel blurred as the guard charged toward Alan. Swords clashed and she flinched at the clang of metal as her heart lurched, her own predicament forgotten as she prayed God would keep Alan safe. The redhead took a step back and pulled his weapon up in a defensive stance as Alan readjusted in one fluid motion.

Stepping in toward Alan, the man swung around and up, aiming for Alan's torso, but Alan met the blade with his own and deflected it easily. Balloch swung in from the opposite side, and the swords collided again and scraped. A blur of red continued toward Alan, even as his sword was pushed out of his grasp and clattered to the floor. The brute clung to Alan's arm and drove him back into the wall. As he did, she felt a tug as Hamish attempted to draw her toward the open door to the other room. She pulled away and his grip tightened painfully on the sensitive skin under her upper arm. Attempting to drive her elbow into his ribs, she thrust toward his midsection, but the vise around her dug in deeper and kept her from reaching the target.

"Do not make me hurt you." His quiet command stopped her for a moment, then she remembered he would hurt her no matter what she did. He honestly thought she would let him drag her out of here without a struggle.

Her gaze shifted to take in his cold eyes, and she pinned him with all the emotion she had. "I willnae be going anywhere with ye, and ye will never lead the Camerons."

Doubt appeared in his eyes for the first time, but before she could savor it, the redheaded guard grunted and cursed.

Her attention returned to the men fighting in front of her.

Alan growled, drew his foot up between them, and pushed out to kick at the man. The redhead lost his grip and flew backward but managed to stay upright. Alan lunged forward, but Balloch had already reached down to scoop up his weapon and skidded out of reach. He stumbled but caught himself on the small table near the closed door to the hall. It creaked and its contents shifted as he nearly tumbled over with it, but when he righted himself, he moved into an offensive stance.

Hamish's iron grip remained firm on her arm as his free hand snaked around her waist and drew her flush to his chest. She tried to struggle, but he pulled her along the side of the room toward the adjoining door.

Despite the threat in front of him, Alan shifted to block Hamish's retreat. The arse took a step back and dragged her with him to stand in front of the window by the bed.

"Look out," she yelled as Balloch charged toward the man she loved.

Movement from the other side of the room caught her gaze as red flames engulfed the side of the room. When Balloch had fallen into the table, the candle must have ignited something. The fingers of fire had spread to the table and chair.

Alan turned in time to block the blow, but Balloch swung around for another attack. Metal clanged and their positions shifted, completely blocking Hamish's escape to the other room.

The redhead caught sight of the flames for the first time. He gaped, and that was all Alan needed to slice through the air and collide with the man's side. He went down screaming as blood poured from the wound. While attempting to pull himself up by the door that had been left ajar, he collapsed and the door clicked shut, sealing his fate as Alan drove the point of his claymore through the man's gut and twisted.

The opposite side of the room crackled with heat as the walls and door of the old inn caught and cut off that means of escape.

"Move now or we'll burn in here." Hamish attempted to push her toward the fiery exit.

Instead of obeying, she dug the heel of her boot into the middle of his foot. He yelled, released his hold on her waist and arm, then pulled back. Before she knew what had happened, his fist struck her cheek, and she fell onto the floor by the bed.

Hamish's twisted rage focused on her, and she flinched into the corner. His hand swept toward her as she shrank away.

"Dinnae touch her."

Hamish turned toward the threat, and her gaze followed his to see Alan poised just a few steps away with a vengeance in his eyes that matched the roaring fire behind him.

A shiver wracked Hamish's body. He lunged toward her but was swept away as Alan collided with him, and they both flew out the window.

• • •

The jolt reverberated through Alan's bones as he landed on Hamish in a thick puddle of mud. He tried to inhale, but the air didn't reach his lungs, so he rolled to the side and then up to his knees; he tried again but almost tumbled over. Checking himself for injuries, he saw blood on his shirt, but when he pulled it up, there was only a small scrape. Not nearly enough to account for the amount of red staining the garment.

Swallowing, he tried to breathe again, and a little air got through. He took in another quick breath, then he remembered the man on the ground in front of him. Shaking his head, he straightened and looked over to assess the threat.

The Covenanter lay with eyes open, staring up into the relentless rain as the storm raged around them. A dark stain coated his clothing, more than what covered Alan's, and the man was motionless. Lightning flashed, and he was able to see a thin flat object protruding from his stomach. It looked like a piece of glass from the window they'd fallen through.

Taking in another breath, he was relieved that this time the air filled his lungs and the pain was easing. Putting his hand in the mud to brace himself, he pushed up to his feet and faced the inn. His heart plummeted.

Flames shot from the window of the room Kirstie was in. The wood crackled and the small bits of rain that hit it sizzled but did nothing to stop the inferno destroying the whole inn.

Kirstie.

She was stuck in that room with her hands bound, one exit in flames and the other blocked by the body of a man he'd just killed.

"Kirstie," he yelled, but there was no sign of her.

A scream pierced the rain. She was still up there. He forced his trembling legs to move faster than he ever had, intent on saving her or die trying.

Chapter Sixteen

Trying to dislodge the icicles that had formed in her veins at the image of Alan flying through the window, Kirstie shook her head. Flames reached the edge of the bed, and the woolen blankets lit with a loud *whoosh* as a new blast of heat barreled toward her. She crawled farther away from the bed and pushed up to standing, but as soon as she did, smoke filled her lungs and she started to choke.

Falling back to her knees, she used the flats of her lower arms to crawl for the door to the other room. Her skirts stretched under her knees as the fabric pulled, and she had to stop to shimmy them up so she could keep going. When she started again, her arms slid on something slick, and she glanced down to see her hands covered in a dark red stain as the coppery smell filled her nostrils. She had to fight back the bile that threatened to spill over.

Blocking her retreat, the guard's body was sprawled in front of her only exit. She attempted to pull at him, but with her arms still bound, she couldn't grip and her fingers kept slipping from his clothes. Her eyes burned and her lungs ached as smoke filled the room. Sitting on her knees and looking around, the helplessness of her situation assailed her. She was trapped. She doubled over coughing as her eyes watered at the pain of the heat and black fog.

Alan had come back for her. She would not die here. Hamish had lied. There was no way he'd have raised a sword to her brothers. Why had she ever believed that arse?

She had to know Alan was safe.

Had he survived the fall? Would Hamish have killed him? She'd set out to save her family, but now, lying in a puddle of blood, she felt helpless. What a fool she'd been to believe she could be the strong one.

The knife.

It was still strapped to her leg. If she could get to it, maybe she would be able to get free. Closing her eyes to the smoke, she reached down and yanked up her skirts. She could reach the sheath but not the hilt to slide it out.

Pulling her hands in opposite directions, she screamed as the rope dug into the skin about her elbows. It worked. She had the knife in her hand.

Twisting her wrist at an awkward angle, she was able to slide the length of the blade between her arms. Slicing up, the tip slipped through and barely touched the end of her bindings.

A bead of sweat trickled down her temple, and she glanced around to see how close the flames were, but it was the smoke that had her gagging and making her eyes sting. It was so thick she could only see a red glow behind it. Positioning the knife again, she pushed as far under her bindings as she could reach. It caught on the rope, and she began frantically slicing, ignoring the pain in her wrists.

The dirk jerked up and fell from her hands, and she panicked because she couldn't see it, but then as she moved, the twine fell from her arms. She was free. But she still had to get out of the room.

Crawling over the body, she centered her back on the wall, placed her feet on the side of the dead weight, and strained to push him away. She was surprised at how quickly it worked. There was a space large enough to open the door, but as she rose up, the black fog invaded her lungs and blocked her sight. Feeling for the knob, she grasped it and yanked open.

A *whoosh* of flames blazed past her head, and she thought they had landed on her as the heat washed over her skin. Leaping to get away from them, she bolted for the other side of the room. Fresh air filled her lungs, but the intake of breath still burned, and she coughed but continued to make her way into the hall.

Running for the steps, she didn't bother to turn around to see the progress of the flames. She slipped on a lump at the bottom and braced for the impact on the hard wooden floor.

Strong, reassuring arms wrapped around her before she collided with the ground.

Alan.

Tears stung her eyes as she realized he was safe. The fear that had engulfed her as she'd seen his body fly through the window gave way to choking sobs of relief.

"Yer alive," she managed to croak as her burned throat fought to release the words and her hand rose to cup his cheek.

"Aye." His head leaned into her touch. "Are ye all right, kitten?"

"Aye, I just need some air." Och, it hurt to speak.

He rushed her out into the night. Cool rain dotted her skin and made her shiver, but she welcomed the liquid as it washed the smoke and heat of the flames and the blood from her flesh. Guiding her toward the stable, he didn't slow until they were a safe distance from the crackling old wood of the building.

As they came to a halt, his hand slid down her arm, and his body stiffened. Holding her out at arm's length, he twisted her from side to side in a frantic appraisal then said, "I have to go back in."

"Nae. Are ye mad?" Her fire-fevered skin froze, and dread clenched at her heart.

"The innkeeper and his wife are still in there." He clasped onto the sides of her head as he dipped to kiss her soundly before continuing. "Stay here."

She nodded and fought back the urge to latch onto him and not allow him to return to the inferno.

She yelled to his back, "I love ye. Be careful."

His retreating form shrank as he ran back toward the burning inn, leaving her, cold, wet, alone, and afraid he wouldn't make it back out.

Moments later, the front of the building collapsed.

· · ·

Alan bounded back into the burning building much lighter, knowing Kirstie was safe. He was determined the couple wouldn't meet the same fate as his mother.

As he reached the steps, the smell of burning wood and smoke invaded his nostrils and made him shudder, but he paused only long enough to drag the body from the bottom. He couldn't risk it being in the way when he escorted the innkeepers down the stairs.

Ominous clouds of smoke filled the open spaces and the flickering reds and oranges on the ceiling. Alan's heart hammered, but he beat back the fear and continued for the second floor to the room labeled private, knowing time wasn't on his side. He was shocked at how fast the flames had engulfed the wall at the top of the landing where Kirstie had apparently left the door ajar in her escape.

Reaching the top, he scrunched against the other side and ran the length of the short hall. Luckily, the door was still shut to the room where the flames had started, but the heat pouring off was hellish and expelled eerie screeching and popping noises.

At the door, he pounded and yelled, "Get up." Pounding again, "Ye must get up!"

An answer did not come quick enough, so he backed a couple steps and ran for the door to ram it. His whole body seemed to shake with the impact, and his shoulder screamed at the brutal use of it, but the door remained shut. The hall was filling with flames and would become impassable in seconds.

He retreated to try the assault again. This time as he braced for impact and expected to hit the hard wood, the door swung in, and he flew through the air to land on the floor. The innkeeper stood over him, gazing into the hall.

Jumping up, Alan slammed the door shut just as the terrible sound of boards collapsing and shuddering in the wake of the inferno's path shook the whole building. Darkness immersed the room in its shroud as the floor tilted forward and he almost lost his footing again; the man standing only in his shirt slammed against the wall.

"We have to get ye and yer wife out. The whole inn is about to collapse."

The man ran for another room, just as his wife came around the corner wrapped in a large plaid and holding a small candle that lit her frightened face.

"Is there another way out?"

"Aye, this way." The innkeeper grabbed his wife's hand and pulled her toward the back of their apartment. Alan followed the couple as they ran, but it was hard to see anything else in the dim light.

They rushed down a set of steps that led to the back

of the inn. Relief washed over him when he realized they wouldn't have to climb out a window. He'd seen enough of those tonight.

He vaguely recognized a kitchen as they rushed to a door that let out to the back of the inn. He took a moment to let the cleansing rain wash over him as his eyes continued to adjust to the absence of light. Sparing a glance for the innkeepers, he saw the man had his arm around his wife as they watched their livelihood burning to the ground.

"I have to get to Kirstie," he yelled over his shoulder as he ran around the burning structure.

The flames lit the night on this side of the building, and he had no trouble seeing her form crumpled to her knees with her head in her hands, not looking at the building in front of her. She must have thought he was still inside.

He knelt in front of her and wrapped his arms around her, drawing her in for a reassuring embrace. Startled, she pulled back, but then her arms flew around him, nearly tackling him to the ground.

"I-I thought…"

He knew what she couldn't voice, the fear that he was gone, the same torturous grip and anguish that had been wrapped around his own heart and stolen his breath from the moment he'd learned Hamish had taken her away.

"Shh," he soothed as she cried into his chest, and he let his hand run down her slick hair as his other hand kept her pinned to him with the need to keep her near. "Dinnae cry. I'm all right."

He tilted her head up so that her gaze met his, and he finally felt whole again, like God had not forsaken him and that his efforts and prayers to save her and all the Camerons had been fruitful.

His mouth covered her lips as he savored the velvety smoothness of the soft flesh and let himself go. He didn't hold back; all the years he'd denied himself her touch had been torture, but no more, they belonged together. Tongue sweeping in to tangle with hers, he lost himself in her warmth and the love, trust, and need he could feel in her response. He was barely aware of the wreckage burning so close. She'd always been able to make him forget the world around him.

This… This, her touch, her adoration was what he wanted to experience every day for the rest of his life. Knowing now he wasn't the monster his father had been, he would prove to Lachlan that he was the best match for Kirstie and he would happily spend eternity keeping her happy. She deserved that.

He let the waves of desire drag him under, let all the insecurities wash away with the receding tide of doubts and fears. Almost losing her today had nearly killed him, and he drank her in now because he'd thought he might never get the chance again.

A thunderous bang exploded, pulling him from the sweet caress, but he kept his arms locked around her. Sparing a quick glance over his shoulder toward the ruins, he became aware of the heat radiating out to where they stood at a safe distance away. Burning beams of the second floor had collapsed in on the first and lay heaped in a fiery mass that lit the yard. His eyes were drawn to Hamish's body still on the ground near where they'd landed. A sudden urge to protect Kirstie and keep the view from her eyes had him averting his gaze quickly so he didn't draw hers to the sight.

When he turned back to her, he sighed with relief that he'd gotten to her in time. She was safe.

Still wrapped in his embrace, a tremble wracked her and his gaze skimmed down to take in her soaked appearance. A dripping dress that left the top of her chest and shoulders exposed clung to her curves. She had no plaid to protect her from the chill of the night or the rain. He cursed himself for not getting her out of the rain immediately.

Unwinding his arms from around her, he took her hand and guided her to the stables a safe distance away from the inferno behind them.

Once inside, the musty smell of wet hay mixed with leather and manure, but he ignored the assault on his senses as he twirled her to face him.

"Look at me, kitten. I'm sorry I couldnae get here sooner. Are ye sure ye arenae hurt?"

"I'll be bruised, but I'll be all right."

He placed a finger to her lips and traced them tenderly. Her rigid frame relaxed, and as her gaze softened, he wrapped his free arm back around her waist to draw her near. She smelled of smoke and rain, and despite or maybe because of the reminder of the events of the day, he'd never wanted to hold her more than he did right now.

Not knowing how to explain the relief and joy he felt inside, he lowered his lips to hers and closed his mouth in a kiss meant to persuade her that she was all that mattered to him. His tongue darted into her mouth and swirled around hers, seeking and giving the reassurance that this was to be theirs, that the unspoken dreams he'd kept locked away in a secret part of his heart he'd never acknowledged to anyone, even attempted to keep hidden from himself. They would always be together, and he would never deny that need again.

His father might have guided every decision he'd made in the past, but now Alan would follow his own heart, not the illusions of a man he'd never really known. He was his own person, and Kirstie was the one who had unlocked the man who had hidden from his past.

His hand slid up her side and shoulder to thread into her hair as his fingers twined and tangled into the soft wet strands and held on as if his life depended on it. Trying to impart all the passion and longing and love that coursed through his veins with just the mention of her name, he poured himself into that embrace. She was his world, and now that he'd given into his desire for her, he could never go back to Kentillie without her by his side, so he let her feel his devotion in his kiss, that she was everything to him.

He only knew he had succeeded when she deepened the embrace as her hands closed around his sides and her fingers dug into his ribs to draw him closer. The slight feminine moan that escaped beckoned for him to release the primal fierce desire he felt to claim every inch of her body and assure himself she was unharmed.

Trailing a hand down to her ass, he nuzzled her to his swollen cock and relished the feel of the way they fit. Shifting his hips to rub against the intimate part of her that he wanted to claim, he groaned with the need that had come on fast and fierce.

He'd forgotten the world around them until he heard a throat clear and felt a hand on his shoulder.

Chapter Seventeen

Kirstie silently studied the roaring flames when a prone figure on the ground caught her gaze. As Alan explained the day's events to the innkeepers, she realized she'd not even had a chance to ask him what had happened and check him for any injuries.

A small woman with vacant, sad eyes, the innkeeper's wife came up beside her and wrapped a blanket around her trembling shoulders. The cold from the rain, cooling her heated skin, had reached all the way to her bones. The young woman's belly was swollen, and her hand absently rubbed it as they watched the men talk.

The lass returned to take her husband's hand and lean into him as his protective gaze washed over her, and Alan continued, "Do ye have anywhere to stay until we can get some men down here to help ye rebuild?"

He'd committed Cameron men to help the couple. She liked that his heart was so large and that he knew her brother well enough that he'd want the same thing and not fear his wrath at the promise of support.

"Aye, my wife's father lives a short distance away. Ye should come with us to get some rest."

"Nae, we will wait here for The Cameron. He willnae be long. He'll want to ken his sister is safe. I will send someone to let ye ken when we can rebuild for ye."

"For now, I need to get my wife somewhere warm and dry. I dinnae wish to make the babe come early."

As the couple rode off, Kirstie shrugged out of the blanket and ran for the cold cleansing drops still careening from the heavens, but he caught her hand before she made it to the door. "What are ye doing?" He followed her.

"I have to wash the smell of the smoke off." She tugged at his hand, but he didn't let go. Smiling, he shuffled his feet and followed her from the stable.

She angled her head up to the liquid and let it run down her face, washing away all the smells that had clung to her today. The sack she'd been wrapped in, Hamish's horrid breath, and the smoke. Breathing in the night air, she twirled in circles.

As the cool drops did their work, they also melted away the hurt that had kept her heart in a vise, the fear that had left her blood cold, and the anger that had almost boiled over. Coming to a stop facing Alan, who eyed the still burning flames, she put both hands on his cheeks and was surprised to see in the dim light that his gaze was filled with a happiness she hadn't seen glow in their depths since before she'd left Kentillie.

"My brothers are safe?"

"Aye. I left before the battle was done, but they had it in hand." His eyes clouded over and his mouth opened, but he shut it just as quickly.

"What? Something's wrong." She shivered and moved in to wrap her arms around him.

"Henry didnae make it."

"Blair. Has anyone told her?"

"No' before I left. When I kenned ye were with Hamish and he was the one who planned it all, I got away as soon as I was certain Lachlan and Malcolm were safe."

"Someone has to tell her."

"Finlay saw it." There seemed to be an edge to his words sounding almost like anger instead of sorrow, but he kept going. "I'm certain he'll tell her."

He scooped her up in his arms, and she squeaked in surprise. Laughing, he carried her back to the stable. Being cradled in his arms heated her cold skin and made her think of the afternoon they had spent in the inn at Edinburgh and all the things he had made her feel.

Walking down the short aisle, he peered into each space they passed. It was dark in the confines of the building, but she was able to make out several horses in the stable. The animals looked up as they passed, and she recognized Alan's and one she thought to be Hamish's; the others must have belonged to the men who had traveled with the tyrant whose body moldered outside in the rain. Only two stalls were empty—the one vacated by the couple's horse and one that was apparently used for only storing equipment.

Alan set her on her feet, and she watched his back as he fumbled around in the near dark. Turning around, he had a mass of something in his arms, but she couldn't tell what it was. "Hold these," he said, and she held out her hands, surprised when soft dry and clean smelling plaids tickled her skin.

Alan took the top one and shook it before spreading it out on what could have been a heap of hay or rushes on the ground. Taking one more, he laid it on top of the other then turned to face her.

Without taking his gaze from her, he took the last blanket and tossed it carelessly on the others and wrapped his arms around her, pulling her in as if he'd thought he'd never see her again. Resting her chin on his shoulder and leaning into the embrace, she whispered into his neck. "Do ye still think of me as a sister?"

"I never did. That was a lie I told myself to keep me from doing this." He drew her flush to his hard chest as his mouth covered hers, gentle and seeking, but at the same time burning with an urgency that screamed out to the primitive part of her and awoke the desire hidden within.

"I want to be the one ye see walking through yer door at night, the one ye go to bed with at night, the one who fathers yer babes. Ye dinnae ken how hard it's been all these years for me no' to come after ye."

Chills spread down her spine and her cool skin heated as he whispered into her ear, all the while his fingers working at the laces on the back of her gown.

"Ye should have."

His lips trailed down, and his mouth brushed her neck. Fire exploded in her core, and her body unconsciously arched into his as the sensations assailed her, and her dress was loosened and fell from her shoulders to gather at the elbows.

Surprising her, he drew back and met her gaze. She couldn't see well but could hear the need and conviction behind the words as his deep, husky voice sent emotions spiraling straight to the soul of the girl who had always loved this man. "I'm here now. Marry me, kitten. I dinnae want to go another day without ye by my side."

Her heart fluttered and flipped as her breath caught, and at the same time, her eyes stung and watered. It was what she had always desired, but how come she couldn't speak?

"I dinnae ken if it's possible."

He stretched back farther and tensed as he studied her with a panicked glaze.

"I could no' bare it if Lachlan sent ye away. I'm happy

anywhere I can be with my animals, but Kentillie is your home."

His shoulders relaxing, a grin spread across his face. "Leave yer brother to me. I think we will work things out."

His warm hand stroked her rain soaked cheek. "When we have Lachlan's blessing, will ye be my wife?"

"Aye, Alan. 'Tis all I've ever wanted."

His mouth crashed down on hers, and another word wasn't said until after they were spent and sated, tangled in each other's arms beneath the blankets that smelled of lavender and reminded her of home and dreams that could come true.

. . .

Trailing a hand up and down Kirstie's soft skin, Alan marveled how at ease he felt despite being in an unfamiliar stable somewhere outside of Edinburgh. She'd fallen asleep after they'd made love, and he spent the time reveling in the view of the top of her head cradled in the crook of his arm with her brown tresses sprawled over his shoulders and chest.

Studying her, he couldn't believe he had waited so long to do this, what he was meant to do; he'd always felt at ease in her presence, but he'd not known until this moment she was what completed him and made him feel like a whole man. All those times he'd sought her out in the stables or when she'd snuck up to the turrets to read or when she found him by the loch and sat next to him quietly when he'd been upset.

Until the day he'd pushed her away, she'd been his pillar of strength and he would hold on to her. He'd be able to enjoy her faith, strength, and love every night from here until they were old and gray with his arms cocooned around her.

He was surprised the Camerons hadn't found them yet, but maybe the boy he'd sent back to tell Lachlan of their location had not been able to find them. Fatigue setting in, he decided to rest before Kirstie and he set out to locate her brothers. She'd probably be impossible to wake anyway, so just as the sun was coming up and his arm was falling asleep, he gently maneuvered her onto her back, snuggled up close, and threw his arm over her to finally fall into a relaxed sleep.

. . .

Familiar voices floated through the air, pulling Alan from a dreamless sleep.

"I'll check in here," Malcolm's voice sounded as Alan glanced to the clothes he'd thrown over the side of the stall to dry before they'd lain down. There was no way to reach them before they would be discovered.

When a warm, chestnut mop of curls matching Kirstie's peered over the partition into the small space, Malcolm's mouth fell open, and Alan would have laughed had he not had the sudden worry Lachlan would be angry at catching them together like this.

Spurring on the dread, the youngest of the Cameron siblings turned over his shoulder and yelled, "Lachlan, I think ye need to get in here."

His heart froze as his laird, the man who had been his brother and best friend most of his life, peered over the railing to see him naked, tangled in a heap with the man's only sister. Luckily, the blankets still covered their more intimate parts, but the old fear of the division between his father and uncle came crashing down on him, and suddenly he was too hot beneath the covers.

Would he have to choose between Lachlan or a life in exile with Kirstie?

He stammered as he tried to think of something to say that wouldn't damage their bond any further.

Surprising him, a dimpled smile stared back at him. "Well, it looks like Kirstie will finally be coming home. 'Tis about time the two of ye came to yer senses."

"Ye arenae angry?"

"Nae. I've kenned all along ye should be together, but the decision had to be made by ye and her. Mother and I discussed it, and we thought it best not to push either of ye."

His muscles relaxed, but that gave in to a flush that spread through his body as he tried to decide how he was going to get to his shirt and plaid.

"I sent ye ahead to Edinburgh because I kenned she would be there. I was hoping 'twould push things along, because with it looking more like war and the uncertainty of the Macnab clan, I was planning on telling her 'tis time she comes home."

Alan felt his brows crinkle together. So Lachlan had planned to torture him with Kirstie's presence. It had worked, and he couldn't be angry because it had been what he'd needed all along and not known.

"Mother will want to ken right away. We should be able to catch up to them in a day or two. Put on yer clothes and get out here so ye can tell me why the building is burned to the ground and what happened to the Menzies man." The brothers turned and walked from the stable, leaving him to ponder how long his friend had known about his feelings for Kirstie.

Rising, he carefully slid sideways, making sure to keep his kitten covered as he snuck from the blankets. As expected, she made a small sigh of protest but kept dozing peacefully.

Stepping out into the midmorning sun, he became aware of the complete devastation of the inn. The rain had subsided sometime in the early morning hours, but a damp feeling clung to the air, despite the promise of a warm, sunny day to come.

"So ye kenned all along?"

"'Twould have had to be blind not to miss ye two always sneaking looks at each other. And all those times ye wouldnae practice with me in the lists only to hear ye'd been up on the turrets listening to her read."

A strong hand gripped his shoulder as Malcolm's laughter split through the air. "We used to make a game of spying on ye two."

They stepped closer to the inn, where Hamish's body still laid prone on the wet earth. "Did everyone make it through the battle?"

"Mostly. We lost Henry and a Fraser." An image of the cowardly Highlander pushing his friend into harm's way intruded, and he couldn't fight the scowl as Lachlan relayed the information.

Looking around, he took in all the Cameron men standing around the burned building. "Where's Finlay?"

"He went to give Blair the news. He should join us shortly."

Alan relayed last evening's events for his brothers, and they vowed to come back and help the innkeepers rebuild.

"Now, go wake my sister. We need to be on our way home. Oh, and tell her we brought Poseidon. She'll be pleased to see him."

Moments later, he knelt over his hope for the future, the one thing he'd never thought he could have, the woman who would become his wife and give life to their children. Waking her with a kiss was easier than he'd expected. She purred with pleasure, then he pulled back. "Time to go, kitten."

Her lazy, hooded eyes widened. "Are my brothers here?"

"Aye, they are safe and ready to head back to Kentillie."

"Damn, I have to talk to Lachlan. He has to ken I want to be with ye." She bolted up, heedless to her state of undress, and the blankets fell to her hips.

"'Tis all right, kitten. He approves." He wasn't sure if he should be looking at her eyes, her assets, or telling her to get her clothes on before someone walked by.

"Ye spoke to him? He is happy for us?"

"Aye."

She threw her arms around him and nearly knocked him over.

"I love ye, Kirstie." He'd been afraid to voice it until now, until he knew that speaking the words wouldn't rip her from him.

"I love ye," she said as he drew her in tighter.

Pulling back, he glanced at her naked state again, pleased he would wake to her this way every day from now on. Tamping down the desire she stirred, he said, "Now, get dressed and let's go home."

Epilogue

After brushing down Poseidon, Kirstie closed his door and walked down the line of stalls toward the exit of the stables. Although it was her last run-through of the day, a warm glow from the setting October sun still cast bright beams through the windows and doors, leaving hints of gold floating through the air.

She still found it hard to believe she was back at Kentillie and that Wallace had asked her to take over because he'd been suffering with a bad back. He'd said, "Yer the only person I trust," and Lachlan had agreed to let her run the stables.

A large dog ran in through the front door, speeding straight down the aisle; she turned as it passed and watched it scoot through the open back door. Brodie, her cousin, yelled from somewhere outside, "Raghnall."

She laughed and was about to turn to leave when arms swept around her, pulling her back into a hard, familiar body smelling of woods and spice.

"Did ye miss me?" Alan whispered in her ear before

nipping at it, eliciting a response she had become well familiar with.

"More than ye can ken." Twisting, she wrapped her arms around his waist and drew him as close as her stomach would allow for a long, deep kiss. Resting her head on his shoulder, she snuggled in and asked, "Is it done?"

"Aye. The inn is rebuilt, bigger and better than before." A satisfied smile turned his lips up. She was happy that he, Lachlan, and a large group of Cameron men had been able to help the innkeepers, especially with Alan's guilt over the loss of the couple's livelihood.

"And they were pleased?"

"They even invited us to stay anytime we want."

"'Twas nice of them, but I think no'. This is the only place I belong." She kissed his cheek.

"I havenae been able to sleep without ye by my side and reading to me before bed."

"I missed ye."

Releasing her, he reached down into a satchel she'd not noticed before. "I missed ye, too, so I brought ye something."

"Books!" she squealed as he drew out three bound leather volumes.

Draping his arm around her as her fingers traced the gold lettering on the cover of the volume on top, he guided her through the door and out into the waning daylight. "Now let's go home. I need my wife, a warm bed, and a good story."

Acknowledgments

Special thanks to:

Robin Haseltine, for her guidance and diligent attention to detail, her continued faith in me, and all the hard work and time she has dedicated to making the Highland Pride series the best it can be. She is a truly gifted editor.

Jessica Watterson, who will drop other things to have wine and cheese with me. She has been my advocate and sounding board. Fate found a way to bring us together, despite my poor choice in footwear, and I will be forever grateful you are my agent.

My best friend, my husband, for his love, support, and for understanding when the story calls and I forget what we're talking about that I still love him and he will always be my real-life hero.

My kids and my parents, Jo Ann and David Bailey, for encouraging me and being proud of what I do.

Eliza Knight and Madeline Martin. There is no way to voice how much these two women mean to me. I treasure our special bond and how we support each other every day. I love you guys.

My writing tribe, for sharing their enthusiasm, love of the craft, and wisdom along with keeping me motivated and on track. I will always be eternally grateful to: Michele Sandiford, Harper Kincaid, Denny S. Bryce, Jennifer McKeone, Nadine Monaco, Keely Thrall, Gabriel Ross, Jessica Snyder, and everyone in WRWDC.

And as always, for you, the reader, who picked up this book and gave me a chance to share a piece of my heart.

About the Author

Lori Ann Bailey is a winner of the National Readers' Choice Award and Holt Medallion for Best First Book and Best Historical. She has a romantic soul and believes the best in everyone. Sappy commercials and proud mommy moments make her cry.

She sobs uncontrollably and feels emotionally drained when reading sad books, so she started reading romance for the Happily Ever Afters. She was hooked.

Then, the characters and scenes running around in her head as she attempted to sleep at night begged to be let out. Looking back now, her favorite class in high school was the one where a professor pulled a desk to the center of the room and told her to write two paragraphs about it and the college English class taught by a red-headed Birkenstock wearing girl, not much older than she, who introduced her to Jack Kerouac. After working in business and years spent as a stay-at-home mom she has found something in addition to her family to be passionate about, her books.

When not writing, Lori enjoys time with her real-life hero

and four kids or spending time walking or drinking wine with her friends.

Visit Lori Ann Bailey in the following places:

http://loriannbailey.com — be sure to sign up for her newsletter for exclusive content and so that you don't miss any news.

https://www.facebook.com/LoriAnnBaileyauthor/

https://www.bookbub.com/profile/lori-ann-bailey

https://www.goodreads.com/LoriAnnBailey

https://www.amazon.com/Lori-Ann-Bailey/e/B01JGPBQSO

https://www.instagram.com/loriannbailey/

Discover more Amara titles…

Six Weeks with a Lord
a novel by Eve Pendle

Grace Alnott must marry a peer to save her brother from his abusive guardian. Soon. Everett Hetherington agrees to a marriage of convenience, but stipulates Grace must live with him for six weeks. She struggles to guard herself against falling for the handsome earl because she has learned the aristocracy cannot be trusted. Major Everett Hetherington, Earl of Westbury, is entranced by the spirited, independent Grace Alnott, but she will be leaving him in six weeks. Unless he can convince her to stay. And she never learns his secret.

Betting the Scot
a *Highlanders of Balforss* novel by Jennifer Trethewey

When Declan Sinclair sees Caya he knows instantly she is his future wife. Caya Pendarvis is on her way to Scotland to wed an unknown merchant. Instead, she ends up betrothed to the far too attractive Highlander who won her in a card game. Winning at cards is one of the many things Declan does well. Unfortunately, the ability to court a woman—a talent he lacks—is the only skill he desperately needs to win Caya's heart.

On Highland Time
a novel by Lexi Post

When someone changes history, affecting the future, Diana Montgomery, the most experienced agent of Time Weavers, Inc., travels back to 1306 Scotland to change it back. Her mission, to find the culprit and ensure a minor clan chief dies in battle as he originally had. What she's not prepared for is Torr MacPherson, the ruggedly handsome warrior with a kind heart and a steadfast loyalty—the Laird she's supposed to ensure dies.

Printed in Great Britain
by Amazon